A SPY IN WINTER

A SPY IN WINTER

Michael Hastings

A TOM DOHERTY ASSOCIATES BOOK

A SPY IN WINTER

Copyright © 1984 by Michael Ben-Zohar

Reprinted by arrangement with Macmillan Publishing Company

First Tor printing: April 1985
Second printing: October 1985

A TOR Book

Published by Tom Doherty Associates
49 West 24 Street
New York, N.Y. 10010

ISBN: 0-812-58350-7
CAN. ED.: 0-812-58351-5

Printed in the United States

0   9   8   7   6   5   4   3   2

. . . The principal character is still missing. In the lives of Burgess, Maclean, and Philby we discern his hand, his influence, his shadow; never once do we see his face or consciously hear his name. He is the Soviet recruiter. For these men were recruited. By whom? Between the ages of nineteen and twenty-one, it seems, these children of Cambridge were recognized, courted, and consciously seduced into a lifetime of deceit. By whom?

. . . Who serviced them, paid them? Who trained, welfared, consoled, and commanded them? Who kept them in play and taught them the clandestine arts?

. . . He understood us better than we understood ourselves: was he our countryman? He recruited only gentlemen: was he a gentleman? He recruited only from Cambridge: was he a Cambridge man?

—JOHN LE CARRÉ

Introduction to *The Philby Conspiracy*, New York, 1968

Part One

1

THE MAN had stepped unknowingly, trustingly, into death.

There had been no struggle, no attempt to escape. And no warning. Maybe just a polite voice asking for directions, or a hesitating approach with an unlit cigarette. He had stopped and bent forward slightly, in the dim yellow stain of a streetlamp. And the snub-nosed dumdum bullet had ripped his face open, shattering the cheekbone and exploding inside the skull. An ice-blue eye, left strangely intact, glowed in the bloodied raw flesh.

"Anything taken?" Hastings asked matter-of-factly as he crouched beside the corpse, carefully folding the folds of his raincoat over his knees. He had rarely seen a face so horribly mangled. The big, heavy-boned body, dressed in a blue suit and a Burberry, was sprawled on its back, the arms spread, the left knee bent inward at an odd angle. A big black umbrella and a derby hat lay closeby, behind the body.

A youthful police sergeant stepped forward. "No sir. I mean, I can't really say, sir. It doesn't look as if anything was stolen." He had a milk-white face with smooth rosy cheeks that radiated an incongruous air of innocence. He hesitated a moment, then woodenly bent over and handed Hastings a transparent plastic bag. "The contents of his pockets, sir. The lab dusted them for fingerprints already."

"Give." Hastings grunted and laid the bag on the ground. He fished in his inside pocket for a cigarette, lit it with a stainless-steel lighter, and left it dangling on his lower lip. "Let's see." He unhurriedly examined the documents in the dead man's wallet. His eyes rested for a second on the name on the driver's license. Anthony Byroade. Flaherty had been absolutely frantic when he had phoned him fifteen minutes before to report the murder. He had repeated the name over and over again, blabbering something about a KGB conspiracy and the Bulgarian umbrella murders. The poor chap had become a nervous wreck lately, after his wife's accident.

"Can we take the body away now, sir?"

"Are you in a hurry?" Hastings grunted and the sergeant clammed up, blushing.

A heavy raindrop fell on Hastings's face. He tilted his hat back and looked up. Over the stark beeches, the London sky was a smoky, cottonlike substance. He squinted in the dazzling glare of the vans' headlights, trained on the body. Converging yellow beams made the slimy sidewalk look like a floodlit stage. Peering above the lights, he could hardly discern the outlines of three police vehicles. Farther down, an ambulance was waiting, its back doors open. The Yard car that had picked him up at home was double-parked behind the vans, and its revolving light revealed the contours of the ambulance in soundless explosions of blue fire. A few blurred figures watched silently from behind the police barriers.

Hastings sucked at his Gauloise. The wallet was padded with neatly stacked one- and ten-pound notes. He delved into the plastic bag, his fingers running over a crisp linen handkerchief, some loose change, a thin Patek Philippe watch, a bunch of keys, an empty leather cigar case, and a Dunhill lighter.

"We've got all those items recorded, sir," the sergeant dutifully volunteered. He started to retreat but changed his mind and remained beside Hastings, awkwardly hovering over the body.

"Who found him?" Hastings asked.

"Two Austrian students, sir. Inspector Flaherty is questioning them now." The sergeant pointed to one of the vans. "The doctor says that he had been dead for only a few minutes when they found him."

"What were they doing here?" Some more raindrops splashed on Hastings's face.

The police officer had his notebook ready in his hand. "They said they were returning from a recital of . . . Jean-Pierre Rampal?" He looked down at his superior, in need of reassurance. "At the Royal Festival Hall. They—"

"Bring them over here," Hastings said, getting up with difficulty. An icy wind was rising from the Thames, and he brushed some sticky ash from his lapels.

"Yes sir," the sergeant responded eagerly. "I'll tell Inspector Flaherty. Right away, sir."

"Good. Do that," he said, but his attention had been caught by a cab that pulled in behind the police vans. Two men got out and, after a muffled exchange with the policeman on duty, hurried to the middle van. A moment later they came into the light, their quick steps resounding on the pavement. The cadaverous, stooping silhouette of Flaherty trailed behind.

Hastings waited for them to reach him. "Well, well," he said sarcastically as he recognized the pale face of Derek Brathwaite, MI-5 liaison officer with the Special Branch. The MI-5 people were in charge of all counterespionage activities inside England; their disregard of the rules of the game made Hastings loathe them cordially. Or perhaps the traditional feud had seeped into his blood. Due to certain nasty incidents with MI-5 in the past—and too many television series and spy novels—both sides had become entrenched in a stubborn, not always rational hostility. "News seems to travel fast in London, Derek. Who's this young gentleman?"

"Good evening, Chief Superintendent," Brathwaite said coldly, peering over his shoulder at the body. His face remained impassive, but his skin turned waxen and his mouth twitched. Behind his thick glasses his short-sighted eyes were huge and liquid. "Inspector Flaherty called me as soon as identity was established." He added with a straight face: "Regulations, you know."

Rain came down in a sudden outburst, ricocheting on the pavement. Behind the wavering curtain of water, the lights pointing toward the body turned into smoldering globes of pale fire. A chalky pallor settled on the face of Brathwaite's companion, a handsome, intense young man with dark brown hair, dressed in a loose sweater and an old tweed jacket. He was coatless and was soaked through in seconds but did not seem to mind. He was staring, mesmerized, at the mutilated face of Anthony Byroade. The rain pounded on the ravaged head, diluting the coagulated blood and snaking away in rosy-colored rivulets.

"Who is your friend?" Hastings asked again, tilting his head sideways. He had to raise his voice to be heard over the rumble of the storm. Two male nurses emerged from the ambulance and ran toward the body with a stretcher and a black vinyl body bag.

"This is Ted Jennings, Thames Television," Brathwaite said, struggling with his umbrella. "I took the liberty of asking him to come along." He looked at the young man and added needlessly: "Chief Superintendent Hastings, Special Branch."

Jennings, who was watching the men in white strap the corpse onto the stretcher, turned. His mouth was drawn. The rain had plastered his hair over his forehead and water was streaming down his livid face.

"So you are Jennings," Hastings muttered, now reassured in his conviction that Brathwaite was a fool indeed. "Well, be our guest and enjoy the show. You might damn well be responsible for this murder."

Jennings stood motionless for a moment, then turned and scurried away in the rain.

The phone in Lynn Kennan's apartment rang several times before she stirred and gazed into the darkness. The faintly glowing figures on the digital clock spelled 5:50 A.M. in modular green. The winter rain furiously rapped on the black windows. She rolled over in the bed and picked up the receiver.

"Lynn, you awake?"

She recognized Ted Jennings's voice. "What's the matter, Ted?"

There was a short silence. "Sorry to call you so early, but there is something I didn't want you to hear over the radio." The anxious voice sunk to a softer shade. "Byroade is dead, Lynn. Murdered."

She gasped. "Byroade? Anthony Byroade?"

"Yes." Another pause. "Somebody shot him dead last night on the Albert Embankment, shortly after eleven. He was taking his evening stroll. He lived quite closeby, you know, across the river."

She sat upright in the darkness, her hands shaking. Cold, it was so cold, all of a sudden. "Did they . . . I mean, was he robbed?"

"No, it was not that kind of crime. The police believe the murder has to do with our announcement of last week."

"Oh God." A violent shiver ran up her spine.

"Lynn, now listen. Lynn?"

She didn't speak for a moment, her mouth dry. "I feel it's my fault," she said finally. "I exposed him, didn't I? It was my story."

"Nonsense," he said angrily. "Absolute nonsense. We were in that together. And he could have refused to appear on television." His voice changed. "Really, I don't understand. A man agrees to divulge how he was forced to spy for the Russians thirty years ago, and a few days later he is shot in the middle of London."

She did not answer, biting her lower lip. In the darkness outside, skeletal boughs reached toward the window, whipped by the wind.

"Lynn? Are you there?"

"I'm all right, Ted. Really."

"Listen, the old man is arriving this morning. I thought maybe I'd go to Heathrow instead of you, and you could stay home today."

"No," she said, vigorously shaking her head. "I'll go. He is coming because of me, isn't he? We are almost family." Without waiting for Ted to answer, she hung up the phone. Her lips quivered and she stared fixedly at the black shapes outside.

2

FAR BEHIND the other passengers, the old man walked stiffly down the vast, cold concourses of Heathrow airport. The bleak London dawn was a drab gray mass clinging to the long succession of rectangular windows. An image of firmness and dignity, he stuck his chin forward and tightened his grip on his new briefcase. Still, odd sensations clawed at his chest and contrasting feelings clashed in his mind, shattering into fragments of anxiety and elation, liberty and entrapment, hope that flowed sourly into premonition. He was back in England after seventeen years of hiding. And for the first time in his adult life, he was traveling under his real name.

"Mr. Alexander Orloff," the clerk in the immigration booth said aloud, as he leafed through the brand-new American passport. The recent photograph displayed the face of an old man: large forehead, deep-set black eyes, leathery cheeks. The mouth was still firm, though, and the long white hair was thick. The immigration officer checked the data against the disembarkation form. Born 1910, St. Petersburg, Russia. Address in the USA, Fort Myers, Florida. Purpose of the visit. . . .

"Purpose of the visit?" the clerk asked casually, feigning not to notice the two men who stood beside the next booth, watching the old man.

"Tourism," Orloff said.

One of the men moved forward. He was lean, balding, with a receding chin. A sweet, heavy smell of aftershave wafted about him. "Will you step aside, Mr. Orloff?" The plastic ID was ready in his right hand. "Special Branch, Scotland Yard."

To Orloff's surprise, the interrogation was rather low-keyed. Yes, he admitted that he was a former Soviet citizen. Yes, he had entered England before under a false name.

"What name, Mr. Orloff?" The bald man was insultingly civil. His companion, big and heavy, wearing a raincoat and a hat, had not moved. A foul-smelling Gauloise dangled from his lower lip. His pale eyes were weary, nestled in a web of wrinkles.

"Alexander Carlisle," he said.

Yes, he had spied for the Soviet secret services between the years 1932 and 1966. Yes, he knew that he had broken English laws. He answered the questions quickly, in a soft voice. He had anticipated them all, had rehearsed the answers in his mind over and over again. He was confident he would not give the English the pleasure of knocking him off balance. Yet, one question made him pause and clench his fists: why had he defected?

"I did not defect," he said firmly, raising his voice slightly. The bald man was watching him closely, a shadow of irony floating on his crooked lips. "I did not agree with the policy of my country anymore, and I applied for political asylum in the United States."

"Yes," the bald man said, unnecessarily leafing through the blank pages of his passport. "Did you spend the last seventeen years in the United States?"

"Yes."

"Under your real name?" Behind the wooden white partition, the hum of the conveyor belt suddenly stopped and the last luggage carts squeaked on the linoleum floor.

"No. I was given a new identity by the American authorities."

"What made you resume your real name?"

He shrugged. "There is no law against that, as far as I know."

"There is a law against spying," the Englishman said with sudden vehemence. Orloff held his eyes for a moment but remained silent. The bald man adjusted the knot of his dark blue tie. His voice was again cold, controlled. "What made you come out of hiding and back here? It could be dangerous, you know."

Orloff answered only to see their reaction. He knew that the British services had been thoroughly briefed by the CIA before his trip was arranged and that the security measures had been approved. "I am seventy-three years old," he said with a faint smile. "At my age, there are not many dangers left."

The bald man handed him his passport and motioned him through. As Orloff stepped by the other man the latter spoke, regretfully taking his cigarette out of his mouth. "Do you know Anthony Byroade, Mr. Orloff?"

Orloff turned to face him. "Who?"

"Byroade. Anthony Byroade." The pale eyes were watchful, alert.

"No, I don't think so."

"Are you sure?"

He nodded. "Should I know him?"

"Yes, you should." In mock salute, the man raised two nicotine-stained fingers, still holding his cigarette, to the brim of his hat. "Enjoy your stay, Mr. Orloff."

They let him go without asking the most important question. But the pack of journalists waiting in the arrival hall threw it in his face as soon as he emerged in the blinding flashes of the press cameras and the floodlights of the TV crews.

"Mr. Orloff, were you the chief of Russian espionage in England?"

"Did you know Burgess and Maclean, Mr. Orloff?"

"Were you their KGB contact? Did you arrange their escape?" In the clamor, he was able to pick out the names of Philby and Blunt. A bearded youth in one of the back rows shouted something about the Prime trial. He wanted to know if Orloff had recruited Geoffrey Prime as well. A dark-haired woman, offering him a microphone, asked in a low but utterly distinct voice: "How many people have died because of you, Mr. Orloff?"

He merely shook his head and let the two police officers clear him a passage in the crowd. The man from Special Branch stuck to him. The last questions were cast at Orloff as the two pushed him down the escalator. He did not look back.

They made him cross several empty departure halls with deserted airline counters, and then let him out on the wet sidewalk. He shivered as a steady drizzle, more like a spray of tiny droplets, enveloped him. England again.

The young woman was standing beside a battered Ford Anglia, and he swayed lightly as he took in the oval face, the big green eyes, the high cheekbones, and the sensuous figure.

"Hello," she said with an uncertain smile. "I am Lynn. How was your flight?"

"God, how much you resemble your mother," he said, his voice choking. And for a split second he was a young man again, in the London of thirty-five years before, infatuated with his American bride, Virginia Fielding. He averted his gaze, striving to cast away Virginia's memory, but it clung to him cruelly, reviving the longing and the pain.

She shifted awkwardly on her feet and motioned toward the car. Her blond hair fell on the narrow collar of her green coat. The cuffs and the belt were frayed. Her knee-high boots were not new either. A black porter emerged from a nearby door and dumped Orloff's suitcase on the back seat of the car, absently pocketing the dollar bill that Orloff, staring at Lynn with a wolfish smile, handed him. The two Special Branch officers had retreated a few yards and stood beside the cab file, watching Orloff and the woman in silence. The heavyset man in the raincoat lit another cigarette.

"Welcome to London," Lynn said. She waited for him to settle in the passenger's seat. After another awkward silence, she said again, in a low, urgent voice, as if she were in a hurry to get this part of the conversation over and done with, "Mother never talked to me about you." She nervously rattled the gearshift, and he stole a quick glance at her face. There were dark shadows beneath her eyes.

As the car pulled out, the two detectives were left behind, two immobile figures rapidly diminishing in the rearview mirror. Two black cabs and an airline bus were behind Lynn's car, but Orloff was interested in the pale blue Vauxhall that followed farther back. There would be a car ahead of them as well.

"So," he said, "how did you learn that your mother's first husband had been a spy?" He gazed out the side window, refraining from looking at her.

"From her sister, Marjorie. Did you know her? She told me that Mother found out about you and divorced you immediately. I was born two years later, after she remarried. I am twenty-six now."

"You know you look very much like her, don't you?" he said abruptly. His voice sounded dry, almost formal. On the A-1 motorway, the blue Vauxhall kept at a safe distance.

She didn't answer, and he went on: "That's why I agreed to come. I had to see you." Before it was too late, he wanted to add, but didn't. She might not understand.

"Oh, come on." She seemed irritated. "You didn't come for me or for anybody else. We were officially informed that you were asked to come. You are here because the American government or the CIA or some other spook organization over there decided that you should appear on British television. You would have come to London whether or not I had written to you."

Her bluntness didn't offend him. "You may be right," he conceded, guardedly. "I wanted very much to see England again. I lived in this country for thirty-four years, and that adds up to a lot of memories. Not all of them bad. When the American . . . authorities asked me to come, I was tempted. That chapter in my life has been definitely closed, buried, but suddenly I had the opportunity to come back."

"A kind of nostalgic journey," she said.

He nodded to himself. "I guess so. Then I started having second thoughts." He didn't tell her what his second thoughts were. He couldn't speak to her, a total stranger, about his fear of facing the ghosts that haunted him. Or of being suddenly exposed, questioned, insulted, maybe even attacked, in front of the television cameras, he who had lived in the shadows all his life. "I was still hesitating," he said dryly, "when your letter came. It was quite unexpected." He had spent a sleepless night pacing about the living room, rereading the letter from Virginia's daughter. "Let's say you just tipped the scales."

She kept silent, her eyes on the wet road. He changed subjects, matching her brusqueness. "When are you going to interview me?"

"The first program is scheduled for Monday night, live," she said, looking relieved, almost grateful. "There will be two more segments over the next week."

"And they are going to disclose that you are the daughter of my former wife?"

She nodded. "That's the deal."

He shook his head. "A high price for seeing you."

"A high price for me to get my first major assignment," she retorted. "I don't take any pleasure in digging up my mother's past."

He turned slowly and looked at her. Her face was dejected, miserable.

"There was an accident last night," she suddenly said.

"What kind of accident?"

"We wanted to confront you with a former KGB spy.

We succeeded in convincing him to appear on the same program with you.''

''Who is 'we'?''

''Ted Jennings and I. Ted is the producer, the man who first had the idea of bringing you over here.'' She paused. ''While we were researching the subject we discovered this . . . this man. He was a former diplomat. He was dismissed from the Foreign Office in nineteen sixty-seven, when a board of inquiry established that he had spied for Russia for ten years, between nineteen fifty-two and sixty-two.''

''I don't remember any trial,'' Orloff said.

She shook her head. ''No trial. The affair was hushed up, like a couple of other cases. The Foreign Office could not afford another public scandal, not after Philby's defection.''

He raised his eyebrows. ''So what made you dig him up?''

''Ted was looking for something sensational to add punch to your TV interviews. He thought that a live confrontation between you two, a former KGB agent and a notorious master spy, would be fascinating.''

A silver Rolls-Royce cut across their path and splashed mud on their windshield. As the wipers laboriously squeaked on the dirtied glass, Orloff felt a wave of anger rising inside him. ''I don't think it's what I would call fascinating. I shall not do it.''

She smiled bitterly. ''No need to worry. The project is definitely canceled.''

He frowned at her. Her knuckles were white on the steering wheel.

''Last night he was murdered on the Albert Embank-

ment.'' A huge billboard praising the virtues of Cutty Sark
sailed past them, as the highway rose on an overpass.

Orloff leaned back on his seat, staring ahead. She stole
a glance at him, but his eyes were deep shadows under
knitted brows.

''What was his name?'' he finally asked.

''Byroade. Anthony Byroade. The former ambassador to
Bonn, you know.''

He slowly shook his head. ''The man at the airport from
the Special Branch mentioned that name. I told him that I
had never heard it before.''

She turned sharply toward him, her eyes filled with
anguish. ''You must know him! You knew all the KGB
agents in the Foreign Service, didn't you? Byroade had
been security officer in Prague earlier and had worked
directly for the Intelligence Service.''

''I am sorry,'' Orloff said gently, without looking at
her. ''I would have known about him if he had worked for
us. But I have never heard his name before tonight, Lynn.''

She left the car under a NO PARKING sign and led him
across the street into the Thames Building. Her original
plan had been to drive him straight to his hotel; but, as
they turned into Cromwell Road, she happened to mention
that Ted Jennings was busy examining the photographs
and the first lab reports concerning last night's murder.
Orloff insisted on stopping at the studio first.

The lobby was brightly lit. The girl at the reception desk
checked their papers and stared at them vacantly. They
found Ted Jennings alone in the newsroom, on the second
floor, sorting a stack of photographs over a large untidy
desk. He got up hurriedly, smoothing down his white
turtleneck pullover. ''Welcome to London, Mr. Orloff,''

...ally, shaking the older man's hand. "We
.../y to have you on our program. It is going to
...ion. I hope you had a pleasant flight." His
sn... ...s engaging, lighting up his strong face. But the
coal-black eyes were reserved, and the voice, underneath
the polite clichés, was guarded, tense.

Orloff instinctively grasped that the young man did not
like him, and felt uneasy in his presence. Not that it really
mattered. He did not fail, though, to sense the tension
between Jennings and Lynn. "May I?" he said curtly,
walking past Jennings to the desk. Byroade's horse-jawed,
well-groomed face was grinning from the front page of the
Daily Mail, spread beside the glossy photographs. SLAIN
DIPLOMAT WAS COMMUNIST SPY, screamed the headline.

Orloff briefly perused the article, then shifted his attention to the grisly pictures of the dead man's face. "I guess
that this gentleman was shot in my honor," he remarked
wryly.

"There is no proof . . ." Jennings began. Lynn was
standing at the far corner of the room, avoiding looking at
the desk.

"I don't believe in coincidences," Orloff said, absorbed
in the photographs. "That's a luxury I could never afford."
He straightened up. "What about the slug?"

Ted dug into the sheafs of paper on the desk and handed
him another batch of photographs; Orloff glimpsed the
flash of a wedding ring on his hand. In the photographs,
the magnified fragments of the dumdum bullet were presented from different angles. Orloff frowned, intrigued. A
memory was slowly shaping in his mind, emerging from
the past. Another face hideously maimed. Another dumdum bullet blown into jagged fragments.

"Did anybody hear the shot?" he asked.

Jennings shook his head. He seemed puzzled by the question. "The police questioned all the neighbors. Nobody heard a thing."

"I understand you have the lab report," Orloff pressed on. "Is there anything about the bullet's angle of penetration?"

Jennings had a photocopy of the report at the far corner of his desk. He flipped through it but did not show it to Orloff. "Yes," he said, raising his eyes. "They say it was forty-five to fifty degrees."

Orloff nodded. "Your killer is a short man, then."

He walked to the window, holding the photographs at arm's length. Across the street, the wind was mercilessly whipping the luscious body of a black model on a billboard advertising Jamaican holidays. The blue Vauxhall was parked by an electrical appliances store, its windows thick with condensation.

"If what you say is correct," Orloff started cautiously, "then this man was shot with a silenced weapon. After the war the KGB developed a noiseless electric pistol. Battery-powered. It fires dumdum or poisoned bullets. It is called the Otmastitel, which means 'Avenger.' " He turned to face them. "This looks like a typical KGB killing to me. That's how they shot Bandera, the Ukrainian dissident, in Munich. He looked very much like this." He threw the photographs on the desk. "Still, I cannot understand why they killed Byroade with this kind of pistol. The last time they used an Avenger was twenty-five years ago. In nineteen fifty-eight."

Jennings didn't answer and an awkward silence settled in the room.

"Well," Orloff said, "I could use some rest. If you don't mind, Lynn, I would like to go to my hotel now."

"Of course. You'll be staying at the Churchill."

On his way out he stopped and turned back to face Jennings. "I know what you are thinking, all of you. Somebody in the KGB, who knew I was coming, was ready to go to great lengths to prevent me from meeting Byroade. But I never saw him in my life."

"Never?" murmured Ted Jennings, loud enough for Lynn to hear.

She shot a quick glance at Orloff. He had heard the question, and for just a moment his calm face colored in anger. His aquiline nose, full mouth, and shock of soft hair bestowed a dramatic aura upon him. Lynn could see now what had made her mother fall in love with this man thirty-five years ago. She could visualize the fervent face, wrinkles and creases gone, the passionate mouth, the intense stare of the black eyes. It suddenly occurred to her that Ted Jennings had the same kind of dark romantic looks. It must be a family streak, she thought, to fall for the same type of men. She shuddered, oddly troubled, and hurried after Orloff without looking back.

3

AN ELDERLY, emaciated butler ushered Peter Snow into the dark vestibule on the ground floor of the manor house. "Is everyone here, Collins?" Snow asked, unbuttoning his raincoat.

"Almost everyone, sir." Collins was obsequious to the point of seeming to play a role. "Mr. Brennan arrived earlier, and Mr. Hodder only just got in." As he took Snow's coat, the doorbell rang. "Excuse me, sir. That must be Mr. MacMillan."

The prime minister's supervisor of the Intelligence fraternity shook his umbrella on the threshold and grimly stared back at the leaden sky before entering. "Ghastly weather," he grunted, and stuck his umbrella in the butler's hands. "Oh, hello, Peter. Any news?"

"Not yet, Ian. We are doing our best."

"Of course you are. Bloody weather, don't you think? Had a rotten drive from London, took me more than an hour. What traffic for a Sunday morning.'' He peeled his camel's-hair coat from his narrow shoulders, took a white kerchief from his pocket, and wiped his horn-rimmed glasses.

"This way please, Gentlemen.'' Collins led the way across the wood-paneled hall into a spacious drawing room. By the French windows, Sir Nigel Sykes, chief of the Secret Intelligence Service, was listening to Andrew Hodder, the new Foreign Office coordinator of the secret services. Snow didn't even bother to return Hodder's effusive smile. Of the two baby-sitters of the services, MacMillan was the man with the real clout. Hodder's position in the shadow hierarchy controlling the Intelligence fraternity was far inferior. Actually, Hodder was nothing but an anachronistic vestige of the time when the Foreign Office had had a decisive influence over the activities of the services. But during recent years a sad succession of espionage scandals had covered the Foreign Office with ridicule; and Margaret Thatcher had shifted the overall responsibility for cloak-and-dagger activities to the newly created function of the prime minister's supervisor. The odd survival of a Foreign Office coordinator in the inner circle of decision makers was due only to the prime minister's reluctance to deal another humiliating blow to her frustrated Foreign Office.

Hodder was a short and frail man, a former ambassador to Brussels and living proof of the Foreign Office's diminishing influence over the services. As he spoke to Sir Nigel, his pallid eyes and tiny hands did not stop moving, as if obeying a force of their own.

Sir Nigel's hawkish face was devoid of expression. His deputy, Jim Brennan, chubby and fox-eared, was nodding his head repeatedly. He saw MacMillan and Snow and hurriedly whispered something to Sir Nigel, who turned around slowly.

"Oh, here you are," Sir Nigel said dryly. "Excuse me, Andrew," he added, smiling absently at Hodder. He crossed the room in quick, easy strides and shook their hands. "Good morning, Ian. Peter. How kind of you to come on such short notice."

Peter Snow flashed a token smile at the chief of the SIS and watched him, tall and lean, move smoothly between his guests. That parvenu had learned to play the game to perfection. Suave mannerisms, morning tweeds, upper-class wife, manor in Sussex, even a thoroughbred grey-hound by the fireside. And last year a knighthood. Who would believe that he had started his career as a colonial policeman in Palestine, and that his sister still ran a grocery store in Manchester.

"Tea, sir?"

"Yes, thank you, Collins," Snow said gruffly, picking up his cup and joining the others in the half-circle of armchairs facing the fire. No one, Snow sadly concluded, symbolized the plebeianization of the British establishment more than Nigel Sykes. Snow had personally interviewed Sykes when he had returned from Palestine in 1948. He remembered the heated discussion within the personnel department about whether such a man should even be considered for employment in MI-5. But twenty years later, they had promoted Sykes over his head, first as chief of MI-5 and later to the very directorship of the SIS. Even Snow's own appointment as chief of MI-5, a few years later, had not dispelled the bitterness he felt toward Sykes.

The Secret Intelligence Service, Snow pondered grimly, was still viewed as the nobility of the Intelligence fraternity. While the MI-5 dealt with counterespionage and security inside England—which exposed it to an unflattering comparison with Her Majesty's police—the SIS was in charge of all covert activities abroad, including espionage, subversion, and special operations. Still drawing prestige and renown from a bygone golden era, and in spite of the scandals that had riddled it in the past twenty years, the SIS carried the aura of an elite order of daredevil, shrewd, blue-blooded Englishmen; a unique assembly of brilliant brains, devious minds, indomitable agents. The chiefs of the SIS had always looked with condescension, often with contempt, at their poor relations from MI-5. And Nigel Sykes certainly was no exception to that rule.

"That will be all, Collins," Sir Nigel said. "Will you please leave the tray on the table so that we can help ourselves? Thank you." Before the butler left the room, Sir Nigel added: "Another thing, Collins. A . . . man from Special Branch will be here in about a half hour. Will you let him in, please?"

"Special Branch? The Yard?" MacMillan arched his eyebrows.

Sir Nigel shrugged. His tone was even, impersonal. "They are in charge of the investigation and have demanded to be present at any high-level briefing. The minister called me personally. I thought it suitable to invite their representative to the second part of the meeting. They should not learn more than need be."

He sat down in the sudden silence and lit his pipe with deliberate slowness. The drumming of the rain on the windows had ceased, but the sky was almost black, and an oppressive atmosphere hung over the obscure, poorly heated room.

"Thank you all for coming," Sir Nigel said. "I do regret having to interfere with your weekend, but I thought it necessary to call an urgent meeting. I believe we are all quite upset over the assassination of Anthony Byroade and the arrival of Alexander Orloff. I thought it important that the director of MI-5''—he nodded at Peter Snow—''Jim, and myself meet with the government representatives to discuss these rather disturbing developments.''

"The two events are linked, of course," Peter Snow said. His voice was sharp-edged. "Somebody in Moscow did not want Byroade and Orloff to meet."

Ian MacMillan frowned. "It could be a coincidence, couldn't it? Moscow might have decided to silence Byroade before he talked too much. It might have nothing to do with Orloff."

"I don't think so, Ian," Snow said softly, smothering the anger that surged within him. The PM's supervisor of the Intelligence community was an able but very vain man, and could be a dangerous opponent. He had to be handled with utmost care. "We have had a few cases of former KGB spies unmasked, and none was ever bothered. We haven't had a KGB killing since the Bulgarian umbrella murders. And I frankly believe that Markov was killed because of his broadcasts to Bulgaria, not because of the secrets he knew."

Hodder carefully unwrapped a thin black cigar. "Was Orloff that important, Nigel? The head of Russian espionage in England?"

"Yes . . . and no. Yes, he was that important. No, he was not the head of Soviet espionage. You see," he eagerly leaned forward, "he was sent to London in a brilliant move by Maxim Litvinov in the early thirties. Orloff's mission was to run an operation parallel to the Soviet espionage network in England. He was the recruiter and case officer of a few selected agents in London.

He worked completely alone, getting his orders directly from Moscow. The resident KGB man did not even suspect he existed.''

"Clever indeed," MacMillan said. "He is half-Russian, isn't he?"

Nigel Sykes nodded. "He was born to a Russian father and an American mother. She was Jewish—"

"Of course," Snow mumbled. "Jewish and Communist. The classic formula in those years."

Sir Nigel marked a pause and continued. "He turned up at Cambridge, in 1932, with the identity of a rich American student, Carlisle. Later he established himself in London as an expert on raw materials and an art collector. He made a few remarkable oil deals."

"I'm not surprised," Snow said coldly. "He was getting his tips straight from Dzerzhinsky Square. This man deserves to hang, and we are letting him parade through London like a movie star." He cast a challenging look at Sykes.

MacMillan put his empty cup to one side. "Nobody saw through Orloff for thirty-four years? That's alarming, Nigel."

"He was very cautious and his cover was virtually foolproof. He must have been programmed as early as his teens for a spying assignment. He was sent here at the age of twenty-two, you see, and that sheltered him from any in-depth investigation."

"When did he defect?"

"In nineteen sixty-six. He arranged the escape of George Blake, and the next morning woke the American ambassador, asking for asylum. My guess is that he dreaded going back to Russia. He had been living in Europe most of his life, and now his career was over. The CIA claims that all he asked for was to go back to America and live quietly in some suburb. He told them all he knew.''

Snow was about to say something, but had a second thought. He knew they would ignore him. Ever since the Geoffrey Prime scandal they had treated him with circumspection, like someone afflicted by an incurable disease, which drove him twice as mad. They behaved as if it was him in person who had introduced the KGB spy into the Communications Center of the SIS.

Andrew Hodder got up from his place and walked to the window, sipping his tea with his small, beaklike mouth. ''I don't understand.'' He had a quick, rather slurred manner of speech. ''Why should the Americans expose him all of a sudden?''

''Excuse me,'' the SIS chief said. ''Would you like some more tea? Ian? Let me replenish your cup.'' He got up and walked to the table, where the teapot had been left with a tray of tiny sandwiches, biscuits, Cheddar, and whipped butter. He poured the tea neatly into MacMillan's cup and his own, and turned back to Hodder. ''The CIA people pretend he can be useful to them as a propaganda asset; consequently they let him out in the open a month ago. They were very keen, though, that his first television appearance be in England, where he operated. My guess is that they got very nervous during the summer, when the Russians broke one of their networks, the so-called Carlovy ring. There were quite a few American diplomats and businessmen involved in that affair; and the Russians, of course, made a jolly nice piece of propaganda out of it.''

''They were always good at that,'' MacMillan said needlessly, gravely surveying his audience.

''I think,'' Sir Nigel went on, ''that the CIA has exposed Orloff now in order to prove that the KGB spies were far worse than their own. The Carlovy scandal was rather disastrous for them, coming as it did in the middle of the SALT talks.''

''Yes, I see,'' Hodder said, obviously not seeing at all but pathetically trying to belong.

''And they have nothing else to do,'' Snow said, ''but toss Orloff in our laps so that, if the KGB boys want to settle their accounts with him, they'll know where to find him.''

''Peter is right, Nigel,'' Andrew Hodder mumbled. ''What do we need with him here? This man is trouble.''

Sykes discreetly caught MacMillan's eye. The bony Scotsman cleared his throat. ''We don't want this aired,'' he started, warily surveying his small audience, ''but the request that we admit Orloff and lend a hand to a good media coverage came from a very high authority in the United States.''

''What authority? The White House?'' Snow asked, smoldering. Nobody had bothered to let him know.

MacMillan removed his glasses and took his handkerchief from his pocket. ''Governmental level,'' he said stiffly. ''We virtually could not refuse. You might be surprised to learn, Peter, that Nigel was very much against Orloff's visit, but I had to overrule him.''

Sykes, his narrow head slightly tilted, was watching Snow. ''On the other hand,'' he remarked, ''I doubt if the KGB would harm Orloff in any way. They have been keeping a low profile these days and wouldn't like to be implicated if anything happened to Orloff.''

''Is that so?'' Snow struck back. ''So how will you explain—''

He fell silent as the double-winged door opened noiselessly and Collins appeared on the threshold. ''The gentleman from the Yard is here, Sir Nigel. Chief Superintendent Hastings.''

The director of the SIS cast a quick glance around the room and nodded. Collins stiffly moved back and let in a heavyset man in his mid-fifties, wearing a good but ill-fitting suit. His sparse hair was brown with a reddish tinge. His face, creased and rugged, wore a vaguely wary expression. He stood awkwardly by the door, his hands gripped behind his back, his small pale eyes taking them in one by one. He did not speak, yet there was something aggressive, raw, in his presence that made them all feel ill at ease.

"Come in, Chief Superintendent," Sir Nigel said with icy politeness. "I expected Robin Coleman, but I was informed this morning that he couldn't make it. Would you like a cup of tea?"

"Thank you. Robin could not come, sir. His daughter is in the hospital. An acute case of peritonitis."

"How awful," Nigel Sykes said absently. "Here you are. Would you sit down. You've got your B-Clearance, of course." He paused, but Hastings did not speak. "Well. . . ." Sir Nigel made short, reluctant introductions. "I understand that you are familiar with the Byroade case."

"Yes," Hastings said. He plunged his hand into his inner breast pocket but withdrew it empty. "I am sorry I interrupted. I was asked to be here at eleven."

"You were exactly on time," Sir Nigel said coldly. "Now, where were we? Oh, yes, we were discussing the danger of a KGB attempt on Orloff's life. I am pretty sure that the KGB would not try anything of the sort, but Mr. Snow . . . Peter, you were saying?"

"I was saying," Peter Snow held Sir Nigel's eyes challengingly, "would you be so sure, if I told you that a KGB team infiltrated this country two weeks ago?'' He paused for effect, took a small notebook from his pocket, and leafed through it unhurriedly. ''They arrived here only six days after Orloff's visit was announced.''

''I don't know a thing about that, Peter,'' Sir Nigel said, and for a second his face seemed to change. The slightly slanted eyes turned dark and mean, the mouth tight, the voice hostile. ''What is your source?''

''A good one,'' Snow said. He had succeeded in tearing that upstart's mask from his face, just once. He did not add that the report had arrived only yesterday afternoon, and by tomorrow a copy would be on Nigel's desk anyway. ''They are hiding somewhere in London. I believe that Derek Brathwaite notified you about that,'' he said to Hastings. ''I have no doubt that they killed Byroade and are on their way to get Orloff now.''

Jim Brennan stooped over Sir Nigel's chair and urgently whispered in his ear. The SIS chief vigorously shook his head.

There was a moment of tense silence. Hodder tried to change the subject. ''Why did Orloff come here in the first place?'' he quipped and added with an apologetic smile: ''I was at the NATO emergency meeting when the decision was made.''

''As I said,'' MacMillan stuttered warily, ''Washington wanted him to appear on British television and other media over here, but they were rather vague about the way it should be done. They had no hold over him to force him to come over. On the other hand, we couldn't force the BBC to bring him over either. Orloff himself seemed quite reluctant. Fortunately, at a certain point Thames Television came up with an idea that might appeal to him.'' He threw a quick look at Sir Nigel.

Nigel Sykes put aside his extinguished pipe, which clanged loudly in the copper ashtray. "There is a producer at Thames named Ted Jennings. Quite a bright young man. He reached Orloff through that American reporter, Lynn Kennan. She and Orloff are related in a way. She is the daughter of his former wife, from a later marriage. Orloff had some earlier offers, but Jennings was lucky to find the girl. She was freelancing for a Boston paper and a couple of magazines. He offered her the job of hosting a three-segment interview if she could convince Orloff to come over. While they were researching their subject, they stumbled upon poor old Byroade. Remember him? The 'sixty-seven scandals?''

"We had promised not to bother him in any way," Snow said. Hastings's eyes shifted between Snow and Sykes, as if following a tennis match.

"Why did Byroade agree to appear on television in the first place?" Hodder asked. "He went too far, didn't he?"

Nigel Sykes and Ian MacMillan exchanged glances. "There was a quite substantial fee involved, I understand," MacMillan said cautiously. "Those private networks can be very generous when they want. They promised him a few thousand pounds, didn't they, Nigel?"

The chief of SIS nodded. "Five thousand. They also told him he could present his own version of his connection with the KGB, without any interference from the network. That was quite tempting, I guess, especially after Thames informed him that they would be broadcasting their own story about him anyway."

"Still, he should have stayed put," Snow insisted.

Sykes shrugged. "What counts is that Jennings convinced Byroade to admit publicly he had been a KGB spy, and made him agree to a televised confrontation with Orloff.''

"And the following week he was done with,'' Hodder murmured. He contemplated the moist tip of his cigar. ''I think we should expel Orloff, Ian. It would save us a lot of trouble.''

Jim Brennan eagerly nodded in agreement but froze at once as the cold stare of Nigel Sykes came to rest upon him.

''I'd rather not. Not yet,'' MacMillan said firmly. ''The CIA could regard that as an unfriendly act on our side. They are interested in embarrassing the KGB publicly.''

''The CIA is not our problem,'' Snow muttered. ''We've got too many skeletons in our closets, and Orloff might easily get killed.''

''That's why I asked you to come this morning,'' Sir Nigel said. ''I propose we establish an ad hoc committee to deal with the Orloff and Byroade affairs. I think it should be headed by Peter Snow. The SIS will be represented by Jim Brennan. We'll ask Coleman to send somebody from Special Branch.''

''They sent me,'' Hastings said placidly.

Sir Nigel turned to face him. ''Yes, of course,'' he replied after a short pause. ''I'd rather like that in writing, though. . . . Well, Peter? What do you think?''

Peter Snow, rather disconcerted, nodded his head.

''Ian? Andrew?''

Hodder hurriedly nodded his assent.

''That sums it up, then. I suggest giving this committee carte blanche.'' Nigel Sykes rose to his feet, followed by his guests. ''You should spare no effort in tracking down Byroade's assassins.''

Sir Nigel cornered Snow and MacMillan by the French

windows, while Hastings and Hodder moved toward the door, herded by Brennan. Waiting till his other guests were out of earshot, he said softly, "I suggest that you keep Orloff under close surveillance, Peter. He might lead us to Byroade's murderers as well." Snow looked at him, frowning. "And if Orloff gets killed in the process," Sykes continued, tilting his head back and staring at his companions, "I don't think anybody here would really care, would we?"

4

"MR. ORLOFF, for most of your life you have been a Soviet secret agent," Lynn Kennan said coldly. "What was your main assignment in this country?"

Orloff did not answer immediately, but watched her eager face under its thin layer of makeup. Above her head, the round lens of the bulky television camera focused on him; a tiny red light on top of the camera started blinking.

"I directed the spying activities of Kim Philby for over thirty years," he said.

He had reluctantly agreed to Jennings's demand to start the interview with that dramatic disclosure. "In television interviews, you either win or lose the audience in the first couple of minutes," Jennings had stated over lunch. They had invited him to lunch at Lynn's apartment, in Chelsea. Ted had insisted on picking him up at the Churchill, but he had flatly refused. He had taken a cab and driven through the bleak, rain-swept streets, dutifully followed by the

Special Branch car, only today it was a black Austin. The doorbell on the second floor did not work; he had to pound on the door to be heard over the desperate beat of Pink Floyd. Lynn had opened the door in faded jeans and a man's denim shirt, a blatant contrast to her cool appearance of the previous day. He had hesitated on the threshold, then had awkwardly handed her a neat package wrapped in plain brown paper: a photograph of her mother in her artist's smock, standing proud and radiant before *Lovers,* which she had just completed. He had had the photograph enlarged and framed in Fort Myers. "I also have a photograph of your mother and me with *Lovers,*" he said gently, "but I thought you would prefer this one." She had looked at him unsmiling, her eyes searching, insistent.

He had been disconcerted, yet seduced, by the carefree disorder of her apartment. Stacks of best-selling novels, memoirs, books on art and politics were strewn all over the place; unframed paintings, most of them outrageous splashes of various colors on huge canvases, lined the floor, along the walls, or occupied choice places, like the ageless sofa and a deep, worn-leather armchair. She had described the unknown geniuses behind those horrors as "Paris friends," and he had not probed further. She did not seem inclined to speak about her student years in Paris. There were piles of newspapers and magazines on most of the chairs, and every table and cabinet in the place was populated with an amazing array of unusual objects: statuettes and pagan artifacts from the South Pacific and Latin America; Indian jewelry; miniature porcelain dolls from Germany; cheap copies of French *images d'Epinal;* Egyptian cartouches and Chinese chops; primitive tribal-music instruments; and two exquisite, egg-shaped pocket watches from the seventeenth century. By the half-open door he had

had a fleeting glimpse of the bedroom, which seemed neat and tidy to the point of belonging somewhere else.

Ted was in the kitchen, Lynn explained, busy with his onion soup. His wife was French, and he had stolen the recipe from her. Was she here? he politely inquired. She was not, and Lynn did not seem to mind. Then she had left him alone for a moment, while she finished unwrapping the victuals. Ted had appeared at the kitchen door, wearing baggy trousers and a checkered woolen shirt, a bottle of dark red wine in each hand. "The Beaujolais *nouveau* is outstanding this year," he had announced solemnly. He definitely knew his way around the house, and unceremoniously swept aside Lynn's private collection to clear off a good half of the table for their feast. And a feast it had been, with delectable oven-baked *soupe à l'oignon*, Italian prosciutto, Swiss dried beef from the Grisons mountains, Greek stuffed grape leaves and coarse feta cheese, ripe French Roquefort and *chèvre*, all served in appalling disorder, while the young, bold wine kept flowing into their unmatching glasses in a cloud of insouciant, mischievous bouquet. The two young people seemed very pleased with each other's company and rather familiar with each other's tastes. But their easy camaraderie was occasionally tinted with the same peculiar tension he had sensed the previous day. Apparently they were not lovers. He sat through the meal, feeling utterly awkward. He was envious of them, being an outsider, only briefly admitted into the bubbling, lighthearted relationship between these two; and at the same time, strangely elated and grateful for this unique opportunity to glimpse a world that was so different from his own. Maybe it had been the wine and the cheerful atmosphere that made him agree to their demands; or maybe those were only his excuses in trying to justify his consent. For so many years he had hoped to meet Virginia's daughter. And here she was beside him now, her eyes sparkling and her cheeks red from the wine, in her happy, blue-jeaned, ruffled privacy, Virginia's rich, musical laughter echoing from her throat.

But in the evening, at the studio, she was once again cool and remote, inaccessible in her strict gray suit and bottle-green silk blouse that enhanced the golden highlights of her hair. As he looked into her watchful face and listened to her firm voice, he again felt the undercurrent of antagonism that she had not been able to conceal the day before, when she had met him at Heathrow.

As he pronounced Philby's name now, she paused, letting the dramatic revelation achieve its effect, then slightly tilted her head. "Are you telling us that you were the man behind Philby, Mr. Orloff?"

His voice came out strangely muffled, and he cleared his throat. "I met Philby in Cambridge, in nineteen thirty-two. I recruited him, instructed him in espionage techniques, and was his controller until his escape to Russia in nineteen sixty-three."

"How did you meet him?"

"I was a student in Trinity College myself. I was reading economics with Dennis Robertson, who was a close friend of Philby's father. I made Philby's acquaintance in the Cambridge Socialist Society, of which he was the treasurer. We had several conversations over a period of a few months. He seemed to be deeply influenced by communism." His life's secrets were coming out in short, concise sentences, like strips of unexposed film mercilessly thrust out of their protective case, instantly turning black when exposed to the outside light. "When I was satisfied that he was sincere in his convictions, I asked him to join the Soviet secret service. He agreed almost immediately.''

"You were twenty-two at the time. You were already acting under cover?''

"Yes. I was born in Russia, but I carried an American passport in the name of Alexander Carlisle. My mother lived in America, and I had ironclad references.''

He sat stiff and tense in his chair, acutely aware that he was stripping himself nude before the eyes of millions of people. In spite of the seventeen years that had passed, and the extensive debriefings by the CIA in America, he still felt he was consciously revealing an inner part of himself, shredding away the shields of secrecy, the layers of make-believe and deception that had become his second nature. He no longer believed in the cause to which he had dedicated most of his life; still, deep down inside, he felt the stinging shame of betrayal. Kim Philby was safe and happy with his fat Nina, in Moscow; still, he feared he might endanger him. Burgess was dead; Maclean, crushed by cancer; even old Blunt was gone and couldn't be watching him now. Among those who would be watching, though, was a handful of angry people who had once known him by cryptic code-names, now grinding their teeth in fury. And there were the others who had been so close to him, neighbors, friends, fellow students, business associates—seeing their good old Alex admit that he had run the most dangerous spy in the history of Britain. And somewhere, in the basement of a safehouse in some London suburb, a video recorder would be purring quietly, while the resident was already feverishly jotting down the coded message to Moscow Center. Tomorrow portions of the interview would be aired all over the United States as well. And some elderly citizens in Fort Myers would skip a heartbeat as they watched the evening news. At least he had warned Nora, and she had hurriedly left for Colorado to be with her son.

". . . No record of any close relationship between you and Philby," Lynn was saying, and he refocused his attention on her. "How did you keep it secret?"

"We used to meet at the house of a mutual friend. Later we met in—"

"Who was your mutual friend?"

"Guy Burgess."

"Did you recruit him as well?"

He nodded. "Guy Burgess was the first. I also recruited Donald Maclean."

"And Anthony Blunt? And Alan Nunn May?"

"I had nothing to do with Alan Nunn May. Blunt was recruited by Burgess, but I avoided frequent contacts with him. I preferred to control him through Philby and Burgess."

"Are you a homosexual, Mr. Orloff?" she questioned him bluntly.

She had not warned him about that question. "No, I am not," he said calmly.

"We know that Guy Burgess . . ." she started, doubt purposefully painted all over her face.

"I also know about Guy Burgess," he interrupted her. "I also know that I was once married to your mother," he added dryly.

She would not let go. "How do you feel about homosexuality?"

"We did not come here to discuss such personal opinions, Miss Kennan." The interview was turning into a curious confrontation.

"You did not mind using homosexuals as an instrument to achieve your aims, did you?" she continued. "We know that the homosexual tendencies of Burgess, Maclean, Blunt, and whoever else were very convenient for your purposes.''

''Philby was not a homosexual,'' he said, irritated. Tiny beads of sweat broke on his forehead. The set was getting too warm, with all the projectors zeroed in on him.

''You must have had other leverage over Philby,'' she said. The wall behind her was covered with blown-up photographs of Philby, Burgess, Maclean, and Byroade, cut like the pieces of a jigsaw puzzle. The centerpiece of the puzzle was a black, enigmatic silhouette with no face.

''How did you feel,'' Lynn continued, ''a sort of master puppeteer pulling the strings behind the scene?''

He did not answer. She shrugged and eyed him critically. ''All of this seems rather astounding, Mr. Orloff. For two decades England has lived in the shadow of the Philby affair. This country still cannot digest the fact that one of the most brilliant brains in her secret service—for a while he appeared to be the likely successor to the chief himself— was a Soviet spy. For two decades everybody has been looking for the man who recruited and controlled Kim Philby. The names of prominent Cambridge dons and of Soviet master spies have been advanced, and all of a sudden you emerge from your secret lair and proclaim: 'I was the one.' Fine. I assume that is the truth. But we'd like to know who else was involved in your spying, Mr. Orloff.''

''As I told you, Guy Burgess and Donald Maclean, who became high-ranking Foreign Office employees; Anthony Blunt, the future curator of the Queen's art collection and—''

''That was not my question. We all know about these four. Who were the others?''

He hesitated. "There were some others, of course, but they have all died or been apprehended since. They were mostly diplomats and Intelligence service officers."

"What were their names?"

"I don't think that's important now."

"Do you refuse to name the KGB spies in England?" she quickly threw at him.

"I did not know most of the KGB spies, Miss Kennan. I was responsible for our networks in the Foreign Office and the SIS."

"Without knowledge of the KGB resident agent in London?"

"Yes. I operated alone, on direct orders from Moscow."

She paused. "Now let me get this straight. You came here in nineteen thirty-two when you were only twenty-two years old. You had spent a few years in America establishing your cover and getting ready for the mission. In England, you went straight to Cambridge. You did not decide to do so on your own, did you?"

"No."

"So there must have been some grand design behind all that."

"Yes, there certainly was a grand design." He felt much easier talking about that. "It was called the World Socialist Revolution." His own words, once uttered, seemed to him pompous, hollow, and he did not have to watch the ironic grin that spread on her face to feel thoroughly embarrassed.

"Come on now, Mr. Orloff," the voice was biting, sarcastic. "World revolution with a handful of homosexual misfits from Cambridge? You can't be serious."

"You asked me about the original design," he said evenly. "You must keep in mind that it was conceived in the early twenties. Soviet Russia had just emerged from a bloody civil war. She had crushed the White armies— Denikin, Wrangel, Petliura, Kolchak. She had expelled the foreign armies from her territory. She was ready for the next stage in Lenin's plan—world revolution. But world revolution would not come. The French were devout Communists, but they cared more about food and sex. The Germans were too disciplined and too subservient. The Italians had found a new caesar in Mussolini. But the British seemed ripe for revolution."

"Did they indeed? What made you think so?"

"Have you ever heard of Maxim Litvinov?"

"Yes, I have," she said. "He was the Russian foreign minister in the thirties."

"Before that he had been Russian ambassador to England and had established our first subversive network in London." The eager, sardonic face of Litvinov emerged before him again, that long-ago night in Leningrad. And his mother standing beside him, her tormented visage flushed with excitement and the enormous eyes burning, alive again. "Litvinov was a man as fascinating as the devil himself. And as cunning. He grasped the political reality in England better than any of his contemporaries."

"And what was the political reality in England, Mr. Orloff?" The cool, sarcastic voice again.

He took a deep breath. "The British empire was falling apart. The old order could not last for long. The British ruling class was desperately looking for a new solution, a new faith. For a while, socialism seemed to be the answer. British intellectuals by the hundreds flocked into Labour clubs and Socialist leagues. But the first Labour government failed miserably, and Ramsay MacDonald stabbed British socialism in the back by crossing the lines and becoming prime minister of a national government. All those good people who for ten years had been devout Socialists felt suddenly betrayed. And that was communism's big chance.''

"That analysis could apply to quite a few other countries as well," Lynn observed. In the shadows behind her, studio technicians were cautiously moving. For a second Orloff glimpsed the tense face of Ted Jennings.

"But England presented us with one key advantage," he said. "Elsewhere, to take over, we had to convince the masses. England was unique because the key to her very heart was the British ruling class. A very small, very select group, with closely knit ties, informal relationships, inborn eccentricities. A few thousand people, the upper-middle-class elite, governed Britain. If we could succeed in winning them to the revolution, we would have England in the palm of our hand. And Litvinov had no trouble locating the hothouse of Britain's future leaders. A few renowned public schools—Westminster, Eton, Harrow. Then Oxford and Cambridge. The young elite of England was there, being bred and trained for the day when it would rule the country. Future ministers and members of Parliament, businessmen, scientists, philosophers, diplomats, journalists; all of them fiercely competing with each other; each one trying to be different, original, unpredictable. Each one dreaming of the Holy Grail.''

"And you were the bearer of the Holy Grail," she snapped.

He nodded gravely. "That might seem pretentious to you, but yes, that was the idea. To get to those people when they were young and rebellious. To get to them not in the guise of a condescending don or a clumsy Russian diplomat. But as one of them. Choose the best, win them to the cause, and stir them in the right direction.''

"So Maxim Litvinov sent you to America to establish your cover and then ordered you to England, as a kind of Trojan horse, to take the fortress from within."

"Yes, I was under his direct orders. A few years later I was placed under the authority of the chief of Moscow Center."

She glanced at him doubtfully. "And *alone* you were—to use your own words—to stir them in the right direction?"

He hesitated. "No, of course not."

"But you do not know of any other young men like you whom Litvinov sent to England?"

"No," he admitted. "When I left for England I was sure there were many others. I was sure that there were others operating in Cambridge, and quite a few in Oxford, maybe in other universities as well."

"But you are not so sure now," she said softly.

"No," he said. "Now I know that nobody was recruited in Oxford. And I doubt if anyone else besides my group was recruited in Cambridge either." He did not look at her now. His eyes were riveted to the multitude of power cables, resembling long sinuous snakes winding on the studio floor.

"What a tragedy," she suddenly said, very gently. "To have wasted your life like this."

It seemed to him that a sudden hush had fallen on the studio, muffling even the low drone of the cameras. "What do you mean by that?"

"It is a tragedy, isn't it, Mr. Orloff? You did not bring the revolution to England. You wound up totally alone. And instead of achieving your Communist ideals, you turned into another common spy, manipulating a handful of neurotic young men into betraying their country. What a sordid degradation for the young idealist you must have been.''

''Philby was not neurotic,'' he said to the cables.

''You really liked him, didn't you?'' she asked with new interest.

''He was my friend.''

''Which did not stop you from manipulating him as well, not as a friend but as a master spy.''

''I did not,'' he flared, raising his eyes.

''Didn't you? Didn't you tell me before we entered this studio that you went to Vienna with him in 1934? That you introduced him to Lily Hartman, a devout Communist, and you talked him into marrying her? That you did that because you needed her close to him, to strengthen his involvement?''

''He was in love with her!''

''Oh, was he? So much in love that when you sent Philby to Spain, posing as a supporter of Franco, you made him divorce her? By the way, is she still alive?''

''Yes, she lives in East Berlin.''

''Anyway,'' Lynn said, ''you went on pulling the strings, and your friend Philby obeyed and did his best to satisfy you. You steered him to the SIS, and you shaped him into your top spy in England.''

''But he believed in what he was doing, Miss Kennan.''

''Even when it involves ordering people killed? You were both responsible for quite a few deaths, weren't you?''

He did not answer.

''We'll talk about that grisly aspect of your work in our next interview,'' she said, and suddenly changed subjects. ''Did you also run Mr. Anthony Byroade?''

"No, I did not," he said, looking at his watch. The interview should end any moment now. At the far corner, two technicians were soundlessly attaching to a screen a rolling celluloid sheet, printed with the credits. Two others were monitoring the screen on a camera marked with a white number three.

"That's strange," she said. "Don't you know that the late Ambassador Byroade, who was murdered in London this week, had also been a Communist during his Cambridge years?"

"I didn't know Mr. Byroade," Orloff replied. "There were quite a few Communists in Cambridge whom I had not met."

"I thought you knew all of them," she said. Then, as if struck by a sudden idea: "Tell me, Mr. Orloff. You know KGB methods well. Will you cooperate with the authorities of this country and help them track down Byroade's murderers?"

He was taken aback. "My knowledge is rather obsolete, Miss Kennan," he said dryly. "All my contacts in this country are dried up and gone. May I remind you that I don't play this game anymore?"

She looked at him, tilting her head. "I wonder," she said. "Don't you really?"

5

"I was too hard on the old man," Lynn said thoughtfully, holding out her empty glass. "He will not forgive me for that."

Ted poured her some more wine, spilling a few drops on the tablecloth. "Nonsense," he announced. "You were super. You gave him exactly what he deserved. That's the way you had to be: tough, aggressive, knowledgeable. You were a real sensation, Lynn." He shook the last drops of the bottle into his glass and beckoned to the waiter for another one.

"Since I met you I've gotten addicted to Moulin à Vent. This one was a little bit tight, though."

She took a tissue from her bag and daubed the remnants of her studio makeup from her eyelids. "He refused to have supper with us. I think he was very upset."

Ted shrugged. "Let him be upset. I couldn't care less, believe me."

"You really don't like him, do you?" She pushed aside her plate, almost untouched.

"No, I don't like him and I don't mind his knowing it." He raised his face, looking at her with a frown. His eyes were narrowed, slightly veiled. "The man is a damn spy with blood on his hands, turned traitor against his own people. Should I admire him for that?" His voice sounded unusually loud in the discreet elegance of the Savoy Grill. "And I am free to dislike anybody I want," he added needlessly.

"It's more than that, isn't it?" she said slowly, watching his face. She saw anger in his black eyes, and his mouth had tightened. Something far deeper than instinctive reluctance haunted Ted Jennings.

"Why do you say that?"

"It's strange that you feel so strongly about the old man. People in this country have a rather perverse attitude toward spies. They did not even care to prosecute Blunt. And Philby seems to be one of the darlings of England. Did you read Graham Greene's preface to his memoirs? Greene spoke of him with such affection he might have been a national hero." She quoted from memory: " 'Who among us has not committed treason to something or someone more important than a country?' " She paused, trying to catch Ted's eyes. "Greene seems willing not only to absolve him but to pin a medal on his chest. How did he phrase it? 'Philby was serving a cause and not himself, and so my old liking for him comes back. . . .' Nobody protested against those effusions, Ted. Nobody reminded Greene that Philby was a traitor, responsible for so many cruel deaths."

"But he *was* responsible, wasn't he?" Ted muttered with abrupt vehemence.

She judged it wiser to keep silent. But her eyes did not leave his face and he finally capitulated. "I never spoke to you about my father," he said quietly.

She winced, taken by surprise. "Your father? I only know he died when you were very young."

"Seven." He planted his elbows on the table, cupping his chin in both hands, his eyes boring into hers. "I barely remember him. Mother says he was a very conservative sort of chap: Kipling, Conrad, king and country, that sort of stuff. He was a linguist and an expert on the Balkans. Bulgaria, Yugoslavia, Albania, you know. Used to teach at Oxford, All Souls College. In nineteen forty, after Dunkirk, Bill Stephenson talked him into joining the Special Operations executive. He was parachuted twice into Yugoslavia, on liaison missions with Tito. Saw quite a bit of action but came back without a scratch. Mother still keeps his photograph with Tito hanging over the fireplace at Uckfield."

"I didn't know he was such a warrior."

"He wasn't. After the war he returned to his books, but was recalled a couple of times for some cloak-and-dagger missions in Yugoslavia." He indulged in a quick, wan smile. "Father was quite active in the negotiations that led to Tito's split from the Soviet bloc."

She nodded, embarrassed by the suppressed pain in Ted's chalky face.

"In nineteen forty-nine he left on a secret assignment. It was winter, there was frost on the windows. They picked him up sometime before midnight. He came up to my room before he left. He had that special smell, mild pipe tobacco and aftershave. His jacket was made of very coarse tweed. He was a very gentle man, very quiet, and I adored him. He never came back."

Spontaneously, she reached for his hand. "He was killed?"

Ted's fingers were limp and cold. He ignored her question. "The CIA and the SIS had mounted a joint attempt to start a revolution against the Communist regime in Albania. The liaison officer between the British and the American services was Kim Philby. He personally supervised the departure of the task force—a few scores of secret agents and Albanian leaders. In Albania, local and Russian secret police were waiting for them. Some were shot as soon as they landed. Others tried to run for their lives. Nobody survived."

She withdrew her hand as a shiver ran up her body. "And Orloff . . ." she started.

He nodded, and she looked away, unable to face his tight, frozen smile. "So, don't get too angry with me if I don't always behave," he said softly.

An awkward silence descended upon them. He displayed sudden interest in two elderly men in black ties who dejectedly munched their mutton chops at a corner table. All of a sudden he turned back to Lynn, trying to sound jovial. "Let's not talk about that, okay? Tonight is your night. You did a splendid job. You should have seen that switchboard, with all those lights blinking. I thought it was going to explode. And wait for tomorrow's papers!" He watched the agile waiter replenish his glass. "THE MAN BEHIND PHILBY. What a headline! Tony Wyatt from the *Times* called twice, not asking but begging for an interview. And that cow from the *Guardian* . . . the Toland woman—"

"Agnes Toland?"

"Agnes, yes. 'You must do this for me, Teddy boy,' " he mimicked. " 'Wasn't I the one who launched you?' "

"Was she?" Lynn asked politely, her mind still locked

on the image of a little boy in a room with frosted windows and a lingering scent of mild tobacco. Ted had grown up haunted by his father's death. No wonder he had become obsessed with Soviet spies and moles in Britain.

"Rubbish." He started counting on his fingers, his face slowly coloring. "Everybody wants an interview. The agencies, UPI, AP, Reuters. The *Mail*. The *Guardian*. The American networks. *Le Monde*. BBC radio. And the *Telegraph*—they've got an entire commando squadron lying in ambush at the Churchill. I told them we might hold a press conference, broadcast live, after the third segment. Till then—*nyet!* Comrade Orloff is our exclusive property."

"And if the comrade decides otherwise?" A middle-aged couple entered the restaurant. The woman stared at Lynn, then urgently whispered to her husband.

Ted chuckled. "See? You are a celebrity already." He drained his glass, and his carefree grin made his whole face light up. He seemed completely recovered, the grim memories of his childhood fading away. "Orloff won't decide otherwise. He cares about you, he came for your sake, and he is still fascinated by you. Just as I am," he added all of a sudden, firmly placing his hand over hers.

"Are you really?" she said wryly.

"Yes, and I don't want this evening to end with the dessert."

She glanced at him with an ironical smile. "What does this mean?"

"It means I like you very much indeed, young lady." The black eyes were suddenly intense and very sober.

She did not remove her hand. His disclosures about his father had moved her deeply, but the game he was playing now had totally different rules. "You have had a couple of drinks too many, Mr. Producer."

He did not smile back. "I might have," he conceded, his grip on her hand tightening. "But I know exactly what I want."

"You want me to take you home," she said, withdrawing her hand. *"Niet, Tovaritch* Jennings."

"And why not?" He shifted his gaze to his plate, and idly stabbed a solitary green pea with his fork. "I like you very much," he said without looking at her, "and I believe you like me too. Is it because I am married?"

"Maybe," she said, rather uncertain.

"Married men are out of bounds?"

She hesitated. "I have been with married men before." She did not like the turn of the conversation, yet she had known from the day she met him that they would reach this stage, sooner or later. "I did not mind, really. It was their problem, not mine. They could give me, at a particular moment, something I wanted. And I don't mean sex. Or only sex. But it was never more than a casual thing, not even an affair."

"Wait a moment," he started smiling nervously. "I did not suggest—"

"Exactly. But I do like you, Ted. And I am very possessive. And I might—I say might—want to go farther down the road with you." She waited a moment, then continued in a different tone: "Now, as far as dessert is concerned. . . ."

He had suddenly become very still, the forehead wrinkled, the black eyes glued to her face. "And what," he said in a low voice, "what if I were ready to take that risk?"

"Oh, come on, Ted," she said briskly, "I've been through all that before, believe me."

"Not with me, you haven't. I might—I said might—be serious."

Panic flickered through her mind as she blindly groped for a verbal weapon. "Don't give me that trash," she said to him with a frown. "You'll make me cry."

But he had that same damn look on his face, and his hand found hers again. There was warmth in his black eyes. The little boy in the dark frosty room. "Try me," he said. "Don't be sarcastic or vulgar. You won't fool me. I've begun to know you a little."

She averted her face. "Please, Ted," she said stiffly, rolling the stem of her empty glass between her fingers, "I hate this conversation. Please."

But he did not budge, and his voice was so persistent. "Try me," he said again. His hand was strong, reassuring.

Hours later, he raised his head from the hollow of her neck, where his teeth had left painful, delicious marks. She was perspiring, her shallow breath slowing down, still feeling his hardness inside her. The room was dark but she had got used to it; and she perceived the roguish smile that settled on his swarthy face.

"May I ask you something?" he murmured.

She put her hand on his lips. "Don't," she said, tracing with the tip of her forefinger the contour of his mouth. "Don't. I know exactly what you want to ask." His lithe body felt good against hers, his skin smooth.

"Tell me," he said, playfully biting her finger. His arms, which were anchored behind her back, pressed her tighter to him.

"Ted, you're smothering me," she moaned. Then: "You'll ask me if you weren't right before, in the restaurant, when you tried to talk me into bed."

"And. . . ." His head plunged again in the hollow of her neck, the bristle on his jaw scratching her skin.

"That's the first question a vain man usually asks. The macho question, subtly delivered. You wouldn't ask: Was I good? Did you enjoy it? That would be too banal. So you'll snuggle and cuddle and sigh and ask: Wasn't I right? Didn't I tell you it would be wonderful? Pure magic?"

"That's not what I wanted to ask." His hand moved down her body and she grew taut involuntarily.

"Oh no?" she whispered, returning his kiss, her fingers plowing through the thick hair on the nape of his neck. "What was it then?"

"Was I good?" he blurted, and she smiled.

"You know what?" Her hands slid gently down his back, along the sides of his body, resting on his hips, locking him against her. "You were surprisingly good." She paused. "For an Englishman."

"What the hell is that supposed to mean?" he said, disengaging himself and rolling on his back. She followed his movement and bent over him, her lips hungry again.

"You Englishmen don't know exactly what you are supposed to do with a woman in your bed." She raised her hand and tossed back some loose strands of hair that floated before her eyes. "You know it is rumored to be divine. So you are very good, as far as preproduction and trimmings are concerned. You might order a bottle of champagne or white wine, sometimes caviar and hors d'oeuvres. You might choose the right music and the proper lighting. Heaven. But when the moment of truth comes—you panic. 'What am I supposed to do?' the Englishman asks himself. 'Where's the fun? Did I miss it?' So you storm through the motions, doing your thing like a blitzkrieg. The charge of the light brigade. The poor woman is dizzy with champagne, mellowed by soft lights, spellbound with the music. And then—*nada!*"

He tried to look at her face, but her mouth was back on his chest, moving downward. "You bitch," he said in mock anger. "This is the most libelous, gross, vicious, ignoble generalization I've ever heard."

She briefly raised her head. "But I said you were different." She suddenly didn't want to jest anymore. "I'd like to say I enjoyed it very much, Ted, but enjoy doesn't seem to be the right word. I loved being with you."

"I loved that too," he said softly, his hands moving gently over her shoulders. "In spite of being English," he added impishly. "And in spite of—"

They were both jolted by the sudden ring of the telephone. Lynn swore under her breath, then reached over him to the night table. He felt her firm breasts against his chest.

"Hello? Yes, Lynn Kennan speaking. Yes, this is she. Who is it? What time is it?" She didn't identify the agitated voice immediately. "Oh, hello, Patrick." She covered the mouthpiece with her left hand and turned toward Ted. "It's Patrick O'Neale," she whispered.

He propped himself on his elbows, startled. He could think of no reason for Patrick to call Lynn at home in the middle of the night. The deputy director of Thames was a rather placid man who rarely deviated from his routine, even when a sensational scoop was in the making.

"Yes, I'm awake," she was saying. "It's quite all right, really. Where are you? Still at the studio?"

Ted could faintly hear the voice of the deputy director crackling in the receiver. Suddenly Lynn's body stiffened and she sat upright on the bed. "Good Lord," she said, inhaling deeply. "I'll come right away. Don't worry, I'll find Ted."

As the line went dead, she turned to him.

"What's wrong?" he asked. Even in the darkness, he could sense the pallor that had settled on her face.

"He was calling from the hospital," she said. "Orloff has been shot."

Orloff had abruptly gotten to his feet as soon as the set manager made the flat, cutting gesture with his left hand. He had walked quickly off the set, averting his eyes from the floodlights, all but tripping against the snaking cables on the floor. A short, fat young woman wearing a bizarre headset and smelling of sweat and cheap cologne had run after him, mumbling apologies, and unclipped the tiny microphone from his tie. He had seen faces, smiles, moving figures, and heard a few cheers of satisfaction. On his left a small group clustered around Lynn, showering congratulations upon her while she stood up, smoothing her skirt. Ted Jennings had called to him from across the set, but he pretended not to hear. Some people spoke to him; a tall bearded man shook his hand vigorously. Orloff did not stop, however. He was driven by one urge: to escape from there. Still, he forced himself to smile and nod amiably. You will not let them divine your feelings, he kept telling himself. You will not give them that satisfaction.

She had caught up with him at the elevator. "Mr. Orloff! Mr. Orloff, wait, please!" Her face was flushed and her eyes glistened. She brushed her hair from her face in a gesture that was becoming familiar. "The interview was excellent," she said breathlessly. "Everybody is very excited. Will you join me and Ted for supper at the Savoy Grill? Please?"

He had shaken his head. "No. I am going back to my hotel."

"You are angry with me," she had said ingenuously,

staring at him closely with that grave, candid look of hers. "You feel I was unfair to you."

"Good night, Lynn," he had said, and the elevator doors had noiselessly come between them. In the lobby, a few employees gawked at him. Through the tall glass doors he could see a small crowd starting to assemble in the street. The security guard, a towering, red-faced Welshman with a bulbous nose and bad teeth, stared at him in open hostility.

"Could you get me a cab, please?" Orloff said. On the portable television set in the guard's booth, two Roman matrons were moaning in delight, spooning their Heinz tomato soup.

The Welshman hesitated for a moment, repeatedly licking his rubbery lips and stubbornly staring off in the other direction. He got to his feet, reached for the phone, then sat down again, suddenly reaching a decision. "I ain't paid to fetch cabs for Communist spies," he blurted, his forehead glistening with sweat. Now that he had said his piece, he thrust his chin up belligerently, proud of his audacity.

Orloff nodded and walked into the street. The crowd parted to let him through. He could sense their hatred. Or was it his imagination? A young man behind him raised his voice, but was shushed. Orloff, hatless in the damp cold, stepped off the sidewalk, turning his back to the crowd. He could feel their eyes boring into his back and knew some of them were experiencing the savage satisfaction of having him, the enemy, alone and within their grasp. A few cars drove past him, slowing down as their headlights caught him in their glare. He did not mind waiting. The cool air and the sudden bursts of icy wind were definitely more pleasant than the small lens of the camera and Lynn's blunt questions posed in Virginia's warm voice.

A cab stopped and discharged a couple of middle-aged men who hurried into the ITV building. "The Churchill Hotel," he said to the driver. "Go by way of Oxford Street." The driver shrugged and turned on the meter. As the cab pulled away, he turned back in time to see the Special Branch car smoothly emerge behind a line of parked vehicles. Farther down the road, another car set out, taking much too long to switch on its lights.

He sat upright in the dank-smelling interior of the cab. The floor was littered with flattened cigarette butts. The enamel sign, warning the passengers to keep their feet off the seats, was broken in two, its remaining half swinging from its loosened bolt like a pendulum. While the streets and lights of London paraded before him, he tried to clear his mind of tonight's experience. He should have expected it to happen. She was Virginia's daughter indeed, but she had no obligation to him, and certainly no reason to like him or to care about his feelings. In a way, she was making him pay for what she felt he had done to her mother, and even to her. He should not have come to London, of course. He knew that now with certitude. But it was true what they said, that old people mellow with the years, and it was his only way to reach back into his past, to revive the memory of Virginia.

On an impulse he decided not to go back to the hotel. Not yet. As they stopped at a red light in Oxford Street, he pulled aside the sliding window of the driver's cabin, dropped a couple of bills on the seat beside him, and, at the very moment when the light changed to green, opened the right-hand door and plunged into the crowd. The car following his own could not stop, pressed by the vehicles lined up behind it. By the time it crossed the intersection, braked, and spilled its occupants onto the sidewalk, Orloff had disappeared and was on his own.

He did not know exactly where he wanted to go. He let the chilly gusts sweeping Oxford Street hound him all the way up to Marble Arch. The underground passage was dim and deserted, and his quick footsteps echoed in the stone-covered vault. Beyond the grilled fence, the dark shapes of the park whispered in the wind. Virginia used to haunt the park at night, alone, pretending she had it all to herself. She had asked him once to come with her at dawn, to see the early-morning mist rise and fade away. Like the last breath of the dying night, she had said; and even that banal remark had sounded so moving, coming from her. Memories—punctual, impatient, overwhelming—dutifully emerged from the past and he abruptly turned away, refusing the pilgrimage to the tombstones of his life. He was almost grateful to the stout Greek whore who brought him back to the present as she strolled toward him, smiling beneath her bleached moustache.

The first snowflakes fell as he hurried past a late-night eatery on Edgware Road. Inside, a group of Thais were soundlessly giggling around a long Formica table. Upper Berkeley Street was dark, hostile. A skeletal Hindu, laboriously locking the ornate door of The Pearl of Punjab, looked at Orloff suspiciously as he caught a whiff of stale curry. Before he reached the corner of Portman Square, the snow had turned into a pale, thick curtain, occasionally torn by the onslaughts of the sharp-edged wind. A black car slowly drove past him, leaving tracks on the virgin snow.

He heard the running footsteps as the elaborate façade of Home House floated out of the dark. The bullet caught him in mid-motion, as he was turning back in the direction of the sound. He distinctly heard shouts, a few dry cracks, and the sudden roar of a car engine. The damp sidewalk closed vertically on him; the huge snowflakes froze in the dazzling brilliance of approaching headlights; then everything became dark again and the acrid smell of black tobacco descended upon him, nauseating, disquieting, yet oddly familiar.

6

THE PUNGENT SMELL was still there, thick and rancid, when he regained consciousness. He smelled it even before he could distinguish the objects in the small white room: the hospital bed, the tubular stand with the infusion, the cocoon-like dressing that immobilized his whole left side. It was not the odor of a freshly lit cigarette but the stale, clinging reek that permeated the clothes and tainted the breath of the thickset figure in the chair beside his bed. As his eyes painfully adjusted to the light and focused, he noticed the deep furrows in the man's face, enhanced by a reddish stubble turning white under the chin and along the heavy jowls. This was the Special Branch man he had seen at Heathrow, the one who had asked him about Anthony Byroade. The pallid eyes, bloodshot and weary, seemed even smaller than before. Another man sat on a chair by the door; he was frail and long-limbed, owl eyes peering out from beneath huge round glasses, tufts of discolored plumage strewn upon the pinkish top of his head. His unblinking round eyes, magnified by the glasses, studied Orloff while his long, narrow fingers anchored by the thumbs in the waistcoat pockets, beat a soft rhythm on their owner's belly.

"I am Chief Superintendent Hastings," the Special Branch man said in a hoarse voice that sounded too loud in the tiny hospital room. "We have met before. My colleague is Mr. Brathwaite from MI-5." Owl-face nodded stiffly, his fingers abruptly ceasing their beat.

"You were rather lucky," Hastings went on, absently brushing his knuckles against the bristle on his jaw. "A flesh wound in your left shoulder. No bones broken. The bullet was extracted in surgery. A proper operation."

Orloff's mouth was thick, sticky, a bitter taste clinging to his palate. He was not going to ask them for a glass of water, though. He nodded his head, struggling out of his drowsiness.

"Did you see the man who fired at you?" Hastings asked.

Orloff swallowed twice before speaking. He looked up at the low ceiling, trying to collect his thoughts. "I heard running footsteps . . ." he began, hesitating. His words came out slurred, and his throat rasped painfully when he spoke.

"You heard my footsteps," Hastings said impatiently. "The man who shot you got out of a car."

"A car?" Yes, there had been a car, he remembered. He asked, inconsequently: "What time is it?"

Brathwaite made a great show of consulting a thin gold wristwatch, holding it between thumb and forefinger. "Eight forty-three." He had a cold, educated voice. "A.M.," he added unnecessarily.

Orloff turned back to Hastings. "Can you tell me how it happened?" As he moved, a sharp pain shot through his right thigh. That must be the fall, he thought, remembering the cold, hard sidewalk smashing into him.

The door opened and a willowy black nurse stuck her head in. "Good, you are awake," she said cheerfully, an easy smile touching her generous mouth. "I'll be back." She left the door half-open, and Hastings, who was about to say something, waited in uneasy silence. In a moment, the nurse reappeared at the door, holding a tall glass of water and a tiny stainless steel bowl containing several pills. She danced in gracefully, ignoring the two dark figures perched on their chairs like ravens at a funeral. "Good morning," she said again, warmly, in the musical accent of the West Indies. "You had a good night's sleep, and in a moment I'll get you some breakfast." He drank the tepid water gratefully. "You are a fortunate man," she chirped, as she adjusted his bed into a half-sitting position. "There is a beautiful young woman outside waiting to see you. I'll let her in as soon as you are ready." She checked the plastic infusion bottle. "Anything else I can get you? No? Here, if you need anything, press the button and I'll be right back. Or maybe you prefer the young lady?" She giggled and minced out, royally indifferent to Orloff's visitors.

"They were in a car," Hastings said, resuming the conversation where it had been interrupted. "Might have picked you out at Thames and followed you. I doubt that, though." He had a peculiar way of speaking—short, clipped phrases. "I was in the car directly behind your taxi. If they had, they lost you at Oxford Street. Where you got out of the cab. They must have driven directly to your hotel. Started making rounds in the streets adjoining Portman

Square, expecting you to show up. Which you did. They saw you at Upper Berkeley Street and stopped. The gunman jumped out of the car and fired at you. When they saw me approaching, they took off. Threw the gun away. We got it.''

"How did you get there?" Orloff's voice was still unsteady. "You also made rounds?"

"I was behind you the whole time," Hastings said matter-of-factly. "You didn't fool me at Oxford Street." He produced a bulky package from the pocket of his raincoat, and took a big automatic pistol out of the transparent plastic bag. "Tokarev 7.62," he said. "No fingerprints. They fired three bullets at you. You were hit by the first. If they had not been interrupted, you would be dead now." The gruff voice was emotionless, factual. Hastings was not trying to brag, Orloff decided.

"Chief superintendents do tailing jobs nowadays?" he asked Hastings, looking at him blankly.

Brathwaite shifted uncomfortably on his seat, and asked Orloff, "Any idea why they didn't use the electric pistol? The one they used to kill Byroade. Had they shot you with a dumdum bullet, they would have killed you."

Orloff shot a glance at Hastings, who was looking at him speculatively, the gun still in his lap. "The electric Avenger has an effective range of barely one or two yards, Mr. Brathwaite," Orloff replied, painfully shifting his leg. "They shot Byroade on the embankment, with nobody around. They could not expect to get so close to me in Portman Square or Upper Berkeley Street. This district is quite crowded, even at night."

Hastings nodded to himself, and for a second Orloff had a fleeting sensation of complicity. "You must have seen the gunman, though," he said to the chief superintendent.

Hastings nodded. "Just a quick glance before he jumped back into the car."

"Did you see his face?"

"No."

"He could not have been very far from you," Orloff insisted.

"He was wearing a hat," Hastings disclosed, unwillingly. He was not the kind to volunteer information. "His face was in shadow." Brathwaite was leaning forward, and Orloff had the impression he was hearing these details for the first time.

"Was he a short man?" Orloff asked on a sudden impulse.

Hastings's eyes narrowed and he slowly tilted his head to the right, closing one eye, as if he were looking through the sights of a rifle. His whole body exuded suspicion. "Now why do you ask that?" he grunted.

"The man who shot Byroade was a short man. Your own reports established that, by the bullet's angle of penetration."

Hastings remained in the same position for a moment, scowling. Then he got up, dropped the Tokarev into its plastic bag, and thrust the bag into his raincoat pocket. "I think we should be leaving, Derek," he said to Brathwaite. "Mr. Orloff is entitled to his breakfast."

Brathwaite was on his feet, pulling his waistcoat down, nervously touching the knot of his tie. "We are reconsidering the question of your further sojourn on British soil," Brathwaite said in a transparent attempt to assert his position over Hastings's. "In the meantime, would you apply for protection?"

Orloff grinned sourly. "You have been tailing me since

I got off the plane. What better protection could I ask for?"

Brathwaite returned a fixed stare, then nodded and walked out.

Hastings stopped at the door, an unlit Gauloise already dangling from his lower lip. "The man was rather short," he conceded.

Lynn walked in almost immediately, carrying his breakfast tray. "Where is the nurse?" he asked before she even spoke.

"You need her?" She looked hurt.

Yes, he wanted to say. She is the only friendly person I've met since I came to London. But Lynn's face looked distraught and her hair in disorder. She must have spent the night behind that door. "That's all right," he said. "Thank you."

She was digging in her bag. "Would you like a towelette? To freshen your face?"

The moist paper napkin had a scent of fresh lemon. "How kind of you," he said, and she frowned, trying to discern a note of irony in his voice.

"I am sorry," she started. "Terribly, terribly—"

He raised his good hand. "Please, don't."

"If you had come with us last night, it would not have happened."

"There was no reason for me to come."

She bit her lip. "I am sorry," she repeated, looking at the wall behind him. "I . . . I seem to mess up everything. First Byroade, and now you. Yesterday, on the set, I was only trying to do my job."

He did not answer, pretending to be busy with his

breakfast. He suddenly realized he was hungry and wolfed down the tasteless food, secretly pleased with her misery.

"Ted left a half hour ago," she said sullenly. "He was urgently needed at the office. He asked me to tell you—"

"I know. That he is very sorry. You'll convey my gratitude."

She fell silent. It would be in order for her to start crying now, he reflected. But she did not. She sat primly on her chair, watching him gravely. "Would you like some more tea?" she asked. Then, unexpectedly: "How many times have you been married?"

He had difficulty keeping up with her sudden transitions. "Three times. Why?"

"Would you mind talking about it?"

"If you wish," he said slowly. He was rather amused. An old-fashioned man like him would never understand the mysterious workings of a woman's mind, and of this one in particular. "I married my first and second wives on orders from Moscow Center."

"Just like that?" A quick smile. He wondered if she was trying to placate him by making him talk about his past.

"I am not sure you'll understand," he said. "I was not free to make certain decisions. I had agreed to that way of life and—"

"Never mind," she said eagerly. "Go on."

"My first wife was English, a pianist. We were married for three, almost four years."

She interrupted him again. "What was her name?"

"Anne. Anne Haldane. She used to travel all over Europe for her concerts. That was very convenient because she was my courier. She brought me instructions and carried back reports." He paused. "She was a nice girl,

77

very warm, very compassionate." He always thought of her as a girl, never as a woman, he realized. There was something waiflike, even ethereal about Anne. The thin, supple, small-breasted body; the grave cameo face with the huge curious eyes; the long, brown hair plaited in intricate, old-fashioned tresses on top of her head, making her look like a medieval maiden; the silent, shadowy movements, so self-effacing, so shy. And the sudden power, the passionate abandon when she would all but plunge into the enormous concert piano. When he came to watch her from backstage, he was always captivated by her delicate profile, so intent, so noble, as it floated above the triumphant tides of her music.

"You loved her?" Lynn was looking at him curiously.

He did not answer immediately. "No, not really. But we got along very well. We were both devoted to a cause, we had our assignment, and marriage was a perfect cover." He rested his head back on the pillow. "I liked her. I went with her a few times to Europe. She was quite active in the Philby operation for a while."

"You had no children?"

"I never had any children, Lynn," he said dryly. "As a matter of fact, Anne wanted a child. There was a time when she became quite obsessed with the idea. But our control said no. She would not have been able to travel as before, and that was what they needed her for."

"What happened to her?"

The sedation was wearing off and a dull pain started throbbing in his chest. "We got orders to divorce. The reason they gave us was that she was under suspicion, and her cover was about to be blown."

She brushed aside her hair, frowning. "But you don't believe that?"

"No. They wanted her out, and she was lucky to get out alive." He noticed the puzzled look in Lynn's eyes. "You've never heard of the purges of 'thirty-eight, have you? When Stalin and Beria massacred thousands of Party leaders, intellectuals, Red Army generals. Many of the best Soviet agents in Europe were recalled to Moscow and liquidated. Among them was Leonid Tolokonsky, the first secretary in the Soviet embassy in London. An old-guard Bolshevik. He had been the chief of Soviet espionage in Britain. Another one was Theodore Maly. A Hungarian. Cunning, sly, and a fanatical Communist. Actually he was a renegade Catholic priest. He had taken over from Tolokonsky in London and later moved to Paris and Vienna. Anne knew both of them, and quite a few other operatives. Well, in the middle of nineteen thirty-eight, Tolokonsky and Maly and a score of others were urgently summoned back to Russia and shot."

"What for?"

"What for?" Her question surprised him for a second. "Treason, deviating from Party line, Trotskyism, whatever. There was never a shortage of pretexts in Moscow. Anne was purged in a more gentle way. Just ordered to divorce and disappear. I think she is still alive somewhere, under a false name."

"And her music?"

"She was told to give it up," he snapped, "so she did." Why should he tell Lynn what really happened, how the sweet, candid girl had been lured to Moscow together with Maly and Tolokonsky and so many others. And shot in the dreary cellars of Lubyanka prison. For him, who for so long had not known the truth, the waifish child-woman had over the years become a sort of *princesse lointaine*, mysterious and beguiling and ever young. He had believed the pack of lies he was repeating to Lynn now, he had truly believed them till the day he had met a certain defector in the CIA's debriefing center in Virginia. The man had said to him: "I saw her die."

Orloff had had nothing to do with her death, of course. Still, a strange uneasiness took hold of him now, and he felt unable to tell Lynn the truth about Anne's death. It was a sort of guilty feeling—for not warning his wife against going to Moscow; for accepting on face value the laconic report from Center about her transfer, for never trying to find her, to get in touch with her. Or maybe he had instinctively guessed what might have happened and buried his head in the sand, running away from the truth, acting as Center wanted him to: docile, obedient, never asking questions.

Lynn shifted on her chair, and Orloff brushed aside the memories. "Until I came into the open," he went on, changing the subject, "the British secret services believed that Maly and Tolokonsky had recruited and run Philby." He shook his head. "If they had, they would be alive today. Moscow would never have touched Philby's controls. He was the crown jewel of the service, and nobody would have dared to upset him in any way."

"And your second wife?" Lynn was doggedly following her course.

"That one was a disaster," he smiled wanly. "A real one. Sweet Emma. A Swiss behemoth. They needed her badly. World War Two had just begun, and a Swiss passport could be very handy. But she was a monster. I couldn't stand her. Thank God she panicked when the spy scare started in England." He smiled again, and Lynn, after a brief hesitation, did the same, uncertainly. "I must confess that I helped Emma, wholeheartedly, in that direction. Frightened her to death with stories about spies being arrested and interrogated in horrid prisons. She cracked up and implored control to let her go. She could not carry on, she said, the British were after her. Moscow Center could not afford an hysterical woman, even a Swiss one. So they sent her back to her cuckoo clocks, and I was the happiest man on earth. We had been married for less than a year.''

''Did you sleep with her?''

He looked up, startled. In her face, however, he saw nothing but spontaneous, boundless curiosity. ''Yes, I did,'' he said. *Tried* would have been a more appropriate word, he felt. ''But don't ask me such questions anymore, Lynn. I don't belong to your generation. I can't take this kind of talk.''

She smiled, shaking her head. ''I did not mean to be rude. I was just curious, that's all. I wanted to know how that . . . arrangement worked. I've never been married to a Russian spy.''

''Your mother was.''

''Tell me about that,'' she said quickly, red patches of color suddenly flaring up on her cheeks. He immediately knew that all her former questions had been intended to steer him to this very point, to make him talk about her mother. She was too proud, too hostile, or maybe too shy to ask him the question that had been on her mind since the moment she had met him at Heathrow the previous Saturday. A question that for her was a mystery, a source of constant wonder: he and her mother. How did it happen? What made it work? *Did* it work? He felt a surge of pity for her. He was not the only one in this room on a pilgrimage to his past. He and Lynn had something in common. They were both striving, each in their own way, to go back in time in their search for Virginia.

"I met your mother in Paris, in nineteen forty-eight," he said, determined to stick to the bare facts. "I used to go there often, mostly to buy paintings, sometimes to rendez-vous with my control. She was living in the Latin Quarter." Lynn nodded knowingly. "She was very involved with the Montparnasse crowd, but I had never seen her before. I met her at a *vernissage,* the opening of a Magritte exhibition. I was totally bewitched by Magritte at the time."

Lynn was leaning forward in eager anticipation. But he knew he would never tell her what he felt that night, when he saw Virginia with her back to Magritte's *La durée peignardée.* There were many people around her, and the sleazy, repulsive Frederic Lacombe moving near her, touching her possessively. At her sight he had felt an odd tensing of his whole body, a sudden physical desire, almost a pain in his insides. He had devoured her with his eyes but had not dared to approach her. He had kept her in sight most of the evening, drinking heavily, reluctant to get too near her, to talk to her. Afraid of the sound of her voice, afraid she might open her mouth and the magic would be gone. When he had finally maneuvered himself behind her, feigning special interest in *La durée,* he had heard her say something to the old lecher, and had suddenly felt grateful. For that husky, sensual voice that did not betray her.

Lacombe had introduced them: "Alex Carlisle, a good friend and a great lover of art. Virginia Fielding, an up-and-coming artist." Orloff had barely suppressed his urge to slap the lewd old man when the latter had whispered to him hoarsely: "*Bien balancée, la petite Americaine. Je vais me la farçir ce soir.*" I'll screw her tonight. The

vulgarity of the tone, of the words, had made his blood
boil. He had asked her about her style, her paintings,
gotten the address of her atelier, promised to come and see
her work. But the whole time he felt convinced she must
not be an artist, not a good one. A woman like her could
not exist on the working side of the canvas. An artist
should have no beauty, no physical appeal. She must be
like a fashion-house model, one of those undernourished,
gaunt creatures who could serve only as hangers for a
designer's clothes. Not somebody to fill them with a perfect body. And make the stubby matrons, the fat, the
angular, the millionaires' plain wives feel so jealous and
humiliated they would refuse to buy the $10,000 gowns
that would make them look like disguised monkeys. Nature couldn't allow a woman as fascinating as Virginia to
be a good artist, for the interest would always focus on
her, not on what she was doing. She had left with Lacombe,
and he had gone to visit her the next morning after a
sleepless night.

"Your mother was a lousy artist," he said, watching
Lynn.

"I know," Lynn agreed.

"*Tu as perdu la tête*," Lacombe had told him. Or
perhaps it was Lasserre. That was true, he had virtually
lost his head over her. In a few days all Montparnasse
knew of Alex Carlisle's sudden passion. He had become
enraptured by Virginia's beauty, her vitality, by the way
she was devouring life, consuming it to the fullest. Her
curiosity had no limits and was equaled only by her lust to
see and experience everything. Virginia's world was clear
and limpid, like a child's; it was populated by real and
imaginary adventures, polarized between good and bad,
friends and enemies. She recognized no shadings, no

nuances. Colors were vivid, black and white, flaming red, poison green, deep blue, yolky yellow, as in those horrid paintings of hers about which he had lied so desperately, so brazenly at first. She had been the only woman he had ever wanted to possess.

"I behaved very stupidly," he said, rather on the defensive. "I married your mother without ever asking Moscow for an authorization. Which I would never have received, of course," he added.

"That sounds like rebellion to me," Lynn said. Her eyes were glued to his face. She guessed there was much more to this story than the dry, factual account that the old man was cautiously phrasing. "They let you get away with it?"

"My control should have recalled me to Moscow and thrown me in prison," he conceded. "It just turned out that I was indispensable at that time. The cold war had just started, Philby was climbing up the ladder—first as head of the SIS station in Istanbul, then as CIA liaison in Washington—and they could not do without me. So they had to learn to live with Virginia."

"And you succeeded in fooling her for seven years."

"Lynn," he reminded her softly. "Since the age of seventeen I had been trained to conceal my feelings and my true identity. It became a kind of a second nature to me. I had always had to control myself and play a role. So if you want to know how it worked"—he stuck his chin forward—"I admit it. I lied to your mother twenty-four hours a day."

"You must have been very much in love with her," she said unexpectedly.

He looked away, disturbed. "Was I so obvious?" As

she did not answer, he asked quickly: "She never spoke to you about me? Even before she died?"

The black nurse walked in without knocking, closed the door, and approached his bed, nodding at Lynn with sisterly familiarity. "Listen," she started in a conspiratorial tone, her face beaming with secret knowledge. "I was told that you are not to see anybody today, see? But there is a lady who insists on visiting you, and she seems quite respectable to me. She says her name is Jane Byroade. The widow of Mr. Anthony Byroade, she says."

Part Two

7

JANE BYROADE, a skeletal, stooping figure in an ill-fitting tan coat, seemed so deeply distressed as she stood in the middle of the small room, Orloff felt the urge to pat her drooping shoulders and take her reassuringly by her clenched, meager hands. This Lynn was already doing, gently leading the aging woman to the second chair, smiling at the plain, long face, placing her bag on the white table to her right. But Jane Byroade remained stiff and tense, nervously touching her bun of graying, wispy hair, readjusting her dark glasses, fidgeting with a crumpled tissue she took from her pocket.

"I am Alexander Orloff. Thank you for coming," he said, hoping to ease her disarray. Her square forehead was mottled with dark moles sprayed over the thinly plucked eyebrows. Two bitter creases descended from her small nose to the edges of her mouth. Her upper lip, which she was repeatedly wiping now with the tissue, was etched with tiny cracks that broke the contour of her mouth, stamping her face with the presage of old age. Her beige-and-brown scarf was expensive, Hermès, as was her bag, which matched her cashmere coat and the brown high-heeled shoes. Still, nothing could dispel the air of drabness and misery she carried about her. Orloff knew unhappiness when he saw it, and constant, profound pain, long antecedent to the recent loss that had afflicted her.

"If you don't feel well," she breathed quickly, pressing her knees and reaching for her bag, ready to leave, "maybe I'll come tomorrow."

"I am fine, really." He managed a smile. "I was shocked to learn about your husband's death."

"I saw you on television last night," Jane Byroade said. She turned to Lynn. "You are Miss Kennan, aren't you?"

Lynn, who had retreated to her chair, nodded morosely. "Yes. I met your husband last week. I sent you a letter by messenger on Saturday."

"Yes, of course. How stupid of me." She removed her glasses, then put them on again, and Orloff glimpsed a pair of red-rimmed blue eyes. "Thank you. Your letter was very touching. It was not your fault, of course. You shouldn't blame yourself."

Lynn abruptly rose to go. "You are very kind. I think I should leave now. I'll be back this afternoon."

"No," Mrs. Byroade said urgently. She seemed to regain some of her confidence. "Please, don't go. It will be easier for me with another woman present. Please." Lynn looked at her, embarrassed, then turned to Orloff, as if seeking help. Finally she sat down, awkwardly pulling at her sweater and running her hand over her forehead.

Jane Byroade stared at Orloff for a long moment without speaking. Behind the dark glasses, her immobile gaze seemed that of a blind person. Orloff did not rush her. She must have rehearsed several times what she wanted to say, and was trying to find the appropriate words. When she finally spoke, her voice was uncertain, wavering with emotion. "You didn't know my husband. That's what you said yesterday on television. I am sure you didn't. But this morning I heard the news about the attempt on your life. I felt that I had to see you. I am sure that the same people who killed Anthony tried to kill you last night. There must be a connection, Mr. Orloff."

"Yes," he said gravely. "So it seems. There might be a connection."

"That is why I wanted to talk to you." She vigorously rubbed her palms with the rolled-up tissue, looked about her nervously, and finally placed the tiny ball on the very edge of the low table. "The people who attacked you last night may try again, and I think you are . . . you are entitled to know anything that may help stop them."

"I appreciate your attitude," he said, anxious to keep her talking. The dark glasses were fixed on him, waiting for encouragement.

"When Anthony spoke to the press last week, after he met this young lady and Mr. Jennings, he did not disclose a very important fact—the real reason why he spied for the Russians."

"He had been a Communist at Cambridge, hadn't he?" Orloff asked finally.

"Yes, but that was not the reason. He had been a Communist in his youth, like many others. That was over and forgotten." She leaned forward, but immediately straightened up again. "You see, he was blackmailed into spying. By the KGB."

"Blackmailed?" His doubtful tone made the poor woman

stir in her chair. Another tissue blossomed in her hand, and she feverishly mopped her brow. "He did it for me, Mr. Orloff. No, I mean, he did not tell the press that he had been blackmailed because he did not want to humiliate me. He thought I would be hurt if everybody knew."

Orloff was nodding compassionately, although he did not understand what she was saying. Lynn was staring at her, frowning in bewilderment.

"Oh my God." Jane Byroade removed her glasses and applied the tissue consecutively to both her eyes, looking down. "This is very hard for me, Mr. Orloff," she said in a muffled tone, on the verge of tears. "It is very painful for me to speak about this." Her voice broke. She took several deep breaths and finally raised her head, hastily putting back her glasses. She seemed to gather all her courage. "The Russians forced my husband to spy for them by sheer sexual blackmail," she blurted out.

"Sexual blackmail?" Orloff repeated after her, perplexed.

His incredulity was the last straw, and the wretched woman could control herself no longer. She buried her face in her hands and burst into sobs. He stared at her with embarrassment, but Lynn was beside her in two quick strides, hugging her, patting her on the back, wiping her cheeks with her handkerchief, and mumbling the appropriate "there, there," and "it's all right now." The widow's glasses slipped and clattered to the floor beside her. Lynn's efforts bore fruit, and Mrs. Byroade gradually calmed down. Her story finally came out, erratically, interspersed with fits of crying. Orloff listened to her in growing amazement.

The Russians had first contacted her husband, Mrs. Byroade's story went, in 1952. He was a security officer at the British embassy in Prague at that time and was in-

volved in much important secret work. The Russians knew
that he had been an active Communist at Cambridge in the
early thirties, a member of the leftist cell at the Apostles
Club, a frequent visitor to James Klugmann's rooms in
Trinity—and they appealed initially to his Party loyalty.
He had flatly refused. The incident had even amused him
to a point; he had expected them to make the move from
the very day he had been posted to Czechoslovakia. But
the Russians did not give up. They had waited, meticu-
lously planning their next move. And at the beginning of
the following year, when he was in Paris, they acted. He
had come to attend a congress on the violation of human
rights behind the Iron Curtain, called by various émigré
and CIA-front organizations. While he was alone in Paris,
the Russians had set him up with a woman, "a cheap tart.
Mr. Orloff, somebody they had picked off the streets, no
doubt, but you are a man and you know how men are,
especially in Paris, and alone," and the trap was closed. She
had lured him into her apartment, and the Russians had
taped and photographed them together. Afterward they had
confronted him with their incriminating evidence and had
threatened him with a scandal if he refused to cooperate.
He felt he was left with no other choice, so for the next ten
years he had worked for the KGB.

Orloff sat very still in his bed, his eyes half-closed,
trying to assess the strange story. The pain in his chest was
much stronger now, and several times he felt a sudden
dizziness, and a warm, prickly sweat breaking out on his
whole body. Still, he was too intrigued by her account to
reach for the button and summon his black angel. "Why
do you say," he started cautiously, avoiding her eyes,
"why do you say the woman was a cheap tart?"

"These were Anthony's words, Mr. Orloff. That's how

he described her when he told me about the whole thing. It was humiliating!'' She started crying into Lynn's handkerchief again.

Anthony Byroade had confessed the affair to his wife but not till years later, after they were settled back in England. The board of inquiry had found out about his betrayal. He had admitted his guilt, then had come to her and made a clean breast of everything. That's when he had told her about the woman. ''He did not lie to me, Mr. Orloff. He had been through hell for years, and he wanted to take that burden off his chest. I knew my husband, and I knew he was telling the truth.''

You knew your husband, he wanted to say, still you did not see through him for all those years. And if there was that woman, there might well have been others. Other cheap tarts. But men always had a knack of downgrading their affairs—once they were caught—labeling the other woman a tart, a whore, an easy catch, stupid, dull, and, of course, a disaster in bed. ''Nothing like you, my dear.'' Still, wives so badly wanted to believe it, to be reassured that the indiscretion was just a casual carnal folly with an unworthy female. That was what they wanted to hear when they had already decided to forgive their men.

''And do you happen to know that French woman's name, Mrs. Byroade?'' he asked skeptically.

To his immense surprise she said yes, she did. She had insisted on knowing every detail, and he had given it to her. ''Here,'' she said, fumbling in her bag. ''I noted it down.''

''Corinne Benedetti,'' he read aloud from the aged piece of paper. ''Sixteen, rue Délambre, Paris.''

The woman nodded once again, seeking refuge behind her dark glasses.

*   *   *

"This is very unusual, Lynn," he said much later, when the young woman returned after escorting Mrs. Byroade out of the hospital. "I have never heard of the KGB using women to blackmail former Communists. Enemies yes, but never sympathizers, even recalcitrant ones."

"Perhaps they needed something very desperately, and he was the only one who could deliver it," Lynn offered.

"Perhaps," he repeated. Still, it seemed odd. Why would they choose Paris, where the operation was much more complicated? Why not Prague? Why not a KGB swallow, one of their own female operators? Why use "a cheap tart"?

"It just doesn't fit the pattern," he insisted stubbornly. The pretty nurse was back with her multicolored pills and dazzling smiles, and the solemn announcement of a forthcoming doctor's visit.

"I think," he said suddenly, when Lynn was buckling the belt of her green coat, "I think that you should not mention this visit to anybody. And as soon as I feel better, I shall go to Paris for a couple of days."

"Why the hell do you want to go with him?" Ted exploded.

She smiled, amused at his outburst. "I don't *want* to," she corrected him. "I am going. There might be a first-class story in Paris, Ted."

"The first-class story is here, for Christ sake!" He scooped with both hands the heap of newspapers strewn on the bed, and, exasperated, threw them on the floor. "Ever seen such headlines in your life? This man is the number-one story in the country today and you are in with him.

95

Your name is in all the papers, your face is famous, every reporter in London wants to interview you—''

''Because of him,'' she said, but Ted was shouting too loud to hear her.

''You have got it made in a single interview, and all you can think about is going with him to Paris!''

''But the next interview has been suspended until he recovers,'' she reminded him. She yawned luxuriously, stretching her arms. ''God, am I tired today. Can you stay? I'd love to spend the night with you.''

''You would, would you? So much that you can't wait to go to Paris.''

''But I told you, dear,'' she said with gentle exasperation, as if talking to a child, which she half-believed every man was in certain ways, ''we might have a sensational story in Paris.''

''So let him go alone and find it.'' He leaned over the heap of hastily discarded clothes, found his package of cigarettes, and lit one with quick, nervous gestures. In the brief silence, the rumble of the tempest suddenly burst into the warm, cozy room. ''You spent the whole day at the hospital. Damn it, Lynn, you don't have to stick to him all the time.''

She moved close to him and traced a sinuous line on his naked back with her fingernail. ''Now, wait a minute, *Tovaritch* Producer. You are not becoming jealous of a seventy-three-year-old man!''

He looked for an ashtray and, not finding one, tapped his cigarette over his cupped palm. ''Your old man is a spy, a cheat, and a double-dealer. And as far as I am concerned, I am fed up with this conversation.'' He reached over her and put out his cigarette in the empty wineglass on her side of the bed, then got to his feet and started dressing. She leaned on her elbows and they faced each other, Ted's face flushed, Lynn's ironical smile slowly vanishing from her lips.

"I understand how you feel after what happened to your father," she said, suddenly serious. "But let me tell you something about this cheat and double-dealer who was married to Virginia Fielding. He is a miserable and lonely man. He is the enemy and everybody in this country hates him. It takes a lot of guts to come out of hiding, fly to England, and face all the hatred and criticism of people like you. And like me," she added after a short pause. "He has come over here not for money, not for pleasure. He has come to see me, because I remind him of the only woman he has ever loved."

"You could star in a soap opera." Ted sneered at her, adjusting his turtleneck.

"How funny you can be. This man almost got killed because of the publicity you and I gave him, and because of the fame you and I are going to acquire on his back. He has no one to turn to. He has never had a friend in his life, except his agents. He has been burning in his private hell for most of his life."

"Oh, so you approve of him now!"

"No, I don't," she flared. He had never seen her so angry. She grabbed the bedsheet and pulled it up over her body, refusing him her nudity. "I don't approve of what he did. But his life is over, and he is reaching out for me, for some human warmth, some compassion. I know I'll never forgive him for the crimes he has committed—and when I say crimes, I mean the people whose deaths he has caused, like your father's. All the rest is bull. But if I can give him, just for a couple of weeks, the feeling that somebody cares about him, I'll do it, no matter what you say.''

"You are breaking my heart," he snapped. "Come on, Lynn, it doesn't become you. Don't be ridiculous."

"Ridiculous or not, I am going with him," she said. But Ted had already gone, slamming the door behind him.

In the week following the attempt on Orloff's life, Hastings was constantly on the move. He virtually deserted his sparsely furnished office at the Yard, occasionally breezing through for an old file or a last-minute report. He did not show up at the morning conferences of the department heads, and twice missed appointments with his doctor. The only meetings he attended religiously were those of the ad hoc committee on the Orloff-Byroade affair. But except for some tedious discussions of the shooting, and an exchange of redundant comments about Orloff's televised interview, the committee accomplished nothing. This only confirmed Hastings's suspicion that the directors of the "parallel" services—Nigel Sykes and Peter Snow—had set up the committee mainly to watch each other's moves and spare themselves unpleasant surprises. The sole achievement—thanks to another call from the home secretary—was to force Peter Snow to report to the committee on how the KGB team had come into the country two weeks before. A local source, Snow said curtly, had advised MI-5 that a minor KGB stringer was setting up a safehouse in London, expecting some visitors. Border surveillance had been tightened and emergency procedures had been activated to net all incoming travelers. This meant thoroughly checking the immigration forms collected at the borders. Foreign agents—KGB, Mossad, Polish and Bulgarian security—would tend to use Austrian, Canadian, Belgian, and Turkish passports. Those countries had no computerized central records, and any inquiry about a suspect passport would take at least twenty-four hours, long enough for the passport bearer to go underground. "Even when we are alerted, we cannot detain any national of those countries, except if he looks really suspect." Nobody did look suspect, but the examination of the landing cards during the week following the tip established that seven people had entered England using false papers: three Canadians, three Austrians, and one Belgian. Suspicions were confirmed when the local addresses they had supplied on their cards turned out to be nonexistent. "This does not mean that other operatives have not come in using French, Italian, or even British passports," Snow said. Hastings asked him how he knew that the group was an operational hit team and not merely an Intelligence-gathering outfit. But Snow looked through Hastings passively, ignoring his question, and Hastings knew that the secretary's call had already been forgotten.

Hastings's other enterprises were at least as frustrating. He seemed to be running into blank walls wherever he turned. The inquiries about the car and the gun used in the attempt on Orloff's life had led him up a blind alley. Mrs. Byroade, remote and entrenched behind her dark glasses, had refused to disclose the subject of her conversation with Orloff. So had Lynn Kennan, who assailed him with questions, until it looked as if she were the sleuth and he the quarry. When he insisted on knowing what Mrs. Byroade had said to Orloff, she found refuge behind a charming smile. "You know that you might be withholding evidence, Miss Kennan, which is a criminal offense in England," he said morosely. She weighed his statement thoughtfully and worded her reply with care. "I am not withholding any evidence, and I am not obstructing justice, Mr. Hastings. All the evidence is in Byroade's file at the Foreign Office.''

But the Foreign Office, after consulting a higher authority, refused to let Hastings see the board of inquiry report on Byroade's case. He suspected that Snow and Sykes had had a part in that refusal. The old-boy network was active again, covering up unpleasant truths, mounting watch over the sepulchre of a murky affair. Still, he had to find out, for sure, if there had been a connection between Orloff and Byroade in the past. As a last resort, he phoned the United States embassy and asked to see Mr. J. J. Kraft.

A huge, straw-haired man, Kraft was the chief representative of the CIA in London. As customary between close allies, he did not operate under deep cover but was buried in the political section of the embassy, a hideous modern block of concrete marring the northern side of Grosvenor Square. But Kraft called Nigel Sykes, who called Robin Coleman at the Yard, and Hastings was immediately summoned to his chief for an acrimonious lecture. The bottom line was that he should mind his own business. He should carry on with his investigations and not step on the "parallels' " toes, Coleman said. He could get all the information he wanted using the proper channels, so why in heaven did he want to meet J. J. Kraft? Hastings could not tell Coleman that he totally distrusted the parallels and attached little value to the meager scraps they would magnanimously throw him now and then. So he just swallowed his defeat and took the first train to Cambridge.

But it was brick-wall week, and Cambridge was not going to be an exception. He had hoped to pick up Orloff's trail from his arrival in England fifty years ago and methodically follow it up to the present day. But there was nothing to pick up and retrace, not after a pack of hungry reporters, obsessed with the banner headlines of the London papers, had swarmed like locusts through the small university town. Every file, room, bench, and punting boat had been thoroughly explored, described, and publicized. All Hastings could find was a photograph of a young Orloff in a rabbit-fur-lined hood, nervously smiling at the camera on graduation day.

It was at Trinity Hall that the phone call reached him, informing him of Orloff and Lynn's sudden departure for Paris.

8

"How DID she die?" Orloff asked as soon as the sturdy Air France Airbus took off from Heathrow. He was leaning toward her, his left hand grasping the buckle of his seat belt.

Lynn looked at him in puzzlement. The ring of earnestness in his voice, the deep concentration in the eyes and the mouth were those of a man in the middle of a passionate conversation. But they had barely exchanged a few banalities in the cab on their way to the airport.

"Virginia," he said impatiently. "How did she die?"

She shook her head. "You are something else," she whispered, and was about to add some commonplace, when he gently put his hand on her arm. "I must know the truth," he said softly.

"I thought you knew. The accident, on Route One in California. She was on her way to Carmel. The car left the road and crashed in a ravine. My father also died in the accident."

"But Virginia was driving, right?" He did not look healthy. He had been released from the hospital only the previous day. He was paler than usual, his eyes were bleary, and his jaws sagged. He looked older and much more vulnerable.

"Yes, Mother was driving," she said and turned to the window.

"I went there, you know," he said in the same soft, choked voice. "It's a straight stretch of road. How could a car suddenly swerve to the left, cross the road, and plunge into the canyon? She was not drinking—or was she?"

"No, that day she wasn't," Lynn snapped. "Why did you go there? What were you looking for?"

"But she was drinking rather heavily at that time," he said, more as a statement than a question.

"What's this, the third degree?" They were just emerging over a mass of dark gray clouds. Somewhere to the right, lightning stabbed the clouds like a dagger of white fire.

"Lynn," he said, and the voice was so kind, so compassionate, that she knew he was going to hurt her. "It was not a suicide, you're sure?"

She hesitated just a split second too long. "The coroner's verdict was accidental death," she said foolishly, avoiding his eyes.

"I was told that they had not been getting along well. Virginia and your father."

She sank into a stubborn silence.

"There was talk of a divorce."

"Yes, there was. You know everything, don't you? You went to the scene of the accident, you poked around. Why? Did you miss your spying?"

His hand was clasping her arm, persistent, demanding.

104

She quickly glanced at him and saw the distraught expression on his face. "She never mentioned my name to you? Really?"

"No, she didn't," she replied sharply. A priest seated across the aisle bent over to catch a glimpse of her. "I am sorry." Her voice dropped to a murmur. "She didn't mention your name." Lynn fell silent. She had been only ten years old when they died; and she still remembered vividly her parents' terrible quarrels those last two years. And her father bitterly shouting something about Alex. "My father mentioned your name, though," she told Orloff. "Several times. When they were fighting."

"And Virginia—"

"Mother did not answer." She added on an impulse, "I loved my father. Very much."

"Did he love you?"

She paused. "Of course. Why shouldn't he?" She lit a cigarette with quick, disconnected gestures. "You went all the way to California," she said in wonder, "and made all those inquiries, because you wanted to know how she died. At your age, Mr. Orloff."

"Alex," he said gently.

"Alex," she repeated, suddenly alarmed. He had opened a door she was not sure she wanted to enter.

Paris was cold and unwelcoming.

She wondered how he felt, coming back to the city where he had fallen in love. But he did not display any emotion when they landed at Charles de Gaulle, on the rain-swept plain that stretched, dull and dreary, to the north of Paris. They went quickly through immigration, and the square-jawed police officer stamped their passports indifferently, without even looking at them. She noticed, nonetheless, the two plainclothesmen who followed them outside. One of the men, heavy and short-legged, wearing black glasses perched on a flat boxer's nose, was breathing heavily and continuously mopped his glistening brow with an untidy blue handkerchief. He looked as if he had run all the way to immigration. The poor Sûreté officer had barely made it, Lynn figured. It was not surprising. They had been identified at the cash ticket counter at Heathrow, only twenty minutes before takeoff. By the time a security agent had been found, a call placed to headquarters, and an urgent signal flashed to Paris, another twenty minutes must have elapsed. The Sûreté officer must have been blissfully digesting his lunch in his office when the frantic phone call had disrupted his lazy afternoon stupor. "Emergency. Air France 137 from London. Orloff and Kennan. *Un vieux et une blonde.*" She pointed out the unmarked Peugeot to Orloff as their taxi darted south on the Autoroute du Nord. *"Les flics,"* she said, keeping her voice low because of the cab driver. The old man shrugged indifferently. From the right front seat of their cab, a huge German shepherd pointed its muzzle at them, its moist flews comfortably splayed on the gray upholstery. "You always take your dog with you?" Lynn asked in broken French.

"Always," said the taxi driver, a bleached blonde in her late forties whose stockiness was enhanced by a sleeveless lambskin that she wore over her blue nylon smock. "He is good protection, and he keeps me company. *N'est-ce pas, Roland?"* She patted his rump.

The uniform-gray sky and the steady drizzle had plunged Paris into premature darkness. Neon lights flickered along the Boulevard Malesherbes, and blurred faces stared out the tinted café windows. The indistinct shape of the Eiffel

Tower loomed above the rooftops of Paris, far down to the right.

"You have been in Paris before, haven't you?" Orloff asked.

She nodded. "For three years I lived off the Boulevard Saint Germain. I was a student of history at the Sorbonne."

Rush hour was descending upon the city, bringing with it another fit of endemic Parisian ill temper. Sour-faced drivers were overtaking each other from all directions, missing collisions by inches, exchanging venomous looks. Their driver metamorphosed into a vengeful amazon, brandishing her plump fist and sticking her head out her window to curse the inept idiots who dared to cross her path. Even the placid Roland shifted on his seat and snarled ominously at the enemy.

"Et voilà. Seize, rue Délambre," the driver triumphantly announced, as she finally pulled beside a six-story nineteenth-century building, the cream-colored facade of which had recently been washed clean. The entrance was flanked on the left by a branch of the Banque Nationale de Paris, its frosted windows lined with savings posters praising a long-term savings plan; on the right side a brightly illuminated bakery was bustling with activity. Two old ladies dressed in black grimaced with pleasure under their black umbrellas as they pointed at the pastries in the shop window. Inside, a huge white-aproned man was stacking fresh-baked *baguettes* and gold-crusted *viennoises* on the double-tiered racks.

"Could you wait for us, please?" the old man said to the driver in good, Paris-accented French that seemed to dispel initial suspicions. "I doubt if she still lives here, after almost thirty years," he explained to Lynn, as they crossed the wet sidewalk into the building.

The entrance was neat and carpeted. A hand-drawn plan of the building hung on the concierge's door, indicating the names and apartments of the tenants. He glanced at it quickly, then knocked on the door. A noise of shuffling feet came from the inside, then faded away. He knocked again. *"J'arrive, j'arrive, un instant,"* a thin voice called acidly. The door opened and a small, frail woman in an outmoded brown dress and a heavy beige shawl raised her head to them. She was about Orloff's age, her white hair coiled into a tight bun, her thick glasses magnifying her cross-eyed look. *"Oui, Monsieur?"* She was wearing thick wool-lined slippers. A whiff of warm air, carrying the smells of cooking, floated through the open door.

"Bonjour, Madame," Orloff said respectfully. "I hate to disturb you, but I am looking for one of your tenants, whose name is not on the plan."

"It is not?" she repeated, ostensibly mellowed by Monsieur's manners.

"No. You have been the concierge here for a long time?"

"I have lived here all my life, Monsieur. My father was the concierge here for forty-seven years. We belong here."

"So you must know Mademoiselle Corinne Benedetti."

The old woman winced and a look of suspicion flashed from her eyes. "There is no Benedetti here," she snapped and took a step backward, about to close the door.

"Maybe not anymore," he said smoothly, "but she did live here, didn't she? I know that."

She cocked her head. "How do you know?"

He smiled, looking embarrassed. "Well, I used to visit her here, once in a while."

"I don't remember you," she said less belligerently, giving herself away.

"That was thirty years ago." He shook his head sadly. "I looked somewhat different at the time."

Her eyes shifted from Orloff to Lynn, who stayed discreetly in the background. "You are not French, *n'est-ce pas?*"

"I live in England," he went on lying. With remarkable ease, Lynn noted. "My name is Alexander Carlisle, and I am an art collector."

"An art collector, *hein*? And what do you want from La Benedetti? You want her for your art collection? You collect antique pieces?" She suddenly smiled, but her left hand quickly shot up to conceal a partly toothless mouth.

Orloff good-naturedly fell in line with her. "One must say she used to be a delight for an artist's eye, in her time."

"She used to be a delight for half of Paris," the concierge said, her face swiftly freezing into the self-righteous expression of old age. "She was a *poule de luxe*, Monsieur, a high-class whore, that's what she was. Thank God she is gone. This is a respectable house, Monsieur. We don't tolerate women like her anymore. What does a gentleman like you want her for? You look very respectable." Respectable was the key word, Lynn decided.

He spread his arms in mock apology. "I haven't been in Paris for many years, Madame. My health, and then my age, you know. . . ." She nodded sympathetically. "I'm here for only a few days and I am trying to meet people whom I once knew. For the sake of old times."

She shrugged. "I can't really help you, Monsieur. You see, she left here long ago. I don't have her address. I only have the address of Solange, you know, the girl who shared her apartment."

"Solange. Yes, of course. She is in Paris?"

"Yes. She kept the apartment for a few more years, then moved to the tenth district. I'll write down her address for you."

In a moment she was back with a piece of yellow paper torn from an old agenda. "Here." She readily accepted the hundred-franc bill that Orloff pressed into her hand. *"Merci, Monsieur."* She threw a last, disapproving glance at Lynn, who understood that she had been assessed and branded as another artistic interest of the old roué. "It's strange, though," the concierge suddenly muttered, more to herself than to them, before closing the door.

"What's strange?" Orloff said in puzzlement. Then he shrugged, and led the way to the cab that was double-parked in front of the entrance. "Thirty-five, Rue des Petites Ecuries," he said to the driver. Roland yawned in lazy indifference.

The tenth district was much poorer. And Rue des Petites Ecuries was a grim, seedy street winding among small North African restaurants, artisans' workshops, clothing stores, and an occasional Armenian or Moroccan grocer. As the cab stopped, Lynn noticed a sign bearing a golden horse's head, the emblem of the almost extinct horsemeat butchers in Paris. She shuddered with disgust. Number thirty-five was a graceless, dirty-gray building with a wide porch leading into an oblong inner court. Most of the court's space was taken up by a wooden shanty, its front covered with faded posters for Dim pantyhose. A rough enamel sign was nailed to the shanty door: SOLANGE—LADIES' UNDERGARMENTS. OPEN 9–1, 4–7. There was no elevator, and a strong, sharp stench permeated the dark staircase. By the time they reached the fifth floor, Orloff was breathing heavily, and his face had acquired an unhealthy red color.

"Are you all right?" Lynn asked, and he nodded curtly, almost angrily. He pushed the doorbell and a strident ring echoed inside.

"Come in, it's open," a woman's voice yelled.

The first thing that struck Lynn as she opened the door was a sweet, somewhat sickening scent of cheap cologne. It almost subdued the sharp odors wafting from the staircase. Almost but not quite, and the combination was a heavy, nauseating smell that was all but palpable. The vestibule was tiny and dark, most of it occupied by an open pink umbrella still glistening with raindrops. A woman's worn coat, sporting a collar of imitation mink, was thrown on a chair under a heart-shaped mirror. A reduced replica of the Venus of Milo was tucked in one corner, the plaster cracked in several places. They walked into the living room, which was sordid: an old sofa and an armchair upholstered in frayed but still flamboyant red velvet; a television set, its top covered with a red lace doily on which there sat three statuettes of naked couples frozen in impossible positions; a fireplace converted to accommodate a gas stove. The walls were covered with pink wallpaper in a pattern of hearts pierced with arrows, plump cupids with tiny bows, and bunches of red roses. The aged drapes adorning the tall French windows were also red. A blue-eyed Siamese cat, stretched on the synthetic rug in front of the blue-edged fire, haughtily ignored them. The cologne odor was even stronger, as if the room were constantly sprayed.

They heard quick footsteps. A full-bodied woman in a vivid green blouse and a black skirt walked into the room. Her slim long legs, out of proportion with the heavy body, seemed to be all that was left of a once attractive figure. She was in her late fifties. Her hair was dyed to a striking platinum-blond and her large face was layered with heavy makeup. Over a thick layer of chalk-white powder, the cheeks were ablaze with rouge; eyeshadow in black, green, and blue shades surrounded the small brown eyes under arched, almost nonexistent eyebrows. The mouth was blood-red, its lipstick smeared beyond its natural contours to make it look bigger, creating an effect of a bleeding wound in the pathetic clownlike face.

"Bonjour," she said in a rasping voice, eyeing them doubtfully. The sleeves of her blouse were drawn beyond her elbows, and she was wiping her arms with a white towel. "You're here to see me? I'll be with you in a minute. I was just washing the . . . the invalid in the bathroom."

She reappeared almost immediately, and Lynn paled as she saw the frail, degenerate shape she was carrying in her arms. It was the underwear-clad body of an old man, bald and skeletal, looking half-starved. His skin had an unhealthy waxen tinge, and his left arm hung limply while the right one was twisted across his chest. The man was grinning foolishly and his mouth was moving soundlessly. A trickle of saliva ran down his chin.

Solange carried him effortlessly as if he were a broken mannequin. Her face was stamped with an expression of disgust. She turned to Lynn. "Would you open the bedroom door for me, Mademoiselle?"

Lynn hurried toward the door, on the other side of the room. "Can I help you in any way?" she asked.

"Oh, you are American?" Solange said. "No, I'll manage. He doesn't need any help." As she walked into the bedroom, the invalid's bare foot hit the door and he moaned, but the woman did not seem to care. They overheard her muttering fiercely in the other room, with strange, wailing sounds uttered in response. The woman reappeared, empty-handed, and closed the door. *"Mon Dieu,* what a calvary,'' she groaned. She approached them now, and Lynn got a closer look at her face. Even the thick layers of makeup could not conceal the creases of bitterness etched in her cheeks and the multitude of wrinkles surrounding her eyes like spider webs.

"You are really looking for me?'' she said again, slightly tilting her head.

"You are Madame Solange Bosco?'' Orloff smiled gallantly.

"Yes. Yes, I am.''

They introduced themselves, the old man again using the name Carlisle. "We came from London today,'' he explained. "Miss Kennan works for British television and I represent a chain of American newspapers.''

She nodded, ill at ease. "Will you sit down? You caught me unprepared. I had to take care of the invalid.'' She wrinkled her nose. "Excuse me.'' She took a big container from the mantelpiece and sprayed the room. "The stench in this house is unbearable. I must apologize. You see, the building belongs to a *maître fromager*—a cheesemaker—and he has his store on the ground floor. He actually makes some of his cheeses in the cellar. And the smells!'' She threw up her arms in a theatrical gesture. "I cannot get used to it. Never! And you should hear my friends complaining.'' She sat down facing them. "What can I do for you?''

"We came to talk to you about Corinne Benedetti,'' the old man said.

"Corinne?'' She stiffened, her eyes hostile. "What's this, a joke? Why should I talk to you about her?''

"We are journalists and we would like to meet her,''

Orloff said. "We will gladly pay you for your time. You know us Americans." He smiled. "Everything goes on expense accounts."

She seemed to consider his offer for an abnormally long time. Finally she shrugged with exaggerated indifference. "All right. What do you want to know?"

"You know her well?" Lynn asked.

"Of course, we came to Paris together. She is from Bastia, in Corsica. I am from Béziers."

"And you . . . worked together?"

She burst into laughter. "Oh, come on, *ma petite,* you know what our work was. We were two young sexy girls, with good connections in Paris, so we specialized in the one and only kind of work. We did not work the streets. Never! Only first-class clients—businessmen, high officials, visiting tourists. A couple of times we were even approached by the government for help. Nothing official, of course. We were asked to entertain some visiting diplomats from these new African states, in the name of France!" She chuckled. "We had a few parties at Rue Délambre, I can tell you that!" She suddenly grew serious. "How did you find me? Who gave you my address?"

"The concierge at Rue Délambre," Lynn said.

"You did not inquire at the *préfecture de police?*" she asked suspiciously. "I don't want any trouble with them."

"No, no. No police," Lynn said emphatically.

"I want no trouble," Solange Bosco repeated. "Life is hard enough for me as it is. You think it is easy to stand on your feet all day long in that shack down there, selling stockings and panties to the stingy housewives of this damn neighborhood? You can't survive on that. And I have two mouths to feed, mine and"—she nodded her head toward the closed door—"and my husband's. So I bring a friend up here once in a while, and make a few francs on the side. The cops here know me, they always close their eyes, but if it gets to the *préfecture*, I'll be in trouble, see?''

"So this is your husband?" Orloff inquired kindly.

"What remains of him." She spoke with bitterness. "Would you believe that he is only sixty years old? When he married me he had about thirty girls working for him at Pigalle and La Madeleine. I thought myself lucky. It was champagne and caviar all the way. And then he fell sick, first paralysis, then complications, tissue degeneration—and in six months he became a vegetable. Now I have to carry him on my back till my dying day. You cannot imagine what I go through when I bring a friend over here. *Quelle misère!*"

"When you were living with Corinne, did you know a man, an Englishman, named Byroade?" Orloff asked in the same soft, compassionate voice.

She was still fuming over her personal misfortune. "When I married him, I thought I was marrying a gold mine. Jean Bosco. Mad Jeannot, they used to call him. Do you remember the murder of Nadine Burin? The girl they found in the Bois de Boulogne? Shot and burned? It was all over the papers. She used to be one of Jeannot's girls. They had him arrested, kept him in jail for three months, then released him. No evidence. His picture made the front page of all the papers. You must remember. That was Jeannot. 'The prostitution king.' And look at him now. Some king! I wish I'd never laid eyes on him."

"I asked you if you remembered Byroade," Orloff reminded her.

She quieted down for a second, staring at Lynn. "Of

course I remember,'' she said less heatedly. ''How could I forget?''

''It happened a long time ago,'' he pointed out.

''Yes, but thanks to him Corinne left Paris. She hit it big with that one.''

Orloff did not speak, and she went on. ''We had a good laugh about that one, Corinne and I. One day, in nineteen fifty-five—or was it fifty-three?—Corinne came home all excited. She had been approached by a man, she said, who offered her a lot of money to seduce the Englishman, Byron.''

''Byroade.''

''That's right, Byroade. He was a businessman. Or an ambassador. Or maybe even a minister. I don't remember.'' She sniffed angrily and darted to the mantelpiece to spray the room again.

Orloff was looking at her strangely. ''Are you sure Corinne was offered money? Wasn't she a Communist?''

Solange stared at him as if he had lost his mind. ''Communist? Corinne?'' She again broke into her rasping laugh, almost choking. ''That's a good one. Corinne, a Communist! My God, she would cross to the other side of the street if she even saw one! She was as normal as you and me.''

Lynn glanced quickly at Orloff, who had withdrawn into himself, a remote look veiling his eyes. ''Go on, please,'' he said.

Solange Bosco was launched, and nothing could stop her now. She told them Corinne had agreed to the deal. She had picked the Englishman up one afternoon at the Palais de Chaillot, where a congress he was attending was taking place. She had introduced herself as a secretary. He had asked her to join him for a cup of coffee, then for drinks, finally for dinner. In the beginning she played the demure, virginal young woman, till the man was almost out of his mind. Then she started teasing him. Finally she lured the Englishman into an apartment that had been prepared in advance for taping and photographing. ''There was even one of those one-way mirrors, the kind they used years ago in the *cinémacochon*, live shows, you know, where you could see everyone in the room without them seeing you.'' Solange described, in ample detail, the orgy that Corinne had staged in front of the hidden cameras. ''She gave him everything in the book, Monsieur, and when she came home the next morning she told me that the poor man had been so excited, so turned on, that he sounded like a slaughtered pig. She rolled on the bed, yelling and moaning and panting the way he had. We had a good laugh about the whole affair. Anyway, she had earned her money, and she was paid up to the last penny. She was not like me, you see. I liked the good life, spending on dresses and food and jewelry. She was the exact opposite. Stingy and closefisted like you've never seen. She was saving most of her money. 'Solange,' she would say to me, 'one day our luck will turn. I want to be safe.' Safe, that's all she wanted to be. So, when they paid her, she comes to me and she says: 'Solange, *ça y est*! I've got the money for my restaurant.'''

''What restaurant?'' Orloff seemed to come out of a doze.

''She had an idea about opening a restaurant in Cannes, on the beach. With all those tourists, she was sure she'd have a guaranteed income for the rest of her life.''

''And . . .''

''And that's what she did. Have you been to Cannes lately? Do you know Le Beau Monde? Just across the street from the Palais des Festivals? That's Corinne's place.

She had it enlarged only last year." Solange was bitter again. "She has it made, La Benedetti, you see? She even changed her name. Nowadays she calls herself Cora de Brétigny. De Brétigny my foot! But look at her and look at me, stuck in this stinking hole with that idiot on my back, counting every penny and considering myself lucky when I manage to fuck an Arab for two hundred francs!"

Orloff walked to the mantelpiece and left a small wad of bills. "I hope things will look up for you in the future," he said without real conviction. He turned to Lynn. "I think we should be going now."

Solange moved behind them swiftly, collecting the money and tucking it into the safety of her brassiere. "So you will be going to Cannes? You'd better hurry up. You are not the only reporters after her, you know."

Orloff turned back sharply. "What did you say?"

"Well, another reporter was here last Friday asking about Corinne. She must have become quite popular in the English press these days. Hey, what are you doing? Are you out of your mind?"

Orloff had grabbed her by both arms. "Who was the man?" he muttered, shaking the frightened woman. "Who was he?"

Solange Bosco was struggling in his grip. "I don't know," she stammered. "Let me go. That hurts!"

"Who was he?" Orloff repeated.

"I swear I don't know. Just . . . just a short, bald man. I don't even remember his name."

Behind the closed door, Mad Jeannot moaned pitifully.

118

9

THEY FOUND Corinne Benedetti the next morning.

Cannes lay sullen and morose in the cold, diffuse light filtering through the low clouds. A salty wind swept over the Mediterranean, angrily whispering in the palm crowns. In the pale daylight Orloff's drawn face looked mean. There was an eerie menace in his behavior, Lynn noted, a grim resignation.

The night before, in Paris, he had insisted on going to Cannes immediately. But they were too late for the last Air Inter flight to the Riviera; the late-evening flight had been canceled because of the bad weather. She had suggested spending the night in Paris and taking the 8:00 A.M. flight. But he was restless. "We'll take the *Train Bleu* and arrive in Cannes in the early morning." After a pause he had added: "She said he was a short man." He repeated it over and over again, as if this constituted the best argument for taking the night train. A short man. Solange had said he was a short man.

It seemed this piece of information was all that mattered to Orloff, but Solange Bosco had actually said much more before they finally left her overscented apartment. When Lynn had torn her from Orloff's grip and sat beside her on the sofa, protectively holding her shoulder, Solange had calmed down and managed to describe the previous Friday's visitor. He was in his sixties, Solange had said, shooting savage glances at Orloff, who stood with his back to them, looking through the window at the courtyard below. A very polite man, soberly dressed—long overcoat, dark suit, with a good-quality tie—beaked nose, prominent Adam's apple, and a scar, a long thin scar under his left eye. Yes, he was English or American. And very generous. He had inquired about Corinne, and Solange had given him the name of the restaurant in Cannes. She did not know Corinne's home number; it was unlisted. No, the reporter had not asked about the Byroade affair.

"He did not ask, because he already knew all about it," Orloff had grumbled when Lynn mentioned this later. They were having dinner in the train's *wagon-restaurant,* and in spite of all that was happening she was thrilled by the quaint atmosphere, unique among the old-fashioned European night trains. "Now, how could he know?" he had continued, while the waiter was filling their glasses with smoky white Pouilly-Fumé to accompany their sole fillets. "The Foreign Office files are closed to the public and the press, aren't they? And Jane Byroade didn't tell anybody but us about Corinne. Even Hastings couldn't make her talk. That's why he came running to you."

Lynn looked into the blackness outside, suddenly imagining Ted alone with her in the carpeted sleeper, but Orloff's urgent speculations caught up with her, pulling her back to reality, racing toward the inevitable conclusion.

"This man knew beforehand about the connection between Byroade and Corinne. He was in a hurry to get to her before I did. He is no more a reporter than I am."

Lynn had slowly nodded, fascinated yet terrified by the implacable logic of Alex's words and the grisly consequence it implied. The short man was racing ahead of them, determined to remove the links between the dead Byroade and his past. He had failed to kill Orloff, and consequently had flown to Paris. He had gone to Rue Délambre. "That's strange," the old concierge had said when they had asked her about Corinne Benedetti. Strange indeed. Benedetti had vanished thirty years before, and all of a sudden two men had popped up, one after the other, inquiring about her. Solange had been surprised too but had played the game till she collected her money. And the short man had had since Friday to reach the Riviera. Ample time.

In the cab, on their way to the Gare de Lyon railway station, Lynn had suggested calling the police; but Orloff hadn't even bothered to answer her. He had tried to call Corinne's restaurant from a phone booth in the crowded departure hall. Nobody had answered the phone. "At this time of year they might be closed," she said halfheartedly, trying to sound casual. But Alex seemed eons away, tense, jumpy, distracted. Only late in the evening, after the waiter had removed his untouched dinner, had he seemed to give in. It was a sort of resignation, admitting his helplessness at least temporarily. They had stayed in the dining car for a long time, talking against the background of flickering lights outside the dark windows and the rhythmic clatter of the train wheels. Lynn had repeatedly looked around, watching the other diners. When they rose to leave the *wagon-*

restaurant, she had remarked in wonder: "I think we've lost our guardian angels."

Orloff had smiled. "You are underestimating the French Sûreté. They're watching us, all right."

A cavernous silence reigned in the fancy sleeping car. The uniformed attendant ushered her into her cabin with an oily smile, obliquely glancing at her older protector, who occupied the neighboring compartment. She slept badly, surprised by her longing for Ted. Twice during the night she got up, intending to smoke a cigarette in the corridor. Both times she hastily retreated when she saw the erect figure of Orloff standing still at the other end of the car, grimly facing his reflection in the black window.

Le Beau Monde wouldn't open before noon, but the cleaning women were already there scrubbing the floor and exchanging news about their grandchildren in the sunny accent of Provence. They straightened up when Lynn and Orloff entered. The two fat figures in dirty sky-blue smocks and rubber boots smirked at the blond girl with a man who could pass for her grandfather. Yes, the manager was already there, one of them said, and the other reluctantly waddled into the darkness. "Monsieur Jérome," they heard her calling. "Monsieur Jérome, it's for you!" A deep voice answered curtly, and the woman was back, shrugging and muttering to herself. She returned to her work without even looking at them. Lynn glanced awkwardly about her. Le Beau Monde was a beautiful restaurant indeed, decorated in the style of "La Belle Epoque"—turn of the century—and lavishly furnished with authentic period pieces: gold-framed mirrors, crystal chandeliers. . . . Lynn thought of how it must look at night: glittering with lights; waiters in black waistcoats and long white aprons mincing between the tables; jewel-studded ladies chatting with studied boredom over their champagne. She had it made, La Benedetti, as Solange had said.

"Bonjour, Monsieur, Dame." The deep voice was polite but reserved. "You were looking for me?" Lynn turned back sharply, toward the man who had soundlessly materialized from the dark. He was of average height, broad-shouldered, with short strong arms and legs, close-cropped gray hair, a small forehead and a heavy jaw. He was impeccably dressed in a double-breasted dark suit and a dazzling white shirt. Only his red-and-blue tie was a trifle too flamboyant. He looked like a former wrestler, Lynn thought. Or a thug.

"You are the manager, Monsieur?" Orloff started.

"Santini, Jérome Santini." Another Corsican. La Benedetti had brought over the entire tribe.

Orloff made the introductions smoothly. "We are sorry to intrude, Monsieur Santini. I phoned several times last night, but there was no reply."

Santini nodded coldly. "In the winter we always close on Mondays." The beady eyes studied them with caution. He did not invite them to sit down or step into his office.

"We are looking for Madame de Brétigny." Orloff used Corinne's assumed name. "It's rather urgent."

"She'll be here tonight," Santini said evenly. "You'll have no problem talking to her. She loves mixing with the guests."

"So she is all right," Lynn breathed.

"Of course she is all right! What a curious remark, Madame."

Orloff stepped forward. He chose his words with care. "We have reason to believe that Madame de Brétigny might be in danger. A man, also from England, has been looking for her in Paris. We are afraid that he might try to harm her. When was the last time you saw her?''

"What are you? Police?'' Santini asked indifferently.

"No, we are private citizens. We'll give you all the information you may require as soon as we are assured that she is all right. Please, can you tell us when you saw her last?''

"On Saturday night, as usual. Why?''

"And you haven't seen her since? Or spoken to her over the phone?''

For the first time concern flashed in Santini's eyes. "We never call her on weekends." He hesitated. "Why don't I call her, and then you'll tell me what this is all about, all right? Come into my office." He made a step forward, then turned back again. "I don't see why anybody should be after her. Are you really serious, Monsieur?''

"The man I'm speaking about,'' Orloff said bluntly, "knew her when her name was Corinne Benedetti.''

Santini pivoted on his heels and moved into the dark with surprising agility. When they caught up with him, he was in a tiny cubicle of an office, papers and ledgers tidily arranged over a small desk, already dialing a six-digit number. He held the phone tightly pressed to his ear, and they could hear no sound. Finally he slammed it on its cradle. "No reply. Well, it doesn't mean a thing, but. . . .'' He stuck his head out of the door. "Yvonne! Call Monsieur Raphael. Quick!'' He grabbed a dark blue raincoat. "Somebody was at the restaurant on Saturday,'' he said urgently. "Somebody she knew long ago. She got very upset.''

"You saw them?'' Orloff grasped his arm. "You are sure she knew him?''

"I was in the office. Our *maître d'hôtel* was there.''

He led the way out of the office. In the dark back room a younger man joined them. He was wearing tight jeans and a brightly colored shirt. "You were looking for me, Jérome?" he asked. Santini whispered in his ear and led the way down the corridor, past the kitchens and out into a cobble-stoned courtyard. A silver Citroën CX and a Peugeot delivery van were parked side by side. Lynn fell in step with Raphael. His youthful face was handsome but effeminate. Undoubtedly gay, Lynn decided, watching the swaying motion of his round little bottom. In a tuxedo, his blond hair combed and a smile on his face, he might be the ladies' darling, gay or not.

But now he stood in the backyard, frightened, wringing his hands in distress as the two men questioned him. Yes, an Englishman had come to the restaurant on Saturday evening. He had sat by himself. Small, bald, sixtyish. Yes, he had a scar. Cora had passed beside him, and he had said something to her. She had sat at his table for a moment; that was not unusual. Quite unusual, though, was the way she had risen, fuming with rage, and walked away. "I asked her what happened, and she said to me: 'The cheeky son of a bitch! How dare he show up here after all these years! Throw him out!' " Raphael turned to Santini. "I asked one of the waiters to get you, but when you came the man had gone. Cora left immediately. She was angrier than I'd ever seen her before, trembling all over."

Santini was already in the Citroën, kicking the engine into life. "Let's go," he snapped. "You too, Raphael." They crowded into the car, backed smoothly into a side street, crawled to the oceanfront, then darted east on the Croisette. The seashore avenue was deserted, and not a soul could be seen on the beaches. A green-liveried doorman shivered miserably by the revolving doors of the Carlton. Farther down, an old couple bending into the wind trudged past the shuttered windows of Van Cleef & Arpels.

"Why did he talk to her at all?" Lynn asked Orloff in English. If Santini understood English, he concealed it very well.

Orloff nodded. "I was thinking about that too. I guess he wanted to make sure that she was the right woman. Even if he knew her, as those people say, he had not seen her for thirty years and had to make sure."

"Maybe he wanted to make her an offer?" They were out of town now, speeding east toward Nice.

"What offer did he make to Byroade? And to me?"

Orloff relapsed into silence as the Citroën left the highway and started climbing a narrow road. They left behind the shopping streets and the last clusters of high-rise buildings. The road narrowed gradually, winding between vast parks, fenced properties, villas surrounded by thickets of pines, juniper, exotic shrubs, and well-tended lawns. Lynn cast a quick glance over her shoulder. A breathtaking view of the beach and the magnificent bay of Cannes was unfolding below. Far to the east, she could see the lighthouse of Cap d'Antibes.

"Here we are," Raphael said as the car reached a large iron gate. The name of the villa was engraved on the fence that surrounded it. MON SECRET, it said. Jérome Santini was already at the gate, ringing the bell. "I think you should call the police," said Raphael. Jérome did not answer. He continued pressing the round copper button. They could not hear it ring. The house was a hundred yards up the sloping lawn, partly masked by a dense growth of shrubs and acacia trees. In the sudden silence, the wind honed to a high-pitched howl, like an approaching siren.

"She is dead, isn't she?" Raphael blurted, his face ashen. "Oh, *mon dieu!*"

"Shut up!" Santini barked.

Orloff turned to him. "Is there any other way to get in? A back door?"

"The cleaning woman has an extra set of keys. She lives in La Valbonne, a couple of kilometers up the road." Santini jumped into the car and drove off. They remained by the gate, three awkward figures observing an uneasy silence.

A black car with two passengers, a man and a woman, climbed slowly up the road. It reappeared a few minutes later, its occupants staring woodenly ahead. Lynn remembered Orloff's remark: their guardian angels were indeed watching them.

A solitary motorcyclist appeared from the opposite direction, his machine coughing in protest. As he approached, they recognized the uniform of a postman. He stopped beside the gate and stared at them, perplexed. He dug into his leather bag and fed a few letters and printed flyers into a slit in the wall. "Excuse me," Orloff said to him. "Were you here yesterday?"

The postman had stupid eyes. His lower jaw was slack, and his small mouth was half-open. He nodded, without speaking.

"Did you happen to see Madame de Brétigny?" Orloff continued.

The man shook his head and remounted his motorcycle. He started it, then finally dared to look back. "Is something wrong?" he asked, his curiosity growing. He received no answer. He advanced a couple of hundred yards up the road, turned off the sputtering engine, and retreated under an oak, watching them.

Santini's car emerged in a screeching of tires. A tall, sullen-faced girl in jeans and a loose red sweater got out of the car, head down, and unlocked the front gate. They all squeezed back into the Citroën and drove up the driveway to the house. In the rearview mirror, Lynn glimpsed the postman. He was by the open gate now, staring in.

The house was a one-story villa in moorish style. A white Chrysler convertible was parked by the front door. They all huddled around the village girl, whose hands were badly trembling as she tried to insert the keys in their separate locks. They all seemed to know what they were about to find, Lynn noticed, and their mechanical, re- signed movements reminded her of Orloff's at the train station. He had known all along, since Solange's disclosure.

She did not follow them into the house but walked instead around it, following a stone path that snaked be- tween the bushes and the flower beds, where a few with- ered chrysanthemum shrubs remained, soaked in yesterday's rain. The path went around the north wing of the house and a cluster of pines. It emerged in front of a small swimming pool, still full of dirty dark water, parts of its surface covered with pine needles and fallen leaves.

She felt no surprise, just a violent constriction in her chest, when she saw the fully dressed body of Corinne Benedetti floating facedown on the water. The arms and neck seemed abnormally swollen. The skirt had slipped up to her waist, obscenely revealing her white thighs. Long brown hair, mixed with the yellow-edged pine needles, fanned out around the dead woman's head.

10

THE FIRST THING that struck Hastings as he entered the graceless gray building sprawled at the southern end of Queensgate was the sepulchral quiet. It lay like a cold palpable mass in the windowless lobby and the poorly lit corridors. It seemed to muffle the furtive steps of the rare employees whose paths they crossed, grave men who sported their plastic badges like the emblems of a secret society; it smothered the ringing telephone and bits of conversation filtering through the thick brown-painted doors along their route. As he followed the bald, stone-faced janitor more deeply into the labyrinth of that dark and still universe, he vaguely remembered a scene from a Hitchcock movie he had seen with his wife. The movie's climax was a strange soundless dream where every visage, every shadow, every dark corridor had a hidden meaning. Things were the opposite of what they seemed to be. Barbara had tried to explain the symbols to him later, but he had refused her

129

interpretation. He had not succumbed to the eerie spell of the dream and had smirked at the suggested conclusion, that behind apparent reality lurked a second, fiendish truth.

The pain at the pit of his stomach tore through him again in the ancient elevator that panted hoarsely all the way up to the fifth floor. Such spells were becoming much more frequent lately and sometimes left him shaking, short of breath. They had to take a narrow staircase to the sixth floor, and he felt a film of cold sweat forming on his upper lip, while a strange numbness settled over his legs. Barbara had gone to bed already by the time he returned home last night, and was still asleep this morning when he left, but she had taped a laconic note for him on the top of the coffeemaker. Dr. Page had called twice, the note said, and it was urgent.

The janitor faded away and a young man, tall and well-fed in a dandyish single-breasted blazer, was ceremoniously shaking his hand before opening the door for him. "Chief Superintendent Hastings," he announced.

"How nice of you to come," Sir Nigel Sykes said icily. "You have met Peter Snow, of course."

Hastings stopped on the threshold and nodded politely at the MI-5 chief, who was uneasily perched on a stiff-backed chair. A forced smile touched Snow's pale, dyspeptic face.

Hastings stepped into the room, taking in Sykes and Snow in a single glance.

"Why don't you sit down." Sir Nigel generously gestured toward the chairs placed on both sides of an oval conference table. He walked around his massive mahogany desk and drew up a chair for himself, in a magnanimous display of equality. "We shall have some tea right away."

His cold gaze rested for a moment on Hastings's livid face.

Hastings gratefully slumped on the closest chair, facing some heavily stacked bookcases and a massive safe tucked in the corner. The invitation to the SIS headquarters had been cryptic and blunt, more like a summons. Nobody had bothered to inform him who would be present. Sykes and Snow alone, waiting for him, meant that they were getting worried.

On Sir Nigel's desk, mysterious green and red lights blinked on a futuristic telephone console. Some leather-framed photographs, a concession to US-made sentimentalism, stood on the polished mahogany and mounted watch over the space-age telephone. Sykes sat at the farthest end of the table, opposite Snow, and both of them half-turned, studying Hastings with condescending interest. Sykes and Snow were sworn enemies, no doubt, but Hastings was lower middle class, which was far worse, of course.

"Our friend is back in London, I gather," Sir Nigel said. "You may smoke if you wish."

These last words made Hastings withdraw his hand from his breast pocket. "Orloff and Miss Kennan arrived at Heathrow an hour ago," he said evenly. "The Nice-London flight. I met them at the airport."

"What did they tell you?"

"Almost nothing that I didn't know. They spent a rather unpleasant night at the Miramar Hotel in Cannes. Reporters from all over France pestered them, but the French police were quite efficient. They blocked access to their floor and disconnected their telephones."

"They did not hold them for questioning?" Snow raised his eyebrows, puckering his lips in doubt.

Hastings shrugged. "What for? The French know exactly what happened. They followed Orloff and the girl to Solange Bosco, the prostitute. Heard from her about the connection between Benedetti and Byroade. And about the short bald stranger, of course. Then Cannes, the restaurant, the villa, and the body. Easy. Anyway, I sent you their report last night and I see that it's all in today's papers.'' Anger suddenly surged in him. ''It's all your fault,'' he muttered, staring at both of them. ''If you had authorized the Foreign Office to give me the Byroade file, Benedetti would be alive now. She is dead because of you.''

''Most unfortunate, indeed,'' Sir Nigel said conversationally, ignoring the accusation. ''She died for what she did to Byroade thirty years ago. A fine example of poetic justice, don't you think?''

''She could have told us about the killer,'' Hastings countered bitterly. ''He is still at large. Maybe already back in England. Poetic justice indeed.''

Sir Nigel had thrown his head back and was watching Hastings between half-closed lids, his sharp face frozen in a slightly sardonic expression. ''I doubt if she could have added anything to the story of that other woman . . . Rosco?''

''Bosco.''

''Bosco, that's right. But the man is still at large, I agree.'' He picked up one of the papers lying on the table. ''A short, bald man,'' he muttered, perusing the document. ''There is quite a detailed description here,'' he said to Hastings, his raised brows forming an unspoken question.

''No,'' Hastings said in quick understanding. ''Our men didn't spot anybody corresponding to that description traveling to France or back. But that doesn't mean a thing. A face like that in a crowd is a needle in a haystack.''

''Yes,'' Sykes admitted. ''Yes, of course.'' He turned

to Snow with a short, unpleasant laugh. "Well, Peter, you have a problem, I'd say. You were the one who reported the infiltration of a KGB team. They seem to be roaming around, killing people here and in France, and leaving an elephant trail behind them. You should have got something on them by now, but you don't seem to have the faintest."

"I told you we should have expelled Orloff in the first place," Snow said stubbornly without looking up.

"Yes, you did. I've talked to the Americans about that before. But to expel him now would be admitting our impotence, wouldn't it?" He busied himself with his pipe while a sour-faced young woman in a green dress brought the tea.

Snow got up and stood by the window, slowly sipping his tea, waiting for the woman to leave. He addressed Hastings without looking back. "Chief Superintendent," he snapped, the two words sounding like a grim accusation, "you said that Orloff and the girl told you almost nothing you didn't know. That implies there was something you didn't know all the same."

Hastings ran a fingernail over the smooth rim of his tea cup. "Benedetti recognized the killer. The night before she died, he came to her restaurant, in Cannes. She asked her chief waiter to throw him out. She said"— he took his notebook from his pocket and read aloud—" 'How dare he show up here after all these years.' "

"Which means?"

"Which means that, besides Orloff, the Russians have had a highly placed mole in this country for at least the last thirty years."

Sykes frowned and spent a few matches in futile attempts to light his pipe. "Would you be so good as to elaborate, Chief Superintendent?'' Snow turned back and glowered at him.

"I am convinced," Hastings said slowly, "that the man who murdered Corinne Benedetti is the same man who came to Paris thirty years ago and hired her to frame Byroade. I am convinced that the same man killed Byroade and made that attempt on Orloff's life. I think that he is acting out of panic. He is taking insane risks out of fear that he might be exposed. The man is running for his life."

"So you don't believe the KGB team is responsible for these murders," Sir Nigel said, his voice heavy with sarcasm.

"They may be involved as a backup team, but nobody has seen them yet."

Sykes was drawing on his pipe without taking his eyes off him. "You think the killer is the mole himself, I gather."

"I guess so," Hastings said. "The KGB would never send the same field agent, thirty years later, to kill Benedetti. The active-duty span of a field operative is no longer than five years. The only man who is still active in this affair is the mole. He is a very secretive man, he must be. A loner. When he sensed danger, he took care of it himself. I already reported that. The man who shot Orloff was not very quick, and probably not very young."

"And what is Orloff's role according to this theory of yours, Chief Superintendent?" Snow's voice was dry, hostile.

Hastings took his time before answering. "The way I see it, Orloff did not know that for a long time there was another mole operating on a parallel level. Moscow Center never told him. That would have been a terrible blow to his pride. Even today, seventeen years after he defected. Anyway, the mole must have felt quite secure all those years. Till Orloff decided to come, and the Thames people discovered Byroade. The confrontation between Byroade and Orloff would have exposed the truth: the Russians had a second man here. And the hunt for him would have started. So he decided to murder anybody who could prove his existence. Byroade, Benedetti, maybe even some other people."

"But why would he try to kill Orloff?"

"If Orloff could convince us he did not know Byroade, it would mean that Byroade had been recruited by someone else. And given the present atmosphere in this country"—he felt a perverse satisfaction in looking straight into the eyes of Snow—"after the Prime fiasco and the Ritchie fiasco, the mole could be sure we would launch the most stringent witch hunt in the history of England. Which might lead us to him."

"Very convincing indeed," Sir Nigel said, his tone in total contradiction with his words.

Snow was watching Hastings with intent dislike. "There is, of course, a second possibility."

"Oh, really? Tell us, Peter." Sykes turned his head slightly, puffing on his pipe.

Snow clasped his hands together on the table and looked at the ceiling. "Perhaps Orloff did not tell everything when he defected. Perhaps he knew there was another mole in England, besides him, but kept the knowledge to himself. He could have done that on instructions—"

"—From Moscow?" Sykes asked, raising his eyebrows.

"Why not? His game was over, his network did not exist anymore, so Center could have fed him to the Americans to keep their other man safe."

135

"It's too farfetched, Peter," Sykes said. "They wouldn't deliver somebody with such knowledge to the CIA. One day he might have a drink too many in a friendly bar and spill the beans, don't you agree?"

Snow's face reddened. "All right. Let's assume the defection of Orloff was genuine. But that he did not report on the other mole, for his own reasons. We know that defectors often keep some secrets, a sort of life insurance, so to speak, I can cite quite a few examples."

"Yes, it does happen sometimes," Sykes admitted.

"Now," Snow continued more confidently, "when Orloff's visit to England was announced, the mole got frantic. Byroade or Orloff or anybody else connected with his activities might expose him. So he turned to murder. A sort of desperate gambit."

The telephone on Sir Nigel's desk purred discreetly, but he ignored it. "You assume it is possible," he said to Snow, "that Orloff fooled the Americans for seventeen years. That he is not exactly what he pretends to be." In the quickly falling darkness that had invaded the office, they looked like a bunch of conspirators, spinning their plot between the black shadows that crept onto the walls.

Snow didn't answer, and an uneasy silence settled in the room. A match briefly flickered, illuminating Sir Nigel's saturnine face. "I'd like your personal opinion, Chief Superintendent," he said in a low, cracked voice. "If Orloff felt threatened by somebody who knew compromising secrets from his past, do you think he would have him killed?"

Hastings scowled. "I don't concur with Mr. Snow's theory, Sir Nigel. I don't think Orloff knew about any other mole."

"I did not ask you for your views on Mr. Snow's theory,"

Sykes said bluntly. "I asked you if in your opinion Orloff might order people killed if he felt threatened."

For a second Hastings visualized the face of the old man, the stubborn jaw, the hard mouth, the inscrutable black eyes. "He's done it before, hasn't he?" he said.

"I missed you," Ted murmured. Her full lips were soft and fragrant. "I really missed you," he repeated and kissed her again, surprised by his own fervor.

She gently disengaged from his embrace. "Somebody might recognize us." Her voice had a hard edge. "You're a married man and, as you said, we are celebrities, both of us."

"I don't care," he pulled her back to him. "I couldn't wait to be alone with you, Lynn."

"I would hardly call this alone," she countered. "Two adults kissing like teen-agers in a car in the center of London. Alone, indeed."

Ted's car was parked a hundred yards down the road from the Churchill's entrance, where they had just left Orloff. Ted had met Lynn and the old man at Heathrow after their short confrontation with Hastings. The chief superintendent, flanked by two of his men, had stopped them in the arrival hall as soon as they had disembarked from the Nice-London flight. He had faced them angrily, sturdy legs planted on the tired linoleum.

He reminded Ted of a bull drinking in the sight of the red cloth before charging. His look had been mean, hostile. "I hold you responsible for the death of Corinne Benedetti," he had said. "If you had talked when I came to see you, she would have been alive now."

"Leave them alone," Ted had intervened, his anger matching Hastings's. "You'd better blame yourself. Had you done your job properly, you would have got to Benedetti long before them.''

The chief superintendent had turned quickly round to him, his stubborn jaw jutting forward. The two had glowered at each other in the middle of the bare Heathrow concourse, to the deep concern of a group of Japanese businessmen who walked past them, their merry chatter dying abruptly. Hastings had seemed on the verge of blowing his top, when suddenly he had taken a deep breath. ''I guess you're right.'' he had admitted, surprisingly, his eyes somber, his voice sinking to a weary tone. ''I am sorry. It's not you I should blame.'' He had turned and walked away. His two men had stayed behind, discreetly escorting them to Ted's car, then hurrying to their own, which had then stuck to them all the way into London.

During the drive, Lynn had done most of the talking, describing their grim experiences in France. The old man hadn't taken part in the conversation. Huddled in a corner of the back seat, he had remained strangely remote, his mind obviously elsewhere. By the time they reached the hotel, he had emerged from his lethargy and parted from them with a terse nod. He hadn't reacted to Ted's reminder that they would pick him up that evening at seven for the second interview.

In the rearview mirror Ted saw the Special Branch car move away from the Churchill's entrance. There was only one man in it; the other must have stayed at the hotel, he figured, to keep close watch on Orloff. Hastings couldn't afford to let him slip away again.

''Let's go somewhere where we can be really alone,'' Ted said to Lynn. ''Let's go to your flat.''

She shook her head in mock exasperation. ''You're like a small boy, Ted.'' She gently ran the tips of her fingers across his face. "No, we will not go to my flat now. I don't want to."

"Why . . ." he began, but she bent quickly toward him and kissed him on the lips. "I also want to be alone with you. But not like that. Not with my eyes on my watch. Why not tonight, after the show?"

"I can't tonight," he admitted sullenly, feeling utterly embarrassed. He avoided her eyes.

"I see," she said, turning away and developing a sudden interest in a printer's shop across the street. After a while she looked back at him and added, with contrived cheerfulness: "So why don't we settle for just a drink, okay?"

In the soothing half-darkness of the Regency bar, Ted asked the question that had been burning on his lips since he'd seen Lynn and Orloff emerging from the arrival gate at the airport. "How was it, Lynn? I mean traveling with Orloff, being with him most of the time?"

She leaned back on the leather cushions of her old-fashioned armchair. "He is a strange man. He can be very violent, even frightening at times. I told you about that Paris prostitute, Solange Bosco. He got so mad at her, I thought he was going to hit her. There were some moments, on the train to the Riviera, when he looked quite sinister. Alien. He would lapse into long silences and make me feel like extra baggage." She took a sip of her kir, and picked her cigarette from the ashtray. "On the other hand, he can also be very gentle, very warm, immensely likable. We had a lot of ups and downs. You know what I mean. One moment I was mad as hell, the next I felt real compassion for him."

"Really?" By the bar, their waiter was whispering something to the bartender, who stared at them openly while he

139

mechanically wiped his glasses with a white towel. "Perhaps you like him because he likes you."

She puckered her brow in thought, like a little girl, seriously considering his question. "Perhaps," she said finally. "I know he likes me. And I know I'm very important to him because of my mother. He is still very much in love with her, poor man." She leaned forward. "Do you know that he traveled all the way to California to see the place where my mother killed herself?"

"I didn't know that your mother killed herself," he said, confounded.

"Mother killed herself in a deliberate car crash," Lynn said slowly, her luminous eyes boring into his. "My father also died in the accident."

"Why?" he managed.

"Orloff seems to believe she did it because of him."

"And what do you think?" he said, reaching across the table. Her hand was slack, inert.

"I don't know," she said. "I really don't."

"How old were you when that happened?"

"Ten. I was raised by my Aunt Marjorie. It was not"—she attempted a smile—"it was not first class all the way."

"You are not as tough as you pretend to be," Ted said.

She didn't answer.

"When did you first learn about Orloff?"

She stubbed her cigarette in the ashtray. "I had heard the name Alex before. My father had mentioned it once or twice. But only when I was fifteen or sixteen did my aunt tell me that he had been my mother's first husband. She told me he had been a spy, and she kept repeating over the years that he had brought terrible misery upon the family."

Ill at ease, Ted beckoned to the waiter for another round

of drinks. "I hated him," Lynn suddenly said in a low voice. "I hated him and his name for years because of all the harm he had caused us. I guess I still resent him at times."

"But at times you're very fond of him."

She nodded gravely. "Fond of him is not the right expression, Ted. I feel for him. I think I understand his pain."

The waiter brought them their drinks. Ted took his glass and looked down at the thick red liquid. "Well," he said, "all that was unexpected. I'm afraid you have a very trying evening ahead of you."

"Why do you say that?"

He let out a deep breath. "You know the subject of tonight's interview. Do you think you can handle it? I mean can you interview him about all those killings? You like him, Lynn, and it won't be easy for you to ask him such questions."

"I agreed to take the job, remember?" she said.

"Yes, you did. But then you didn't expect to get friendly with the old man."

"I'll do what I have to do," she said stubbornly. "Don't you worry. I've got my first real chance and I won't blow it."

"Listen," he said. "Let me do the interviewing with you, all right? I can take some of the heat off you and ask the—"

"—the vicious questions?" Lynn's face was flushed.

"I want to help," he insisted. "Really."

She stared at him, doubt and uncertainty painted all over her face. "Just to help," she repeated. "That's all you want?"

"Yes," he said seriously, a lump in his throat. "I'm on your side, Lynn. I told you I missed you. I really did."

She shook her head. "Somebody told me once that you can't miss something you don't have."

"Lynn," he said, taking her face between his hands. "You can't know how much I missed you. I didn't expect what happened between us to happen that way. But if you want to know how I feel, I—"

"Don't." She put her finger softly on his mouth. "Don't say things you might regret later. Please."

"How many people did you order killed, Mr. Orloff?" Ted Jennings asked. From the darkness behind him, Camera One sailed forward soundlessly and focused its unblinking eye on Alexander Orloff.

Orloff looked at Jennings thoughtfully. The question didn't surprise him; the person asking it did. Lynn's phone call had caught him at the door when he was about to leave.

"Would you mind terribly, Alex, if Ted joined me for the interview? He has a lot of experience and is quite knowledgeable on the subject." He had hesitated. There was something odd in her voice, a hint of weariness and some sort of implied plea.

"If it is all right with you, I have no objection, of course," he had said, cautiously. What did this mean, he wondered.

In the studio, before they went on the air, Ted had been very civil, a handsome young man in a dark suit and a dazzling white shirt. Lynn was rather withdrawn, quietly sitting in her armchair while the makeup girl hovered about her. Her face was studious and grave again, the high collar of her immaculate blouse singularly pristine under her velvet jacket. Virginia had looked like that once—very solemn, very still, when they had met at her lawyer's office to sign the divorce papers. She had been very beautiful and subdued that day, and he had felt she was trying to tell him something, but she never did.

Ted Jennings was looking at him insistently. "Would you like me to repeat the question?" he inquired.

"I did not order anybody killed," Orloff said. "I reported to my superiors the names of people who threatened the activities of Philby or constituted a danger to the vital interests of my country."

"But all those people died, didn't they?"

"Many of them did, yes."

"So you were responsible for their deaths." Ted's voice was respectful but cold.

"Yes," he said firmly, stealing a glance at Lynn's pale face and understanding why she did not ask the questions herself, why she had let Ted do that. "I was responsible."

"As in the Volkov case, for instance," Ted said, leaning forward. "Do you remember Konstantin Volkov?"

Konstantin Volkov. "Yes, I remember the name," he said. Grim memories suddenly swept over him; the fears, the fever, the urgency of those faraway days came to life in his mind. The sudden phone call to his flat that balmy evening in August 1945. Philby's anxious voice: "Is this the Faversham Pub? Oh, awfully sorry, wrong number. . . ." The crash meeting, an hour later, at Hampstead Heath. Philby's stutter, aggravated by his distress. His story, told in disjointed sentences. The report that had just arrived at SIS headquarters from their man in Istanbul. A KGB officer, vice-consul at the Soviet mission, wants to defect with his wife, offers as price of his ticket the names of three Russian moles in Britain: two in the Foreign Office; the other, the head of a counterespionage organization in

London. "That's me, Alex. The bloody bastard knows about me!" The following hectic hours, interspersed with bouts of heavy drinking, till they'd hatched the plot. "Stall them, Kim," Orloff had urged. "Talk Menzies into taking his time till we take care of Volkov." In the wee hours, after he had dispatched his coded message to Moscow Center, Kim had suddenly had a stroke of genius. He would volunteer to go to Istanbul and debrief the Russian himself. Wasn't he the head of Section IX, the anti-Soviet counterespionage department? Philby was sure Menzies wouldn't suspect a thing and would charge him with the mission.

It had worked perfectly. Philby had convinced Menzies, the gullible chief of the SIS, to send him to Istanbul; and, after a series of delays including a flight via Cairo, he had landed in Turkey in mid-September. By then, Alex recalled, he had received the laconic message from Moscow Center: "Volkov taken care of." When Philby had at last called the Russian consulate in Istanbul, he had been told that a man by the name of Konstantin Volkov did not exist. Which was a sort of black humor; Volkov did not exist indeed. Not anymore.

"Is it true," Jennings was asking, "that you alerted the KGB after a meeting with Philby? And that they had Volkov sedated, tied to a stretcher, and flown to Moscow aboard a special plane? That they told the Turkish authorities the man was sick and needed urgent medical treatment?" Ted paused and leaned forward, his eyes deep black pits in the chalky face. "And that Volkov was tortured and shot with his wife in the courtyard of Lubyanka prison?"

"I believe your description is correct," Orloff replied woodenly.

144

"Thus, you directly caused the death of Volkov and his wife."

He made an effort to control his voice. "I had to protect Philby, Burgess, and Maclean."

Lynn intervened, her voice low, hesitant. "I would like to ask you about another man. Jordania." Jennings looked at her sharply.

"Jordania was the leader of the Georgian émigrés in Europe," Orloff said. "He lived in Paris." He added, somewhat defensively: "He died there of old age."

"But when he was alive you considered him a threat to the Soviet Union," she went on, showing a sudden interest in the pad on her knees.

"Yes," Orloff quickly said, determined to spare her the next questions. "My superiors in Moscow were rather upset about the émigrés, especially those from Georgia and the Ukraine."

"Was there any particular reason for that?" she asked.

"Moscow Center wanted to disrupt the émigré organization abroad and crush any subversive network it might have established in Georgia. Georgia was something of an obsession with them, as it was the birthplace of Stalin." He smiled faintly but, seeing no reaction, continued. "The opportunity came when Philby was appointed head of the SIS station in Turkey. He convinced the chiefs of SIS and Turkish Intelligence to mount a joint operation and get several of Jordania's agents across the Turkish border into Soviet Georgia. We hoped that Jordania himself would swallow the bait and go with his men."

"But he didn't," Lynn said.

"No. He sent two young men, boys in their twenties. They were trained and equipped in London and flown to Erzerum. They crossed the Russian border at—"

"You say they were in their twenties," Lynn interrupted. "How old were they when they left Russia?"

He felt Jennings's insistent gaze upon him. "They had not left Russia. They were born in Paris to émigré families and had never seen Georgia in their lives."

"Nevertheless, they went straight to their deaths there," Jennings commented.

"They crossed the border close to Akhlatsikhe, which is a Russian garrison town," Orloff continued, ignoring Jennings and focusing on the dejected face of Lynn. "The Turks who escorted them to the border heard some bursts of machine-gun fire a few minutes after the crossing. One of the boys was killed. The second was captured the same night, interrogated, and finally executed."

"You arranged that, didn't you? You were there," she said.

"I had flown to Istanbul. I had come for the formal reopening of the Topkapi museum. They had some rare pieces on display. Philby was in Erzerum supervising the operation. He kept me informed of the infiltration attempt, and I notified Moscow."

"Two more dead," Jennings said quietly and made a show of turning a page on his pad. "Would you please tell us now what happened in the Ukraine between nineteen forty-nine and nineteen fifty-one?"

"Many thing happened in the Ukraine during those years," Orloff said flatly.

"We mean events in which you and Philby were involved, Mr. Orloff." Lynn's voice was hollow now, devoid of feeling.

"In nineteen forty-nine, a party of Ukrainian dissidents belonging to the Fascist Bandera group were parachuted by the British into the Ukraine. They had to establish contact with the local resistance movement.''

''What for?''

''What for? The British intended to start a revolution that would lead to the secession of the Ukraine from the Soviet Union. The infiltrators carried arms, money—in napoleons and sovereigns—and wireless transmitters. They were never heard of again. Two more parties entered a few months later, with the same result. The following year, the British Intelligence Service dropped in three parties of six men each. These infiltrators were transported in unmarked planes that took off from the Royal Air Force bases in Cyprus. The first group jumped close to Tarnopol; the second was dispatched to the shores of the Prut; as far as I remember, the third was dropped close to the source of the San River, inside the Polish border.''

''And they were never heard of again,'' Jennings said. The eye of the camera was on Orloff, stalking his reaction.

He nodded.

Lynn turned a leaf on her pad. ''In his memoirs, Kim Philby writes the following: 'I do not know what happened to the parties concerned. But I can make an informed guess.' '' She looked up at Orloff, her face suddenly showing its rage. ''I think that his cynicism is disgusting, Mr. Orloff, and I want to ask you: can you, too, make an 'informed guess' about the fate of these wretched people?''

''Yes, I can,'' he said. ''And, if I may add, those 'wretched people,' as you call them, were sworn enemies of my country.''

''A country you have since deserted and betrayed,'' Jennings said in a patient, slightly bored voice, like a teacher correcting a child's too frequent mistake. ''Now, let's talk about Albania.''

11

SHE CAUGHT UP with Orloff when he was about to cross Euston Road. He held his hat in his hand, letting the icy drops of rain stream down his burning face. Lynn did not seem to mind the rain either, and her only protection was a thin black cape she clutched under her chin with her left hand. The two Special Branch plainclothesmen, who had stuck to Orloff like shadows since the attempt on his life, did not interfere. They must have recognized her, he assumed.

"I must talk to you," she managed, breathless, as she fell in pace with him.

He stopped and turned toward her. Her wet hair fell in clumps on her shoulders, and her makeup was dissolving into dark smudges that descended her cheeks. "You just did," he said. A sports car roared by, splashing muddy water on his legs.

She shuddered. "Alex, I have to talk to you." Her

voice was insistent but not pleading. "Let's go into a pub or a bar or a restaurant or something. I need lots of people around me."

"No," he said. "No people. Where is your car?"

"Around the corner. Why? Where do you want to go?"

"Nowhere. Just drive around town."

She looked at him doubtfully, then nodded. "Okay."

They did not speak until they were in the car. The cold engine refused to catch and the starter shrieked in protest as she somewhat frantically pushed down on the accelerator. Finally she gave in. "Let's wait a moment," she said. The interior of the car smelled of damp cloth and stale cigarette smoke. A film of condensation swiftly crept up the windshield.

"Where is Ted?" he asked.

"He went home to his French wife," she muttered furiously, and tried the starter again. "He is a married man." The engine coughed several times and came to life. She clumsily maneuvered out of her parking space, missing a Dairy Maid van by inches. The car lurched forward. Huddled in his seat, he watched her pensively. The rearview mirror reflected the discreet lights of the Special Branch car.

For a while she drove recklessly, without speaking. Finally, as she braked before a red light, she spoke without looking at him. "How could you, Alex? All those deaths."

He had been expecting the question. "Do you really want to know?"

She did not answer.

The light turned to green and he leaned back in his seat. "Lynn, since the day I was born I was brought up to be a devout Communist. Today one might say that I was conditioned. Maybe. It doesn't really matter. I was eight when my father was killed in the civil war. My mother told me that he had been shot at Romanovka, near Vladivostok, by American soldiers.''

"American soldiers? In Russia? Come on."

He smiled bleakly. "You find it hard to believe, of course. But it's true. You certainly must know that when the White armies launched the counterrevolution against the Reds, they were assisted by foreign intervention forces. Now, in most history books one would read that the expeditionary forces that attacked Soviet Russia were British, French, Japanese—''

"—and Czech?" she suggested.

"And Czech, of course. The truth is there was also an American unit, dispatched by President Wilson.''

"I really can't believe that Wilson would do such a thing. What about his principles? Wilson joining the Whites against the revolution?''

"It's true, though. The Yankees had even composed their own battle song.''

"They actually sang a song about the war in Russia?" Disbelief was painted all over her face.

"They did. They used the tune of the 'Battle Hymn of the Republic.' '' He quoted the lyrics easily: " 'We came out from Vladivostok to catch the Bolshevik / We chased them o'er the mountain and we chased them through the creek / We chased them every Sunday and we chased them through the week / But we couldn't catch a gosh darn one.' '' He paused, casting an absent glance at the bright entrance of the Red Parrot Club. "Well, there were a few they did catch at Romanovka, and my father was among them. That's what my mother told me.''

"Was that true?"

"I guess so. I know he was in the Far East with the Red partisans, fighting against Kolchak's troops."

"That made you hate the Americans?"

He pondered the question, pressing his fingertips together. The neon signs of Piccadilly were projecting multi-colored patterns over the windshield. "No," he said firmly. "Not really. My mother was American herself. She made me hate the imperialists, the enemies of the people. Not the people themselves." He smiled in apology. "It might seem to you that I am speaking in slogans. But don't forget that in a way I absorbed communism with my mother's milk. My father was a Bolshevik revolutionary. My mother was a dedicated Communist. Someone is writing a book about her now." He chuckled despite himself. "American Communists seem to be very fashionable lately. You know"—he half turned to her—"before the revolution, in nineteen seventeen, Mother left me in Saint Petersburg and traveled to Switzerland to join Lenin and the other exiles. She used her American passport. Later, she was one of the only three women who returned to Russia on the famous sealed train, together with Lenin. All the way across Germany, to start the revolution! And I was her only child. I grew up in a house where the revolution was ever present. All the great leaders used to hold meetings in our house—Molotov, Trotzki, Bukharin, Zhdanov. . . . At my father's funeral Red Marshall Budionni walked behind the coffin, his hand on my shoulder. I was a child of the revolution. Do you understand?" He suddenly felt he wanted her very much to understand, to see things from his point of view. "Do you understand?" he repeated.

"How did all that bring you over to England?" There was no compassion in her voice.

"Didn't I tell you? One night Maxim Litvinov came to

our house in Leningrad. He had just returned from London; he was not foreign minister yet. I was fourteen. He was very kind to me that night and looked at me in an odd way. I remember that his look frightened me a little. Then he shut himself up with my mother. They talked most of the night. Before I fell asleep, I saw my mother go to the kitchen a half dozen times to prepare fresh tea. Litvinov was drinking gallons of it.''

She lit a cigarette. ''What did they talk about?''

''I can only guess. The next morning my mother told me we were going back to America. In America they started my training.''

''Who are 'they'?''

''Some instructors I had. A couple of Russians, an old American spinster, and an Englishwoman, Mary.'' He smiled to himself. ''She was adorable. Taught me English manners, customs, forms of speech.'' He marked a pause, rubbing his eyes with his left thumb and forefinger. ''Mother assumed a new name—Carlisle—and we moved to New England, where nobody knew that she was one of 'those Communists,' like Louise Bryant. It was only years later that I understood how, during that winter night in Leningrad, in nineteen twenty-four, the course of my life had been decided.''

''Litvinov had talked your mother into making a spy out of you?'' she said bluntly.

He took no offense. ''In effect, yes. That night they decided to make a spy out of me. But they didn't use that term and didn't see it that way. Neither did I. I never felt manipulated, or conditioned. I believed for many years that I was fighting for a noble cause. A better world, thanks to communism. A French poet, a Communist, wrote about *Les Lendemains Qui Chantent—The 'Morrows That Sing.''*

"Isn't that touching," she said bitterly, accelerating up a dark, empty street. "In the name of the 'morrows that sing you ordered people killed. Didn't you ever feel any remorse?''

He sighed and tried to suppress the patronizing note that had slipped into his voice. "Throughout history people have murdered other people in the name of a better future, Lynn. For the sake of a better future, America sent the Rosenbergs to the electric chair. The US supports some of the cruelest regimes in the world, for a better future. In Saudi Arabia they are still chopping off thieves' hands and stoning adulterous wives. In El Salvador and Chile torture is a state monopoly. Those regimes are America's friends, and America helps them for a better future.'' He took a deep breath. "I did all I could to serve Soviet Russia. If you ask me if I did it knowingly, the answer is yes. I knew people would die because of what I was doing, and I did it anyway. I thought I was doing the right thing.''

"So what happened?'' she said. "What made you change your mind?''

For a time he said nothing. He looked fixedly through the windshield down the dark street, uncertain whether or not he should share with her the ugly memories her inevitable question had suddenly raised from the past. The name of the woman had been Vera Zaritzkaya, but for more than a year he and Philby had known her only under her code-name. Source Charade. They had first learned about her from an urgent telegram from Moscow Center: "Top priority—Report identity SIS agent Moscow named Source Charade, probably female.'' For many months all they could report about her was that she was a loner, a Muscovite, and the best agent the SIS had in Russia. It was 1959, Philby was no longer head of the anti-Soviet counterespionage department and had no free access to the agents' files. And despite the insistent, frantic demands transmitted from Moscow Center, at the rate of one a week, Kim was unable to pin a name under the enigmatic code-word. He was in half-disgrace already, after the flight of Burgess and Maclean, and had only glimpsed some of her reports. Moscow Center had ample reason to be worried. Her material was first-rate and she seemed to be privy to the most secret intrigues inside the Kremlin.

It was only in September 1959 that Philby had achieved a breakthrough and come up with a name. Vera Zaritzkaya. Surprisingly young—only twenty-seven—and daughter of the former Russian military attaché in London, she was presently employed as a researcher on the private staff of Chairman Khrushchev. There was a grainy picture of a willowy girl with luminous eyes and a flowered dress in the middle of a group photographed in the embassy garden in London.

Orloff had triumphantly transmitted the details to Moscow. The same evening Vera Zaritzkaya was arrested and imprisoned at Lubyanka. Starting that night, and for the following six weeks, she was intensively interrogated, three teams of investigators working in shifts around the clock. Still, the investigation failed to yield the expected results; at the beginning of November, Center let him know that a confrontation was necessary. Philby couldn't go to Moscow, of course, so Orloff flew to Leningrad, after having memorized Kim's detailed report. Center had gone to great lengths to provide a cover for Orloff's visit to Russia. They had organized a special display of Czar Nikolai's art treasures in the Leningrad Hermitage, inviting noted art critics and collectors from the West. The enormous effort, just to establish cover for an agent's visit to Russia, didn't surprise him. In 1956 Moscow had called an emergency congress of the World Peace Movement in Belgrade, just to make possible a short meeting between a German journalist, working for Center, and his KGB case officer.

Orloff had not been prepared, though, for what awaited him in Russia. Images of his version of Danté's journey to hell and back flickered through his mind as he now recalled the nightmare he had tried so hard to forget but never would. Playing the main role in its grim culmination, he had been taken secretly to meet the chief investigator at KGB headquarters in Leningrad, while most of his colleagues had been sent to a showcase kolkhoz to see some samples of local art. The investigator was young, gray-faced, with prematurely white hair and thick glasses that gave him a wooden, fixed look. Orloff assumed he was very important in the Center hierarchy, as only a half dozen people were acquainted with his secret functions in London.

"Because of security problems," the investigator had said, "we can't hold the meeting here. You must meet the suspect at the detention facility."

Alex had protested meekly, only to hear the cold, detached answer. "Yes, we know it's highly irregular. Every measure has been taken to guarantee your personal security." The conversation was held in English, as he was explicitly forbidden by Center ever to use his rather rudimentary Russian.

He should have understood, then and there, the implied meaning of the chief investigator's statement, but he hadn't. Thus, he had embarked upon his fateful trip to the secret recesses of his country. They had taken off that same afternoon aboard a military Tupolev and headed east toward the dark, frozen spaces of the Arctic Circle. He recalled the bumpy landing at Vorkuta at dusk, with the jagged Ural mountains looming over the heavily guarded airbase; the night ride aboard a military Pobeda through a snowstorm that rolled down the bare hillsides. He remembered the convoy they had overtaken—big, uncovered trucks with hundreds of prisoners squatting at the back under the armed guard of Red Army soldiers, their cigarettes glowing like fireflies above the drivers' cabs. At the double-fenced labor camp, with its watchtowers and floodlights and machine-gun nests, guards in full combat attire circled on their skis, like ghostly apparitions doing their *danse macabre* around that home of the damned. Dogs were barking, and there was the smell of sweat, cheap makhorka tobacco, and urine on the blanket somebody threw on his shoulders to protect him from the polar cold. He recalled the walk through the prison corridors, the sighs, the pungent smell of hundreds of exhausted, unwashed human bodies. And finally the confrontation in a tiny office with a coil-shaped radiator, a window with bars and a huge picture of Marx on the wall. And the inscription in Russian: ALL ROADS LEAD TO COMMUNISM.

And the girl.

The girl. That shapeless dull-green bundle of coarse prisoners' clothes; the dirty, wispy hair; the hollow cheeks; the bloodless lips. Her eyes were dull and clouded. The skin on her small hands was so thin, so pale, that one could see her tiny blue veins through it. The laughing girl in the flowered dress he had seen in the photograph must have been somebody else. But the oblong yellow patch on her uniform, over a starved left breast, carried a number, PP 398441, and a name, Vera Zaritzkaya. He couldn't avoid thinking about what they had done to her.

On the chief investigator's cue, he had addressed her, disclosing his secret trade in London. For the first time in years he was speaking Russian. He quoted passages from her reports, detailed accounts of Kremlin meetings, inside information only she and a few other employees had known. She had listened in silence, her head bowed in a strange posture of resignation, but not of surrender. He quoted internal SIS memos identifying Source Charade as Vera Zaritzkaya and pointing out that she had been recruited while her father was serving in England. She had maintained her silence despite the angry interruptions of the investigator.

And then Orloff had produced his trump card, the main reason for his trip. "We know all about you," he said, exactly as had been rehearsed in the Tupolev with the chief investigator. "We know who seduced you and recruited you. He has been bragging about it all over SIS headquarters. Remember him? Captain Sandy Hallandale?"

"We bought him three weeks ago . . ." the investigator viciously began. But the girl was already all over Orloff, screaming, writhing, scratching his face with her nails, madness and despair burning in her eyes.

In the plane on the way back he had sat by himself, holding his bloodied handkerchief against his face. Only then had he understood why he hadn't been allowed to run any risk of exposure by flying east to meet the prisoner. She would never tell anyone about him, because she was going to die. She might have been shot already, even before the plane had taken off from Vorkuta. They didn't need her anymore, not after she had broken down under Marx's benign gaze in the camp office and told them what she knew. It struck him that even if the confrontation had failed, they would have shot her all the same. Just because she had seen his face. Her life had been expendable from the very first moment. He had only been an instrument in their hands, a precursor of death dispatched to the very heart of that icy Hades to get the wretched woman's confession before they took her life. The decision had probably been made even before they summoned him from London.

Before returning to London, he had spent a few days in Moscow. He had walked the streets aimlessly, mixing with the throngs in Red Square, noticing for the first time the drab clothes and the unhappy faces, the miserable peasant women shoveling the snow on Taras Shevchenko Quay, the chauffeured limousines waiting in front of the lavish residences on Kutuzovski Prospect. And the popular slogan painted on huge billboards in golden letters on long strips of red silk fluttering over the Lenin Mausoleum: ALL ROADS LEAD TO COMMUNISM.

Back in London, Philby had listened to Orloff in silence one long evening, frequently refilling his glass. "You are an incurable romantic, Alex," he had finally said. "You knew these things existed, didn't you? You knew they were necessary." When Orloff made no reply, Philby had added: "You should learn to face the truth, Alex. She is not the first person who has died because of us. The only difference is that you haven't seen the others; they were just names and statistics in your reports."

It was not only the death of Vera, he wanted to shout back, it was how and where she had died. And why. But he kept quiet. Philby was much stronger than he was, he suddenly realized. He had recruited Philby and made him into a hard-core Communist. While Alexander Orloff,

Litvinov's great hope and the man sent to take the fortress from within, had remained a dreamer. A believer in a pure and humane revolution where Vorkuta could never happen.

He could never tell this truth to Lynn, he now thought as he looked back at her intense, questioning face. He feared she might cut him with a sarcastic remark and irreparably destroy the fragile bond between them. "What made me change my mind about communism?" he repeated slowly, biding his time. "What made so many Communists repent, I guess I lost my faith for the same reasons as the others. Stalin's crimes, the labor camps, the show trials, the oppression. . . . I made a few trips to Russia, and each time I returned more disoriented. But I guess Philby kept me going. Our friendship meant much to me. After he escaped to Moscow I was suddenly left alone. And I did a lot of thinking. A sort of delayed reaction."

"If Philby . . ." she began, but he suddenly leaned forward, peering through the windshield. He would have recognized that red brick house under any conditions. "Wait! Lynn, please, turn right. Here. Then take the second left, then left again."

She seemed baffled but followed his instructions. Minutes later, they came into a mews. He got out of the car and crossed to the opposite sidewalk. The rain had turned to sleet, but he didn't mind. He heard her steps behind him and pointed to the neat cottage that loomed in the darkness, half-hidden by some oaks and shrubbery.

"This is the house where I lived with your mother," he said. "Seven years. It used to be white." There was a soft light downstairs in the living room, and he had the feeling of prying into his own life.

"My mother left you," Lynn said angrily.

He turned back. "She did. But she never betrayed me."

"I don't understand."

"She found out about me, and she left me. She could have gone to the police or to the American embassy. She never did."

Lynn slowly shook her head. "I . . . I can't cope with you," she murmured. "You fascinate me and you revolt me. There is so much love and warmth in you, yet such ruthlessness, such fanaticism. One moment I approve of my mother, and the next I hate her for having married you. Sometimes I wish I had never met you."

A man walking a hairy Afghan dog and sheltering under a large black umbrella trudged past them. Orloff shook his head and got into the car. They did not speak all the way back to his hotel. She parked by the curb and turned off the engine. He sensed that she did not want to leave things this way. She was staring ahead, both her hands on the steering wheel. When she finally spoke, her voice was very soft. "Ted's father was killed in Albania in nineteen forty-nine. I guess he holds you responsible."

For a moment he didn't speak. So that was the reason for Jennings's hostility. He had had the feeling, since his arrival in London, that there was something personal in the young man's animosity. "I am sorry," he finally said, but a slow, cold anger seeped into his voice. "I am sorry for Ted Jennings, Lynn, but I don't feel guilty. You can be mad at me, but I did not come here to ask forgiveness for my crimes." He opened the door of the car and felt the cold night air on his face. "Philby told me about the Albanian project and I was very happy to thwart the coup. You can tell Ted that if the operation had succeeded many more people would have been killed. Innocent people."

She looked at him gravely, seeming to consider his words. "How did you start working with Philby in the first place," she asked.

"When I arrived in Cambridge . . ." he began, then suddenly fell silent. "Good God, Lynn," he said in wonder. "You just gave me a great idea."

As he walked past the uniformed doorman, a tremor of excitement shot through his body.

12

CAMBRIDGE did not stir any emotions in his heart. The city that he had loved so dearly in his youth looked hostile and squalid in the rain, and its ancient monuments, once so magnificent, seemed to have shrunk with the years. The train journey from King's Cross had been surprisingly uneventful. One of the passengers in his compartment had apparently recognized him but had been civil enough to leave him in peace. Another one, a woman, was too busy knitting a hideous green-and-yellow pullover to spare him a look. His third companion for the trip had been one of the Special Branch plainclothesmen, already a part of the scenery. At Cambridge station he found the name and address in a badly abused phonebook and took a cab to Chesterton Lane. The house of Mary Ellis was near the Jesus lock on the River Cam. He vaguely remembered a punting excursion to Grantchester Meadows for tea, and the easy, silvery laugh of a girl. He could not recall her face, though. She had been sitting at Kim's feet while he punted. Kim had been very proud that day. Not because of his conquest ("She is just a good friend, Alex," he had stressed rather anxiously, "nothing but a friend, really."), but because of what she had given him: the first document the freshly recruited Kim Philby had passed to his case officer. A paper they would christen "the secret list of Mary Ellis," with the carefree irreverence of two young-sters still hardly aware of the grim, cruel nature of the adventure they had embarked upon.

When Kim had met Mary Ellis in the spring of 1933, she was the secretary of the Colonial Office Liaison Bu-reau in Cambridge. The bureau, run by a florid, flabby Welshman by the name of Randall, recruited talented young students for overseas positions. The walls of Mary's small cubicle were covered with posters offering jobs in the Thrilling Capitals of the Dark Continent, or praising the Untold Mysteries of Fabulous India. But the truth, as Mary revealed it to Philby, was that Mr. Randall did not actually give a damn about any recruiting, and practically no re-cruiting was ever done. Randall was an employee of MI-5, and the bureau was a counterespionage agency. Its true task was to keep a close watch on Communists and left-wing activists among the students and the dons of Cam-bridge. The secret list of Mary Ellis, which she had passed to Philby, and he in turn to Orloff, included about fifty names of leftists. The list had been compiled by Randall and his aides over the previous three years. Orloff had been immensely pleased that Kim's name was not on the list; he had included the list in one of his first reports to Moscow.

Almost fifty years had passed since; and last night Lynn's offhand question had triggered a sudden recollection. What if Byroade's name had been on that list? And what if Moscow had instructed someone, perhaps even Philby without Orloff's knowledge, to recruit Byroade and other Cambridge graduates into a parallel network? A week ago Lynn had spoken to him about a few high-ranking diplomats who had been dismissed from the Foreign Office in 1967 for spying. They had been Communists in their youth, she had said. Perhaps Moscow had made use of Mary Ellis's list? If he got his hands on it, he might find the names of other diplomats apprehended at the same time as Byroade. And if he dug deeper, he might reach the man who pulled the strings of their network, the murderer of Byroade and Benedetti. It was a long shot, no doubt, but in his line of work the wildest hunches sometimes brought the choicest trophies.

The dull bronze plaque on the gatepost read ELLIS. Orloff paid the cab and walked into the tiny garden, between two hedges of myrtle shrubs. A second cab discharged his two bodyguards, who kept back, watching him morosely. Mary Ellis had never married, he recalled. A few years after their paths had crossed she had become involved in a scandal that had shaken the conservative establishment of Cambridge. She had become pregnant after a short affair with a Pembroke student and had brazenly decided to have the child and raise it under her name. By then Philby was a war correspondent in Spain, while Orloff had established his rear base in Hendaye, on the French side of the border. They had discussed the girl's bravado one night over a bottle of Alicante in San Sebastian. But after the scandal, Mary Ellis had been forced to resign from MI-5 and they had lost their first agent.

The man who opened the door was tall and gaunt. His

sparse hair was gray but he was no older than forty-five. He was dressed in baggy worsted trousers and a brown pullover of coarse wool. His weak chin and the pale, nervously blinking eyes betrayed a timid character and profound, ever-present anxiety.

"Good morning," Orloff said politely. "I'd like to speak to Mary Ellis, please."

But the man facing him was staring back in surprised recognition. "Goodness gracious," he blurted out. "Weren't you on the telly last night?" And when Orloff nodded, he smiled with embarrassment. "The Russian . . . the Russian agent." He seemed reluctant to use the word spy. "Ornoff, Alexander Ornoff."

"Orloff."

"That's right. Good morning." He suddenly stopped, obviously unable to decide what to do with a dangerous foreign spy who had suddenly materialized on his doorstep.

"I'm looking for Mary Ellis," Orloff repeated gently.

"We just saw you on the telly last night, and here you are," the man went on foolishly. "My wife would have been amazed. We discussed your . . . your interview till late. Such a pity she is out for the day. She will not believe me when I tell her. I can hardly believe it myself." He shifted awkwardly on his feet.

"Are you a relation of Miss Ellis?" Orloff asked.

"I am Phillip Ellis. Mary Ellis is my mother," the man said, suddenly suspicious. "What do you want with her?"

"Is she home?"

The man shook his head, and retreated a step backward, into the reassuring darkness of the tiny vestibule. "My mother is in a nursing home," he said. "She has not been very well during the last two years. I live here with my

family. We hope to have her back soon." He paused.
"You know her?"

Orloff had prepared a cover story for Mary Ellis. Not
for her neurotic son. He had to improvise. Phillip Ellis was
frightened.

"Mr. Ellis, I believe you would like to help your country," he said in a low voice.

The man blinked at him, perplexed.

"If you have followed my interviews, you should know
that I was granted asylum in the West seventeen years ago
and I have been cooperating with the American and British
secret services ever since."

The man nodded, unconvinced.

"I am now working with the authorities of your country," Orloff continued in the same conspiratorial tone. "I
have undertaken to reconstruct, for their benefit, every
stage of my activities here; that way, with my help, they
might discover other Communist agents who are still alive."

"What do you want with my mother?" Ellis repeated.

He was fighting a losing battle. "When I was at Cambridge, in the thirties," he tried, "I made an application
for service overseas. Your mother worked then for the
colonial office."

"Did you know my mother?"

"She was in charge of the applications," he said noncom-
mittally. "Now, I promised the British authorities I'd find
my application papers. I thought perhaps your mother
might have kept some of the documents from that period."
Philby had boasted once that Mary was copying entire files
for him. She kept a record of every paper that passed
through her office, he had said.

"What do you want?" the man repeated stubbornly.

"I would like your permission to go through your mother's

papers. Perhaps she has kept a copy of my application. You do know, of course, that the archives of the colonial office were destroyed during the war. Our only hope is that your mother has kept some duplicates.''

The man shook his head vigorously and took another step backward. ''I am not going to show you any papers,'' he said. ''Please go away.''

''Why not?'' Orloff tried again. ''You can be present and see exactly what I look for.'' He pointed at the street. ''You see those people there? They are from Special Branch, Scotland Yard. They came to protect me while I look for the papers. It's official business, you see.''

The man gaped curiously over Orloff's shoulder. For a second he seemed to hesitate. ''Those are detectives?'' he asked, unable to conceal his interest.

''Yes, they came with me from London.''

But the moment of grace had passed, and Ellis retreated into the obstinate entrenchment of the weak. ''I shall show you nothing,'' he said, and his hand gripped the doorknob. ''If the government needs something, they can come themselves.''

He was left alone on the porch. There was no use knocking on the door again. Ellis would not let him in. He might even call the police.

Back on the street, Orloff spent a moment staring at the Cam. Then, his decision made, he walked briskly toward the Special Branch agents. He had never spoken to them before. ''Something has come up,'' he said. ''I wonder if you could get in touch with Chief Superintendent Hastings?''

It took Hastings barely fifteen minutes to find the list.

The large study of Mary Ellis was a model of order and tidiness. On the racks, the books stood in neat rows, classified by subject and then by alphabetical order; pens and pencils, duly sharpened, lay in a tray on the small desk in the corner; letters and documents were arranged in fat blue files marked with the year and stacked in a spacious cupboard. Orloff stood in the corner, watching Hastings peruse the papers, his forehead wrinkled in concentration. From the dark doorway of the living room, the face of Phillip Ellis would occasionally appear, and he would anxiously peer over the sagging shoulders of the chief superintendent or shoot quick, poisonous looks at Orloff. An aging child he was, obviously waiting for his mother to die to take possession of the whole house but not daring to step into her private realm as long as she was alive, even though she was a doomed invalid.

The list was exactly where it should have been: in the file marked "1934."

"I guess that's it," Hastings grunted as he straightened up, his eyes glued to the rectangular folder. He hesitated a moment, and Orloff detected droplets of perspiration on his livid face. Hastings finally handed the list to him. "Do you make anything of it?" The list was headed: "Scholarship candidates—1933," in an amateurish attempt to conceal its real meaning. There were forty-seven names in it. Byroade was the third one.

"Byroade," he said. "That's what I was looking for." The other names were unknown to him, but that was to be expected. "I suggest that one of your men check with the Foreign Office to see if any of these people were employed there after graduation. My hunch is that we'll get a few positive answers. Then you should find out if any of them were involved in an espionage affair, as Byroade was."

"And your hunch is that we'll get a few positive answers again?" Hastings grunted. "What will that mean?"

Orloff glanced at the blurred figure in the doorway and shook his head. "Not here," he said.

Hastings seemed at a loss. For a long moment he stood in the middle of the room, a heavy block of a man, clumsy as a bear, his small eyes fixed on Orloff, spelling a mixture of suspicion and embarrassment. When he finally spoke, his voice was tentative. "Let's have tea somewhere," he said, and made for the door.

In the small tearoom at the Lion's Yard, Hastings gruffly insisted that Orloff sit with his back to the entrance. One of his men took the next table, while the other, a blond, broad-faced man named Wells, was dispatched to the local police station to phone London. The tearoom was almost deserted. In one corner two bearded Americans ate cheese sandwiches and guffawed at each other's jokes. Farther down, a boy with rimless glasses and a college scarf was pretentiously explaining Wittgenstein to a pert little blond in a tight sweater.

The waiter brought two Indian teas and a tiny plate with lemon slices. Hastings pushed his untouched cup aside. Orloff noticed that his hand holding the Gauloise was trembling slightly. "Now," Hastings said, "what's this all about?"

Orloff felt a sudden lassitude pervade his body. He had had some curry and a glass of wine in the Akbar on Wheeler Street, while waiting for Hastings to arrive from London, and walked in and out of several bookshops. Hastings had immediately responded to his call and promptly used his authority to get the list from Ellis's house. He had stuck his neck out by consorting with him and searching the Ellis house without first conferring with his superiors. Orloff himself was not very happy about getting Hastings in on the operation, for the chief superintendent's intervention might seriously impede his own activities later on.

"The list might be the key to the problem," Orloff was now saying, taking a sip from his cup and trying to sound matter-of-fact. He told Hastings about Philby and Mary Ellis, and the MI-5 list he had sent to Moscow. "When I remembered the list," he said, "it occurred to me that Byroade was a Cambridge man. There is the possibility that at a certain point Moscow Center decided to make use of that list. They might have instructed somebody to find out if any of the Communist sympathizers on that list had reached an important position in the government here. Let's assume that it was discovered that a few of them had joined the Foreign Office. They might have been recruited to form a new network."

"Without your knowledge?" Hastings seemed surprised.

"Without my knowledge. It was the height of the cold war. Center desperately needed more intelligence about the West. Perhaps they did not want to jeopardize me or Philby or our group. So let's say they set up another organization, either by appealing to former sympathizers or by using some muscle, as in the case of Byroade."

"I didn't know the KGB used blackmail or prostitutes to recruit their agents," Hastings remarked, surveying Orloff through half-closed eyelids.

"They most certainly didn't," Orloff confirmed. "But they might have been desperate, as I said."

"So desperate that they wouldn't ask you or Philby for the information they needed?"

Orloff shrugged. "I don't know. Compartmentalization is the first commandment in that trade. But that's not the point, not now. In nineteen sixty-seven, several diplomats, including Byroade, were suddenly apprehended." Seeing that Hastings was about to speak, he hastily added: "Don't ask me how I know. We are not playing games now. Lynn Kennan and Ted Jennings told me. I'd advise you to check and find out who smoked them out and how. But if they were part of a ring, there must have been a ringleader behind the scenes. The man who pulled the strings. As far as I understand, no arrests were made in 'sixty-seven. The diplomats were simply fired, and the affair was hushed up. If you get back to them, and put some pressure on them, they might lead you to the man you're looking for."

"The short killer with the scar," Hastings said. For a moment he retreated into thought, occasionally wiping his sweating brow. He suddenly leaned forward, his eyes drilling deep into the old man's. "Why the hell are you mixed up in all this, Orloff?" His voice was rough but controlled. "It's none of your bloody business."

"I want to find the man who shot me, and I want to find out why," Orloff said flatly.

Hastings shook his head. "Rubbish. Where you're concerned, the KGB is merely trying to settle an old account with you. Period. You should be satisfied with that. And let us do our job. But you don't." He leaned back on his chair. "So let me tell you, Mr. Master Spy, why you're in this. Not because of a blasted attempt on your life. You don't care much about your life. You told me that when we first met. You don't care very much about the identity of Byroade's killer either."

"Now what . . ." Orloff began, but Hastings raised his hand.

"You have one and only one motive: your wounded pride. You are a very proud man. You don't like being called a defector. You almost blew your top during that television interview when the girl called you a common

spy. You came back to this country, after seventeen years.''
He was speaking in his strange, characteristic way, hacking his sentences like chopping wood, punctuating his prose at the most unlikely places. ''After seventeen years, as the greatest spy Russia has ever had. The super-mole. The mole behind the moles. Compared to you, Philby looked like a choirboy.''

He suddenly grimaced. He seemed to be in pain. ''And what did you discover when you came to England? That you might not have been the greatest after all. That there was somebody else, someone you did not know about. That your masters in Moscow did not trust you enough. That they planted *another* mole here. With another network, right behind your back. That's why you have no peace of mind. And you run around, playing Sherlock Holmes. At your age. Just to find out if there really was somebody else.''

''Nonsense,'' Orloff said. His face was on fire. ''Absolute nonsense. If there was somebody else, Moscow Center had their reasons.'' His voice sounded hollow to his own ears.

Hastings drew hard on his cigarette, as if it were a life line. ''Of course,'' he said. ''But back there on the telly, you were the most humiliated man I've ever seen.'' His voice was suddenly conciliatory. ''You don't have to glare at me like that. I understand what wounded pride is.''

He leaned back, apparently exhausted. Orloff averted his eyes, looking out the window at the effigy of the red lion in the middle of the square. An awkward silence settled between them. The tea was lukewarm and left a bitter aftertaste. A premature dusk was stealthily invading the far recesses of the square.

Hastings suddenly raised his head and looked beyond Orloff's shoulder. The old man turned back. Wells, the

Special Branch man who had gone to call London, had just walked in. His jaw was grimly set. He approached their table and bent over Hastings. "May I have a word with you, Chief?"

Hastings heaved his bulk from the chair and moved with Wells to the far corner, where they conversed in whispers. Hastings shook his head angrily several times and strode back to Orloff. "Will you excuse me? I have to drop by the station to make a few calls. I won't be long."

Orloff looked up. Anger was stamped all over Hastings's face. "That's all right, Chief Superintendent," he said with a dry smile. "You've got your problems. I understand wounded pride."

Hastings blanched and was about to say something, but changed his mind and walked out. Orloff turned and watched him leave. The tearoom was suddenly very quiet. The American students were gone, and the couple at the far table was already past the Wittgenstein stage. They were holding hands now.

When Hastings returned to the tearoom, darkness had fallen and Orloff was having his third cup of tea. The chief superintendent held an open notebook in his hand. "I wanted to tell you," he began in a strange, almost formal way, "that your assumption was correct. Our inquiries have revealed that nine of the men on Mary Ellis's list—in addition to Byroade—became career diplomats. Four of them were approached by the KGB between nineteen fifty-one and nineteen fifty-two. For a while they passed information about their work to the Russians. Two of them, one based in Prague and the other in Sofia, had access to top-secret material. All four were interrogated by MI-5 in the sixties. They confessed. To avoid scandal the Foreign

Office decided not to prosecute, as in the Scott and Byroade affairs. They were discharged from the service, roughly at the same time Byroade was.''

Orloff was on the edge of his chair. "Does that mean that all the diplomats exposed in the 'sixty-seven scandals as KGB spies were on that list?"

"Yes."

"Do you know which four?"

Hastings nodded. "I am not supposed to reveal them to you, but Ted Jennings could get them in one phone call." His voice was bitter again. "One of them, Rodney Shaw, left for Canada last Thursday to visit friends. His present whereabouts is not known. Another one, Llewellyn, lives in Maldon. We have been trying to phone him, but there is no answer at his cottage. Roger Darcy moved recently to Hertford, and I've sent someone to look him up. The last one, Archibald Westlake"—he took a deep breath—"is dead. He was killed in an automobile accident ten days ago." He threw his notebook on the table. "After Byroade's murder, that is."

A quick, urgent exchange at the door made them both turn around. Wells and an elderly middle-aged policeman came into the tearoom. Wells was disheveled, out of breath. Hastings stepped toward them and stood slightly hunched, his head bent, as they both spoke to him. He came back to the table and retrieved his notebook. His face was blank. "They just found Darcy," he said. "They had to force the door of his house." He glanced at his watch. "I'll stop by there on my way to London."

Orloff stood up. "I guess your superiors would crucify you if you took a Russian spy along."

Hastings scowled at him and stuck his chin out. "Be my guest," he grunted.

13

THE STENCH was unbearable. The bloated body of a fat, bald man, lay on its back in a dry stain of coagulated blood, some of which had soaked into the pale gold rug. The man had bled to death from a nasty wound to his throat. The bullet had ripped the jugular, and the scorched edges of the torn skin curled upward, a grisly brand of death on the livid, puffed flesh. "He was shot point-blank as he opened the door," Hastings muttered. "I'll bet we'll find a Tokarev slug in the wall." He stepped aside and Orloff caught full sight of the corpse. The mauve silk kimono was wide open, exposing a flaccid chest, swollen belly, and shrunken penis. One foot was bare, the other still encased in an expensive suede slipper. "An old queen, if I ever saw one," Hastings commented. "Here's your blackmail motive."

The policeman on duty, an elderly constable who held a kerchief to his nose, moved aside to let Orloff in. The big living room was furnished in exquisite taste. The rugs were of Persian silk, the furniture genuine Louis XVI. Pale gold draperies and voile sheers hung at the high windows. On the table and the two matching cabinets stood crystal vases, but the blood-red roses they contained sagged over their rims, limp and withered.

"The other one is over here, sir," said a young detective, who came in by a door at the far end of the room. He was pale as a sheet. "Rather messy, I'm afraid."

Hastings stopped by the door and let pass the police photographer, a burly man with a dirty-blond beard and white Adidas sneakers. "Jesus!" he groaned, then let out a string of curses. He moved along the near wall and went to work, his flash bathing in cruel light the sight that unfolded before their eyes. The posh bedroom, a tasteful blend of different shades of white, looked like a butchery. Large stains of blood were smeared all over the silk wallpaper, the ankle-deep carpet, and the satin sheets spread over the round bed. An immense wall mirror had been cracked into thousands of broken strips, emanating like linear filaments of a spiderweb from a bullet hole in the upper left corner; some splinters were strewn on the carpet, shining like precious stones in the cold light of the photographer's flash. On the carpet, by the back door, lay the body of a man in a tight-fitting, dark blue velvet shirt and modish white trousers. The man lay on his face, his arms sprawled. He had been shot twice in the back, as witnessed two tiny holes in his shirt, encircled by large dark stains. But he had not died from these wounds. The back of his head was smashed, almost beaten to a pulp. The murder weapon had been thrown on the carpet, beside the body; a heavy chunk of ebony primitively carved into the shape of a naked man. The head of the effigy was smeared with blood.

"You are through?" Hastings asked the photographer. He was already packing his equipment, only too happy to get away. Hastings turned to the police inspector. "Lab and fingerprints are through?"

The man nodded hurriedly.

"When did they die?" Hastings went on.

"The pathologist said about a week ago. But he refused to be more specific before the postmortem."

Hastings was listening glumly, fumbling in his pockets. "You can turn him on his back," he said to the detective.

The young man looked at him as if he did not understand. Hastings, who was lighting a cigarette, slowly shook his head and threw the burnt match into a Sèvres china bowl over the marble fireplace. He bent over, his head briefly enveloped in gray smoke, caught the body by its shoulder, and turned it over. The young detective covered his mouth with one hand and darted out of the room, brushing against Orloff.

The dead man's face was turgid and distorted but bore no wounds. The eyes were wide open, dark and long-lashed. He was very young, almost a boy, and the swarthy skin, the thin curved nose, and the full mouth faintly suggested Arabic origins. His velvet shirt was slit almost to his midriff. A heavy gold chain with a twenty-gram gold bar mounted as a medallion hung 'round his neck. Hastings turned back, walked to the open door and beckoned to the elderly policeman. "Do you know him?"

The constable threw a quick look at the body, still holding his handkerchief against his face, then looked again. He dared to take a step inside the room and slowly lowered his hand a few inches. "No sir. I don't think he is a local, sir. Mr. Darcy lived alone. Sometimes he brought over visitors in the evening, but they left early in the morning. Most of the time there was nobody but Mr. Darcy in the house.''

Hastings nodded repeatedly. ''As I thought,'' he said. ''All right. Why don't you open the damn windows?'' The constable quickly retreated, and a moment later they heard the clatter of the shutters in the living room.

''The killer didn't expect Darcy to have a visitor,'' Hastings said. ''He must have come early in the morning. The fag was in the bedroom, dressed and ready to go. Darcy opened the door and he shot him. Then the Arab must have appeared at the bedroom door, and the killer took a few shots at him.'' Orloff followed Hastings out of the bedroom and watched him run his fingers over the dark wooden panels beside the door frame. ''Right here,'' he said, pointing at a neat round hole about a foot to the left of the door. ''There might be others as well. Our man is a rather bad shot. He followed the boy into the bedroom, shooting. Wounded him twice, blasted the mirror. The boy fell by the door but was still trying to get out. The killer must have run out of cartridges, so he grabbed the statue and finished him off. Seemed to be in panic. That's butchery, not murder.'' He suddenly winced, and his hand darted to his belly.

''Are you all right?'' Orloff asked.

Hastings slowly straightened, wiping his forehead with his sleeve. ''Let's go,'' he said.

The windows were open. The cold evening wind blew welcome freshness into the fetid rooms. They were met at the door by Hastings's driver. ''London evening papers, sir.''

Hastings unfolded them, one by one, holding them at

arm's length for Orloff to see as well. The *Evening News*'s main headline dealt with the mackerel war in the North Sea. A second article, adorned with Orloff's picture, was entitled: DEFECTOR DESCRIBES PHILBY'S BLOODY TRAIL. Last night's TV interview would keep them going for weeks, Orloff reflected.

Hastings spread open the *Evening Standard:* KGB MUR-DER TEAM HAUNTS LONDON STREETS. screamed a banner headline. The subtitle read: "Russian agents linked to Byroade's death."

Hastings veered back sharply to catch Orloff's reaction. The old man shrugged.

"Bull," Hastings said. "No professional team would do such a lousy job. And on two terrified fags. Agreed, Mr. Orloff?"

The old man looked at him briefly and walked to the waiting car.

Hasting dropped Orloff off at the Churchill and instructed his driver to proceed to Dr. Page's clinic. As he got out of the car, he glanced at his watch. He was fifteen minutes late and the pedantic Page wouldn't miss the opportunity for some vicious jab below the belt. He threw his cigarette away and was halfway across the sidewalk when he heard the distinctive pitch of the transceiver above the whine of the engine. He turned back. The driver stuck his head out the window. "They want you at the PM supervisor's office, sir. At eight sharp." Hastings shook his head. He would hardly make it to Whitehall in fifteen minutes. He had to cancel Dr. Page once again.

The outer office was empty. He knocked on Page's door and walked in. His breath was shallow and he mopped his moist brow with his crumpled handkerchief. His sweat had a sharp, unpleasant odor.

Dr. Page nodded at him from behind his desk. He had a boyish mouth and a smooth complexion, but his china-blue eyes were wary, secretive. "Good evening," he said. Hastings waited for the inevitable sting, but there was none. "I only dropped by to apologize, Doctor," he said. "I hate to cancel the appointment again, but I was just summoned to an urgent meeting. I must be on my way."

Dr. Page looked at him gravely, as if he had not heard him. His rosy, well-manicured hands lay on the desk, on both sides of a pale blue file. He said cautiously: "This is also rather urgent, Mr. Hastings." He never called him chief superintendent.

"I do understand," Hastings said. "I can even feel it is." He grinned faintly. "The bloody pain never stops lately. Reminds me of you. But I must go. Excuse me for being such a nuisance, really." He was thinking of a short bald man hounding a frightened, screaming boy in a love nest of silk and satin.

The doctor seemed rather embarrassed. He opened the file and closed it, then rubbed his hands as if he were washing them under an invisible faucet. He was the tidiest person Hastings had ever seen—a starched white smock, placid face, silvery hair combed with care to one side. Hastings suspected he used some kind of oil or maybe a coloring shampoo to keep the silvery sheen. "I think you'd better sit down, Mr. Hastings."

"I really haven't got the time," he repeated, the damn sweat breaking out on his forehead again. Still there was something in Dr. Page's voice that made him hesitate, his hand on the doorknob.

And that was how he learned, as he stood restless and uneasy on Dr. Page's doorstep, that he was going to die.

The good doctor, anxious to ease the shock, plunged

into a hurried recitation of the trite formulas of his trade. Hastings was staring at him in a strange stupor, his hand gripping the cold doorknob, his mind refusing to digest the ominous platitudes. "I guess I have to give it to you straight," he heard Dr. Page saying. "Unfortunately the results of the tests are conclusive. It's too late to operate, I'm afraid. You are strong, Mr. Hastings. You should take it like a man." He failed to grasp the ghastly truth immediately and the doctor went on blabbering about incurable diseases and the frustrating helplessness of medicine. Hastings slowly surfaced back into reality and heard himself asking a couple of silly questions, including the inevitable "how much time have I left?" He had the strange feeling it was all a kind of game. Page and he were going through a well-rehearsed rite, both of them bound by secret connivance. It was like repeating a scene one had seen so many times performed on the screen, like the deathbed confession of a Mafia don or the last words of a mortally wounded cowboy. One knows all the questions and answers and the gestures and the mannerisms without really comprehending what they actually mean. His eyes locked on a chrome-coated clock on the doctor's table, dumbly following the incessant metamorphosis of the luminous digits. Page was speaking again, telling him how much he admired his attitude; Hastings was putting on a good show and taking it splendidly indeed. He produced some charts and lab reports, which Hastings did not gratify with a single glance. Unfortunately, Page sadly admitted, he could not really predict when it would happen; he knew it sounded very dramatic to tell someone he had six months or a year, but that was all mumbo jumbo, of course; no doctor could say such a thing except in those foolish TV serials. "It's generalized and terminal, that's all I can tell you," Page added, needlessly shuffling his papers and suddenly unable to look at his patient. "Let me get you some pills. They are marvelous for your condition, do wonders for the pain. A German formula. It's amazing what those Germans have been doing lately. The Germans and the Japanese won the war, don't you think?" And Hastings said yes, they did, the bastards.

The truth hit him only in the street when he stopped to light a fresh cigarette, wasting match after match. The pain had subsided—those wondrous Germans, really—and he felt better for the first time in weeks. He looked at his watch and was amazed to find out that he had spent barely seventeen minutes in the doctor's office, listening to his death sentence. Many verdicts he had heard in the courts of England had taken longer to read. He finally managed to light his Gauloise. The coarse smoke tasted of paper. He thought for a moment about not going to the supervisor's office, but the car was waiting, and he suddenly realized he had nothing else to do. Where was he supposed to go in such a situation? Get drunk? Weep on Barbara's shoulder? Walk the streets, returning to places he had known in his youth? He thought of all those stories about condemned men like him, who would start running about, determined to enjoy themselves as much as they could before their time ran out. The news had caught him totally unprepared. And it happened so quickly, so suddenly. The real shock was yet to come, he assumed.

A woman passed by, chased by the icy gusts, and her brown coat reminded him of Barbara again. Poor girl, to be left like that, all alone at her age. And no children, no relatives, not a blasted soul to take care of her, except her deaf aunt in Cornwall, who was half-dead anyway. Dr. Page had made a very decent gesture by promising to tell her himself. Page had devised an even better approach. He would let Barbara in the know, but would pretend he hadn't told Hastings. He would advise her to carry on as if nothing had happened, keeping the secret from her husband. That would spare both of them a few months—or weeks—of excruciating torment. Barbara would be forced to keep a stiff upper lip. And start to get used to being on her own, while he was still around.

As for himself, he felt neither fear nor sorrow. Maybe that would come later, along with the shock; but that was life and he had always thought one shouldn't waste time and energy on things one couldn't control.

"Whitehall." He was surprised that he was talking to his driver in his natural voice. Stranger still, as he thought of the meeting that awaited him now, the conversation with Page made him feel better. Definitely better.

A portrait of the queen when she had been much younger and had to worry neither about the exposure of Lady Di nor about that of Koo Stark hung over the supervisor's desk. Under it, in perfect symmetry, another portrait was suspended from which Mrs. Thatcher resolutely looked on the world, a martial expression painted all over her makeup. Ian MacMillan himself was lighting a long, lean cigar as Hastings walked in. MacMillan peered at him owlishly through his thick glasses. "Oh, here you are, Chief Superintendent. Bloody weather, don't you think? So glad you could make it."

Sykes nodded at him, puffing on his pipe. He had pulled his chair back, close enough to MacMillan that he seemed to share his desk. Jim Brennan, his deputy, was nestling in his master's shadow. Looking at him, Hastings recollected all of a sudden that the ad hoc committee on the Byroade affair, with Brennan as its SIS representative, had not met for ten days. Nobody seemed to deplore that irregularity, not even the fourth person who had joined the closely knit group clustered behind MacMillan's desk: Andrew Hodder, the Foreign Office coordinator, was proudly seated on the supervisor's right. All four of them looked as if they expected a photographer to take their family portrait. Only Snow was sitting alone, in splendid isolation on the green leather sofa, his face sour and arrogant as usual.

"We've been waiting for you since eight o'clock," Snow said.

"I was busy," Hastings grunted, not really caring. He was still deep in thought, trying to visualize the meeting between Barbara and Dr. Page.

"But of course," MacMillan said hastily, looking vaguely upset. "We know you've had a rather eventful day, haven't you? Cambridge and Hertford, I understand. We heard some bits and pieces, of course. I spoke to the prime minister not long ago, actually . . . but we'd really appreciate it if you could fill us in." Andrew Hodder eagerly nodded in agreement.

Dr. Page suddenly seemed to him very far away, almost unreal. He pulled a chair up opposite MacMillan's desk and talked for the next fifteen minutes, without being interrupted. He described the day's events in detail, starting with Orloff's call from Cambridge and ending with the discovery of the bodies in Hertford. His narrative apparently irritated Snow, who furiously scribbled on a pad, shaking his head. As soon as he was through, Snow was at him. "I heard you called the home secretary to complain, Chief Superintendent."

"Yes, I did. The Foreign Office refused to give me the names of the diplomats investigated in nineteen sixty-seven."

186

"It was an MI-5 investigation. You could have called me."

"You are not my superior, Mr. Snow. I shall continue to call the home secretary. Any time when I encounter difficulties coming from the parallel services."

Snow pressed his lips in anger, while Sykes, surprisingly, seemed to gloat maliciously for a reason Hastings was to understand only later.

"I also hear you are working hand in hand with Orloff," Snow went on.

"Orloff called my attention to the list," Hastings said coldly, and for the first time allowed himself to hit back. "Did you see the evening papers, Mr. Snow? Somebody in your service must have leaked the story of the KGB team. Most unfortunate."

The head of MI-5 shifted his dismayed look from Hastings to MacMillan and back. "That's preposterous," he said, his voice rising to an unpleasant falsetto. "How dare you!"

As nobody else spoke, Hastings allowed himself a further step. "There is one question that I wanted to ask you, though, Mr. Snow. What precautions did your service take to protect the other compromised diplomats after Byroade's death? The good old boys seem to be dying like flies."

"Now, now, Chief Superintendent," MacMillan intervened, avoiding looking at the smoldering Snow, but his tone much milder than Hastings would have expected. "Nobody could foresee that those . . . those poor fellows would be in real danger. I understand that there is no news of Mr. Llewelyn yet."

"No sir. His cottage was found empty. We are also investigating the car accident. In which Mr. Westlake died."

"Yes, quite right. Well. . . ." MacMillan seemed to hesitate, shuffled his papers, and needlessly shook the ash of his cigar into an ashtray.

"Nigel, I think you wanted to say something."

Sykes leaned forward and took his pipe from his mouth. "I have to report to this committee that my services succeeded in locating the safehouse that serves as shelter to the KGB team we're after." Having made his announcement, he leaned back, his face blank.

Snow half-rose to his feet. From his seat Hastings noticed the swelling vein that throbbed in the man's neck. "Your services? What had your services to do with it?"

"We just found it," Sir Nigel replied, displaying sudden interest in the moist stem of his pipe. "After I heard your views, Peter, during our last meeting, I became rather skeptical about the chances of finding those Russians. I admit that I was quite impressed by the theory of Chief Superintendent Hastings." He nodded amiably at Hastings. "His main points were that the mole himself—and not a KGB team—had been carrying out these murders, and that the KGB team might have been sent to this country only for the purpose of collecting information."

"Who gave you the authority . . ." Snow began, but Sykes had turned to address MacMillan. "You see, Ian, we have some experience with the modus operandi of the KGB. When they dispatch an operational team, they never get in contact with any existing network already in place. They send in their own independent organization in order not to jeopardize their resident agents. But when they send a team of experts only to collect and process accessible information, they don't take such elaborate measures. They used to rely on the existing infrastructure. I instructed Jim Brennan"—he pointed to his deputy—"to place under surveillance all KGB-front organizations—Aeroflot, Sovtorg, cultural mission, science academy, peace movement bureau. We also tapped some embassy phones and got in touch with our informers.''

"I did that too, the very day we met in your house," Snow interjected heatedly.

Nigel Sykes nodded. "Nobody blames you, Peter. I guess I was lucky with my informers, that's all."

"Where is this house?" MacMillan asked, and Hastings had a vague impression that his surprise at the revelations of the SIS chief was rather mild.

"In London," Sykes said cautiously. "We're keeping it under close surveillance. I would like to request your permission, Ian, to raid the house at the earliest convenient moment."

Andrew Hodder, who had kept silent all this time succeeded in catching Sir Nigel's eye and flashed at him a dazzling smile of encouragement.

"I protest," Snow said. The man was seething but tried to control himself. "This is the most revolting interference of SIS in our domain. You had no right to do what you did, and I certainly object to any further SIS intervention in this matter."

"I found them, didn't I?" Sir Nigel asked casually.

"Even if I assume you did," Snow retorted, "I must make a formal request that you hand over to me your report so that my men can carry out any further measures. Counterespionage on English soil is our responsibility, and the SIS has no right to interfere."

"Well . . ." MacMillan began, and Hastings looked up in surprise. "I think, Peter, that the official regulations are rather vague on that point. It's a borderline case and we should give it some thought together." He glanced at

Sykes, seeking support, and Hastings had no more doubts. Sykes and MacMillan were in this together. Snow had been chosen as the scapegoat, to be blamed for the sloppy handling of the affair up until now. Hodder and Brennan had been summoned as witnesses to the slaughter.

"I suggest that Chief Superintendent Hastings and his men carry out the operation," MacMillan was saying, "under the supervision of Sir Nigel. You'll be more than welcome to join them, Peter. That goes without saying." He leaned back, obviously pleased with his idea of what seemed a compromise, but which wasn't one.

"Good idea," Hodder managed to squeeze in, obliging everybody present with his fraternal smiles. "Jolly good idea, really."

Hastings felt a strange surge of pity for Peter Snow, who had been cornered like a hounded fox. He was watching Sykes, who suavely nodded at MacMillan's every word. There was no doubt in his mind now that Sykes had been the one to leak the KGB story to the papers. The sly bastard was carefully laying the groundwork for his future triumph, when he would hand the Russians' heads on a platter to MacMillan.

"What do you say, Chief Superintendent?" MacMillan asked hurriedly, anticipating a new outburst from Snow. "Would you command the raid?"

14

THE PHONE CALL reached Ted Jennings shortly before midnight. He was working late at his office, sorting the stills for a TV special to be broadcast the day after Orloff's last interview. It would be entitled "The Other," and tell the story of the phantom mole who runs the Foreign Office network. It would start with a quick succession of photographs on the screen, accompanied by dry camera clicks. Byroade. Benedetti. Westlake. Orloff in his hospital bed. Darcy. He still hadn't got the name of the Arab boy.

"Yes," he said, picking up the receiver. It was the Thames stringer in Maldon. He listened to him in silence, crushing his half-consumed cigarette in the overflowing ashtray. He was taut as a bowstring. "Okay, we'll be there," he said finally.

He called the first floor. "I'll need a crew in Maldon at five A.M. No, there is no mistake. I said five A.M." He shook a cigarette from his pack and lit it with one hand.

His mouth was thick, sticky. "I know it's on the other side of Foulness, and I know it's forty bloody miles from London." The agitated voice squeaked in the receiver. "You can order the van for whenever you wish," he said, "as long as you get them to Maldon by dawn." He spent five more minutes arguing with the faceless dragon on the first floor, and when he got his way he turned on the charm and told her how much he appreciated what she was doing. Really, she was super.

He dialed Lynn's number. "Guess who," he said.

He picked her up in front of her house at a quarter to four. She was cowering on the porch, seeking shelter from the hail. Her face was cold, her lips tight, unyielding. He had not seen her since they had interviewed Orloff.

"I thought you spent your nights with your wife?" Her voice was sarcastic but strained.

He slammed the car door and switched on the wipers. "My wife flew to Paris this afternoon," he said. "She wants to stay with her father till we sort out things between us." Lynn winced and seemed to move away from him, shrinking into her sheepskin.

"If we sort out things between us," he added.

She didn't speak. "I told her about you," Ted said cautiously, keeping his eyes on the road.

"You what?" She stared at him in disbelief. "Are you out of your mind?" She paused, shaking her head. "Do you always share your affairs with her?"

"That was below the belt, Lynn, and I didn't deserve it." He swerved the steering wheel rather abruptly to avoid a garbage truck that emerged from a side street.

But she did not answer, and her stubborn silence made him blow up. "Well, say something! Maybe I shouldn't have told her after all. I should have kept screwing you until we got sick and tired of each other, right?''

"I am sorry." He felt the hesitant touch of her fingers on his burning cheek. "I did not mean that. I guess I am too tense."

He let out a deep breath. "We both are." He tapped his pockets with his right hand, searching for his cigarettes. She promptly lit two of her own and placed one between his lips. "Tell me what happened."

"I did not want someone else to tell her," he said, angrily sinking his teeth into the soft filter tip. "She would have found out sooner or later. I think she suspected something anyway. After she saw you on TV."

"What did she say? Ted, I must know."

"I told you," he said, "she flew to her daddy in Paris."

Lynn retreated again into her corner, cupping her cigarette in her hands. "I don't know what to say, Ted. You must be going through hell, both of you. Oh, shit!" She violently shook her head. "I am supposed to feel guilty, aren't I? Well, I don't. But I dragged you into a fine mess."

"I asked for it," he said stiffly. "But you wanted this to happen, didn't you?"

"Yes," she said gravely. They crossed an ambulance, its red lights flashing urgently. "I wanted this to happen. You don't know what it is to long for someone at night and not be able to reach out and touch him. But I didn't want to force you into anything."

The dark street was stretching before him, swept by the hail that fiercely drummed on the car roof and ricocheted off the pavement like tiny flames of cold white fire.

"Nobody forced me into anything," he muttered. He

smashed down on the accelerator as they emerged onto the deserted motorway. He stole a quick glance at Lynn, trying to make up his mind, and finally said: "She won't come back if I don't call her, I guess."

Lynn did not answer for a long while, leaning back on the headrest, eyes half-closed. When she finally spoke, her voice was very soft, very private. "But you will call her in the end, Ted. One day you won't be able to cope with this mess anymore, and you'll go back to her."

"Why don't you . . ." he began, but just then the lights of an approaching truck swept over her chalky face, and he fell silent.

They drove in continued silence the rest of the way to Maldon.

The gale subsided shortly after dawn, but the storm had not blown itself out yet and was whipping the waves of the North Sea into a bubbling froth. He was surprised to find the van on the beach already, the boys busy setting the equipment on the sand, checking the microphones and adjusting the mobile spotlights. The Maldon stringer was there too, a rather grotesque figure in vivid orange oilskin, hopping around in a flurry of excitement. He recognized Ted as he got out of the car, and darted toward him, hood, sleeves and immense trousers flapping. "Good morning, Mr. Jennings." He stole a look at Lynn, who had stayed in the car, her face in shadow. "Welcome to Maldon. I am Ron Baldwin."

Only when he came nearer did Ted notice that he was a very young, short lad with an acne-ravaged face, tallow hair, and round, inquisitive eyes. "It's over there, Mr. Jennings," he said, pointing down the rainswept beach to where a small group of policemen and civilians miserably huddled beside three police cars. They slogged through the heavy, sticky sand between small heaps of black seaweed and broken pieces of wood.

One of the civilians turned to face them. He was wearing a brown driving coat and looked soaked to the bones. A pair of regulation navy binoculars hung on a leather strip around his neck. "Inspector Guest," Baldwin breathed hurriedly, "this is Ted Jennings from Thames Television. You know, the Russian spy story."

"How do you do," Inspector Guest said, the rain pouring down his craggy face and soaking into his imitation-fur collar.

Ted nodded. "Good morning, Inspector." Beside one of the cars, two men in black wet suits and pink life jackets were busy over the outboard engine of a Zodiac dinghy.

"It's supposed to be down there," Baldwin volunteered, pointing toward the sea. A few hundred yards from the shore, a line of black, jagged cliffs rose above the water. "On the right side, you see?"

Ted strained his eyes. The broken contours of the reef, ugly black teeth enveloped in opaque spray, etched a blurred outline on the low sky. The waves were exploding over the cliffs with a continuous roar. "No," he said. "I don't see anything."

"Here." The inspector offered his binoculars. "On the right of the big rock. The horn-shaped one. A little above water level."

Jennings carefully adjusted the knobs and scanned the black rocks rising from the sea. He finally spotted it, a big bundle wrapped in gray-and-brown fabric, sprawled under the protruding edge of the cliff.

He handed back the binoculars to the inspector. "We

sighted it in the late afternoon,'' Guest said, becoming more talkative. He had a coarse accent, rather similar to the Irish brogue. ''I guess it was washed over there by the tide. We think that's him but we can't be sure.''

''They tried to get over there twice last night,'' Baldwin broke in, eyes shining with excitement. ''Used big navy searchlights and the dinghy. They overturned both times, and one of the blokes almost drowned.''

''Bad storm.'' Guest nodded and squinted malevolently at the dark clouds. ''Had no choice but to wait till dawn.''

The dinghy was already in the water. The engine caught immediately and sputtered as the tiny boat hopped over the waves' crests. On the beach, Ted was suddenly aware that Lynn was not beside him. He turned to the right and saw her standing about fifty yards away. The wind was whirling her golden hair 'round her face, and beating her skirt about her long legs. She was staring into the sea, one hand clutching her coat over her chest, the other striving to remove the strands of hair from her eyes. She suddenly seemed utterly inaccessible to him and isolated. He felt a surge of warmth, and desire, and raw, inexplicable anxiety.

He walked toward her, aware of the persistent stare of Guest and Baldwin, and took her by the hand. ''Come,'' he said softly.

''Your hand is cold,'' she said in a small voice. Her boots crissed in the rough sand. She followed him, but he felt her reluctance to come too close to where the policemen and civilians were all gathered now, awaiting the return of the dinghy. One officer was bent over the open window of a prowl car, speaking urgently into a microphone. They heard behind them the noise of engines. More cars were arriving. A white ambulance turned and backed up, its open rear doors swinging heavily. The cameraman and the sound engineer, bent under the weight of their equipment, ran in front of Lynn and Ted.

The returning dinghy touched the beach, and the small group of people involuntarily moved back. The faces of the two frogmen were red with effort as they hauled their load onto the wet sand. A sudden wave, higher than the others, splashed the beach, driving the dinghy into the sand, but pulling back the shapeless object that had just been discharged, as if the sea were trying to reclaim it. As the water retreated, swirling in small eddies around the feet of the unfortunate bystanders, Ted felt Lynn's hand shivering in his. He held her close to him. She was trembling all over, her face waxen. The policemen were pulling out of the water the gruesome bundle that had been a human being. A few wet wisps of yellowish-white hair protruded from the tarpaulin in which they wrapped the cadaver before they laid it on a stretcher and loaded it into the ambulance.

The TV camera was focused on the face of young Baldwin, who stood with his back to the sea, talking quickly into the microphone. He in turn offered it to Inspector Guest, who said a few words. "It's him," Lynn murmured. "I'm sure it's him."

Guest walked toward them. "It's Mr. Llewellyn, all right," he said, reading the mute question in their eyes. "One of the constables identified him immediately." He pointed to a bony, lean Scotsman with a gnarled face. "It seems he has been in the water for a few days."

"That means ever since his disappearance," Ted said.

"That is a correct assumption," a familiar voice said. They turned back. Chief Superintendent Hastings stood behind them, wearing his shapeless raincoat and saggy brown hat. "Good morning, Miss Kennan," he said gravely. "Guest, I want an immediate autopsy."

Inspector Guest nodded and trudged toward the ambulance. Hastings wiped his forehead and made a few attempts to light his cigarette. His fingers were trembling. Finally, he gave up. "Well, Mr. Jennings," he said, looking intently at Ted. His voice was muffled, low. "We meet again. Foul weather, foul play, another body. Life's getting monotonous lately, don't you think?"

He didn't wait for an answer, but clumsily plodded after Guest. Ron Baldwin ran after him, but he shook his head.

As the car sped toward London, Lynn sat upright on her seat, her hands tightly clenched in her lap. She seemed to be very far, lost in a strange reverie. When she finally spoke, her voice was bitter. "Why did I write that damn letter to Alex in the first place?"

"Come on, Lynn, who could have imagined—" he tried.

"Six people have died already," she went on. "It's a nightmare."

"Don't," Ted said, taking his hand off the wheel and reaching for her wet cheek.

Shortly after 6:00 P.M., a delivery truck from Fulham's Groceries backed into the reserved space of the Paddington Supermarket, at 124 Edgware Road. The driver and his assistant, dressed in heavy gray coveralls, delivered a few crates at the service entrance, then, arguing loudly, strode toward the White Unicorn pub, on the corner of Boscobel Street. At the pub door, the truck driver collided with a thin, hawk-faced man who was on his way out, fumbling with the buttons of his leather coat. "Watch your step, mate," the truck driver grunted, and the other man quickly walked away mumbling under his breath. He climbed into the cab of a smart blue van, parked in front of the Edgware Laundry. The name BAYSWATER CLEANERS LTD., followed by a phone number, was stenciled in bold yellow letters on both flanks of the van. The man with the hawkish face lit a small cigar and drove away.

In a second-floor flat down the road, Chief Superintendent Hastings lowered his field glasses and backed away from the window. The change of shifts watching the KGB safehouse had been flawlessly performed. The van and the truck belonged to the surveillance department of Special Branch. The blue van had been parked all afternoon across the street from the safehouse, an off-white two-story building at 113 Edgware Road. The compact video camera, mounted behind the dark side window, had taped all the comings and goings at the neat brown door of number 113. Hastings had dispatched several agents to tail two men and a woman who had left the house in the early afternoon. But the woman and one of the men had returned; the second man, after lingering for a couple of hours in the lobby of the Churchill, was presently being watched buying toys at Hamley's on Regent Street.

The truck's position was slightly farther down the road, but it still offered an adequate view of the house. The Branch had no night-filming equipment, and so the two agents concealed in the truck relieved each other watching the house, using SIS night glasses, and manning the transceiver. Hastings intended to move his command post to an automobile-accessories store offering a good view of the house; but he would do that only minutes before the assault.

He ran his hand over the bristle on his jaw. He hadn't shaved since the day before. He could have dropped by his home that morning for a couple of hours, after returning from Maldon. But at the very last moment he told his driver to proceed straight to his office at the Yard. He had remembered that he had a lot to do to lay the groundwork for tonight's raid—fill in search warrants; brief the agents; issue bulletproof vests, firearms, and ammunition. Of course, all those duties could have been entrusted to his assistants. But it was his only excuse for staying away from home. He had to admit to himself that he feared the encounter with Barbara, and was going out of his way to postpone it. He knew she had met with Page that morning; he had not yet found the courage to start playing his part in the cruel charade the doctor had conceived last night.

As he swallowed another of Dr. Page's wonder pills with a sip of tepid coffee, he heard steps in the corridor, and Wells stuck his head around the door. "We just got the report on Westlake's death," he said.

"Westlake?" It took him a moment to place the name. Another of those diplomats, of course. The car crash. "What about him?" he grunted, slumping into a battered chair. The flat they had requisitioned that morning had been empty except for a few chairs and desks that had served a defunct modeling agency.

Wells sat across the desk, taking a sheaf of papers from his pocket. "He lived in Tetbury, in the Cotswolds, as you know. Last Wednesday he drove down to Cheltenham. It's a winding mountain road, rather steep. It had rained during the night, and the road was slippery. The car missed a turn and hurtled down the slope. Westlake was flung out of the car. He died of multiple fractures. It was an open-and-shut case."

"But you asked them to check the car," Hastings said.

"I asked them *if* they had checked the car." Wells

separated another crumpled sheet of paper from the sheaf and started smoothing it on the table. "The same question must have worried them, because when I called they already had the answer for me."

"Don't tell me," Hastings muttered. "No brakes."

"Wrong," Wells said, shaking his head. "The steering mechanism was sabotaged. It was no accident. The old boy didn't have a chance."

The radio set in the other room was crackling, and a blond young man wearing a padded nylon jacket, Wrangler jeans, and cowboy boots peeped through the open door. "Changing of the guard on Hatton Street completed," he announced, an amused glint in his blue eyes.

"Thank you, Hallam," Hastings said. Hatton Street ran parallel to Edgware Road, and the back courtyard of number 113 could serve as an escape route for the Russians: over the low fence into the courtyard of 8 Hatton Street, and then through the service entrance straight into the street. Thus, Hastings had blocked all exits, even posted a few men on the roofs. "By the way, Hallam," he called after the blond boy, who reappeared in the doorway. "Could you get some sandwiches and beer for the boys up here? We still have a long wait ahead of us."

"I sure will, boss," Hallam quipped, thumbs in his belt. The boy was obviously watching too many American movies.

Hastings turned to Wells. "Where is Orloff, by the way?"

"Spent his morning in the archives of the *Times*," Wells recited effortlessly. "Lunched alone at Wheeler's in Soho, and was back in his hotel at two. Hasn't left his room since."

Hastings nodded. "All right," he said. "What else have you got on Westlake?"

Nigel Sykes arrived at 10:40 P.M. He was wearing a dark blue cashmere coat and a white silk scarf over a velvet dinner jacket, bow tie, and dress shirt. His narrow, swarthy face and sardonic leer reminded Hastings of the devious villains described in Edgar Wallace's thrillers. "I hope I'm not too late," he apologized dryly. "Awfully long play at Windham's. Can't cope with Pinter, really. Where is Snow?"

"We've asked him to be here by eleven," Hastings said.

"In time for the show, right?" Sykes said with a rather forced smile. There were a couple of knocks on the outer door, a shuffle of feet, and a quick, angry exchange. Hallam burst into the room, his face flushed.

"Chief—"

But Sykes was looking over his shoulder, smiling benignly. "That's all right, young man. Those are my boys, right on time."

Hastings pushed young Hallam aside and walked into the adjoining room. The flat was suddenly full of people, as if taken over by an enemy organization in a bloodless coup. Fifteen men, maybe more, had smoothly positioned themselves throughout the various rooms, all of them looking brisk and efficient, clustering in small groups by the situation desk, the wall charts, the radio sets, the operational switchboard. He veered back angrily. "What's this supposed to be?" he said sharply.

"I brought some reinforcements," Sykes said. His voice was soft, but the eyes had hardened. "My people are experts in this kind of operation. I'm sure you won't mind if we carry on from here, or would you?''

Hastings beckoned to his improvised office and moved aside to let Sykes walk in ahead of him. He was perspiring profusely, and the pain in the pit of his stomach had erupted again, worse than ever. "The thing is, I do mind." His words seemed to squeeze out from between his teeth as he closed the door behind him and leaned on it. "I was instructed to carry out the operation with my men and that's what I intend to do. You are supposed to supervise it, no more, as far as I remember."

Sir Nigel, very much in control of himself, pulled up a chair, unbuttoned his coat, and sat down, crossing his legs. "Why don't you call Ian MacMillan?" he asked softly. "I am sure you'll get the appropriate instructions." He took a leather pouch out of his pocket, unzipped it, and produced his pipe.

Hastings nodded and reached for the phone. Wells was manning the switchboard. "Get me the home secretary," he said into the mouthpiece. "On the double."

Sykes's fingers, holding a burning match, froze in mid-motion. He regretfully took the pipe out of his mouth and slowly shook the match. "What's that supposed to be?"

"I get my instructions from my superiors," Hastings said. "I did not accept the supervisor's offer last night, before I had it cleared with the home secretary. Any change is subject to his approval."

A mean, almost hateful look flashed in Sir Nigel's eyes. But it dissolved as quickly as it had appeared, and the SIS director leaned back, staring at him with a scheming expression. Finally he shrugged, as if he really did not care. "No need to get upset," he said in the same voice. "You can cancel your call. We shall proceed as agreed." He paused, then lit a new match. "I gather you won't mind some of my people taking part in the operation."

"Under my orders," Hastings said. He could not believe Sykes would give in so easily.

The SIS chief exhaled a long, contented puff of bluish smoke. "But of course, my dear fellow," he said.

15

A SHARP but not unpleasant odor of synthetic rubber hung in the dark interior of the accessories shop. Hastings squeezed his bulk between a rack laden with colorful mats and a display of hinged rear-window louvers. The light filtering in from the street fell on a glossy poster of a sparsely clothed blond invitingly stretched on the roof of a sports car. He had a good view of the street, between two pyramids of spark plugs rising from the showcase. Across the street, the ground-floor windows of number 113 were still faintly glowing. The lights on the upper story had gone off a few minutes before.

A whiff of static erupted behind his back. Wells, comfortably positioned behind the owner's desk, was softly whispering in his walkie-talkie. They had entered the store from the back door, following the precise instructions of the owner, a retired sergeant from a Chelsea police station. The old policeman had even left on his desk a bottle of gin and two glasses, but all that Hastings wanted now and could not risk was a cigarette.

On the opposite side of the street, an elderly couple walked past the entrance to number 113. The man was animatedly speaking, and the woman, a white-haired lady with an outmoded little hat, was possessively holding his arm with both hands. Hastings ran a finger inside the collar of his shirt. It was too tight, or maybe that was his imagination. He had finally phoned Barbara, a half hour ago. The poor girl was such a lousy actress. Her laughter rang phony; her questions were phony; her desperate attempts to deliver a humorous account of the day's trivia sounded pathetic. She did not mention that she had seen Dr. Page, of course. What was she doing, now that she knew, all alone in the small cottage, moving about in utter stillness, as she would for so many years to come? He only wished she were prettier or younger, could remarry, start something new. They had had a fight once, when she had wanted to buy a cat. He had said he loathed the bloody animals, why didn't she buy a dog instead.

Across the street, the lights on the ground floor went off. Wells was already beside him, pressing the walkie-talkie to his ear and nodding repeatedly as the reports flowed in. "They are ready," he said. "The men have already moved to the roofs and backyards. The cars just arrived." Hastings took a step forward and stared to the right. At the far corner, he could make out the indistinct hulks of a few vans. The operational team was there, ready to move in.

"What about the back entrance?" His thoughts were drifting away, carrying him back to the eerie encounter at Dr. Page's office.

"Five people at Hatton Street, inside the house. They can cross the backyards in forty-five seconds."

"Let's start then," Hastings said with sudden urgency.

Wells whispered into the tiny transceiver. There was a smooth movement on the left, and two dark figures disappeared into the shadows beside the service entrance to number 113. Wells stepped forward, holding his walkie-talkie with both hands outstretched as if it was a holy cross or a magic talisman. "The Cheetahs are in the yard already, heading for the back door." Christening the various detachments with names of animals had been his idea. The two other break-in units were named Antelopes and Rhinos. Wells was Tiger, and Hastings, Hippo. It could not be a coincidence, Hastings suspected. He would have chosen Hippo himself.

"Synchronization is twenty-twenty so far," Wells said behind his shoulder. "They'll be inside on the dot, all of them." A group of five or six men, dressed in jeans and leather jackets, hurried southward on the opposite sidewalk. They breezed past the porch of number 113. One of them said something and they burst out in loud, hoarse laughter. Suddenly the last in the group veered sharply to the right and darted, quick and silent as a ghost, up the five stairs and onto the porch. He bent over the lock for what seemed to be a split second, and then the outer door was wide open, and the shadows in the leather jackets were pouring in. As more figures were being swallowed into the gaping black rectangle of the service entrance, two unmarked cars smoothly braked in front of the house, discharging six or seven more people, who took positions outside the doors and under the windows. Tiny white beams—probably pen lights—briefly flashed from the adjoining roofs.

"What do you call those?" Hastings asked. The pain in his stomach was dull but persistent.

"The backups? Hyenas."

"How awfully nice," Hastings grunted. "They must be overwhelmed."

Wells looked at him uncertainly. Across the street, electric lights were exploding in the windows in quick succession. They heard muffled shouts, a dry crack—a pistol shot?—but it was not followed by others. A second group of men crossed the street and swarmed up onto the porch. The white silk scarf of Sir Nigel floated like a banner over his lean figure.

"You have a name for the parallels too, don't you?" Hastings asked, teasing Wells.

"Bastards," Wells mouthed viciously. His hatred for the parallels was well known in the service.

"Let's go," Hastings said and unlocked the front door. The bite of the wind was icy, violent. As they crossed the street, they saw young Hallam blocking the way to two perplexed policemen. "That's okay, fellows," he was drawling in his best Texas accent. "Nice surprise party. No booze, no grass, no women."

Hallam was misleading the law, of course, for there were two women in the house. They were kept in one corner of the narrow sitting room on the ground floor, already separated from the men, who had been herded to the upper story. All the lights in the house were on, and several men, both Special Branch and SIS, were purposefully moving about. Repeated flashes of dazzling white crudely bathed the stairwell. The photography team was already at work upstairs, as were the investigators. They seemed to be going systematically through the bedrooms.

Hastings heard the familiar sound of doors being slammed, cupboards emptied, beds overturned. Somebody was protesting loudly, but his words were distorted by his foreign accent.

Hastings stopped in the middle of the sitting room, enjoying his first inhalation of smoke as one of his men, Bartlett, sped down the stairs. He was carrying a big cardboard box full of video cassettes. Behind Bartlett, a young man he did not recognize was cautiously descending, one step at a time, holding a video recorder. Bartlett noticed Hastings's inquisitive stare and came over to him. "We're doing fine, Chief," he announced. His face was flushed with excitement. "We've got five men upstairs and two women over there. We took them by total surprise. A few were asleep. One of the Russians was in the loo."

"How do you know he is Russian?" Wells interrupted. He was sticking close to Hastings, defending him jealously as if he were his own property.

"What else could he be?" Bartlett shrugged, somewhat confused. Hastings stepped closer to him to clear the way for two more men who carried boxes and files to the cars outside. Other men were hurrying up and down the stairs, and Hastings noticed young Hallam walk in, a triumphant expression painted all over his face. Two more SIS men drifted inside, conversing in low tones, but they abruptly fell silent when they noticed Hastings. He watched them retreat discreetly toward the back of the house. "Take care that none of the bastards are left alone," he murmured to Wells. "Not in a room, not with a prisoner." Wells stared at him in bewilderment, missing the message. "None of the bastards," Hastings repeated, stressing the last word. Wells's eyes registered comprehension at last. He nodded solemnly and hurried up the staircase.

"Was that a shot we heard before?" Hastings asked Bartlett. Behind him the boy holding the recorder had become red in the face with effort. "You can go," Hastings grunted at him.

"One of our chaps," Bartlett said. He stepped aside to let two women officers, dressed in civilian clothes, get across to the female prisoners. "A warning shot. One of the Russians"—he glanced at Hastings for reassurance—"made a threatening gesture, and he fired into the air. No damage done."

"Found any weapons?" Hastings asked.

"We're checking now, Chief," Bartlett said. A handsome blond man with an effeminate mouth—one of Sykes's operatives—stuck his head out of the kitchen door and called cheerfully: "Tea, anyone? Genuine Russki *tchay*?" Getting no response, he regretfully retreated.

Sir Nigel strode casually down the stairs, nodding repeatedly as Jim Brennan whispered in his ear. He stopped beside Hastings. "Where is Peter Snow?" he asked in a low voice, then stepped back as if readying himself for the answer. He tilted his head slightly, watching Hastings with narrowed, hostile eyes.

"He didn't show up," Hastings said. "He might have been offended by the supervisor's decision, don't you think?"

"He did not show up," Sir Nigel repeated, disregarding the second part of Hastings's answer. He exchanged angry glances with Jim Brennan, who seemed to be there for that very purpose. "First," Sykes said, "Snow does not report when he should about the infiltration of a KGB unit into this country. Second, he does not find the safehouse. Third"—he was hitting the cupped palm of his left hand with his right middle finger—"he blows his top when I find it. And fourth, he disappears on the night of the raid. That's too much, Chief Superintendent. Don't you think?'' As Hastings did not answer, Sykes said nothing more and went out.

Hastings dismissed Bartlett with a nod and approached the two women prisoners. One was a big, graceless matron in a quilted nightgown and wool-lined slippers. She looked like a vengeful Gorgon with her hate-filled eyes, thin bad mouth, and brown greasy locks curling about her face like tiny snakes. She was the one who had gone out that afternoon.

"Good evening," Hastings said politely. "What is your name?"

"Inge Schreider." She had a strong foreign accent. "I am Austrian tourist and I demand to be released immediately." He nodded and turned to the shorter woman who stood beside her, feverishly winding her long black hair around her fingers. She was a slender flat-chested girl with a hungry mouth and tired doe eyes. He detected the weakness and the fear in her dejected look, and in the slight trembling of her small chin.

"Get her over here," he said to the female officers, turning back and opening a door at random under the staircase. It was a sort of storeroom—a few crates, a closet, a couple of suitcases. The girl and one of the female officers followed him in. The policewoman was quite young, plump and fair-skinned. Barbara had had such a smooth, fine complexion when he had met her. She used to tease him that he had married her only because of her country-lass look. He took a pile of dirty bedclothes from the single chair in the room, tossed them in the corner, and beckoned to the girl. "Sit down." Then, turning to the rosy-cheeked officer, he added: "Her rights. Let her learn

about her rights.'' The young policewoman started reading the girl her rights in a melodious voice that sounded rather out of place. Hastings lit a fresh cigarette and blissfully inhaled the stinging smoke, then removed his hat, opened his raincoat, and loosened his tie, as if he had a long night ahead of him. The girl was staring at him with growing fear. He settled heavily on the edge of a crate. Wells peeped inside. ''Later,'' he told him, and Wells retreated hastily. ''What's your name?'' he asked the girl. ''You're English, aren't you?''

''Anne. Anne Harrison.'' She fumbled in the pockets of her worn jeans and produced a banker's card.

He did not even look at it. ''Your name,'' he repeated.

''I told you, Anne Harrison.'' But the hand offering him the dog-eared card was shaking, and her eyes, blinking nervously, avoided his.

''I have no time for you,'' he said bluntly and started buttoning his coat. ''I know a lie when I hear one. Your papers are fake. You'll be accused of complicity in five murders.'' He turned to the policewoman, who looked as shocked as her prisoner. ''Take her away.''

He was at the door when the girl called after him, right on cue. ''Wait, don't go, please!'' He turned back and watched the panicked girl go to pieces before his eyes. ''My name is Joan Valero,'' she cried. Her fingers plowed feverishly through her hair. ''I can prove it, I really can. I am not mixed up in any murders, honest, I swear it, I. . . .'' She burst into tears, burying her birdlike head in the loose sleeves of her gray pullover.

He nodded at the policewoman and returned to his crate. He knew from experience that she would talk now. But he also doubted if the people captured in that house could have killed anybody. No killer team would employ this kind of amateur, ever.

An amateur she was, indeed, devoid of any serious motivation, lacking the protective shield of fanaticism or devotion to a cause. Once her defenses were breached, nothing could dam the flow of her confession, her subconscious effort to please her interrogator and redeem herself in his eyes. At first she stammered, wept, and whispered in turn; but as she gradually became more coherent and the spells between her outbursts of whining sobs grew longer, her narrative slowly took shape, its triteness lending it a ring of credibility. A secretary in the Chelsea Public Library, her story went, she had been dragged into this Russian mess by her boyfriend, a boy younger than her by four years, named Kevin Gregory. Kevin was working for Intourist, the Soviet tourist bureau, as driver, messenger, and jack-of-all-trades. The oddest of his miscellaneous duties had been this last one, when he had offered her a way to make some quick money on the side. People were coming from abroad, he had said, reporters from Central Europe assigned to cover the visit of the Russian spy Alexander Orloff. They had rented a house to cut down on expenses and needed an English researcher who would transcribe TV and radio programs and keep files of press cuttings. The pay was good—one hundred pounds a week for as long as it lasted—so she took her long-due leave from the library and moved to number 113. Yes, she readily admitted when he pressed her, of course she knew there was something fishy about the whole affair; all the secrecy, code-words, counterfeit papers, and mysterious phone calls. Of course she understood they were Russians; their Austrian passports and Canadian names had not fooled her for one second, but she was not doing anything illegal,

213

was she? Anybody has the right to tape TV programs and radio news bulletins and collect press cuttings. It *was* legal, wasn't it? So what if she ran a few errands for them? They wanted somebody English to do the job, and so two or three times she and Kevin had tailed Orloff in the streets. The Russians said that a couple was less conspicuous and an English couple was the best. But then that was surely not a crime either. Private dicks were shadowing people all over London, weren't they? Of course she knew Kevin's friends were not journalists, but she didn't care what they really were, as long as they did not ask her to do anything against the law. No, she never saw Byroade or Darcy or the other diplomats. She learned about them from the papers; she kept a separate file on each. Hastings made her repeat this, and she confirmed that the files were in the house, on the second floor. They could ask Kevin. He was upstairs. If she had only known he'd involve her in such trouble she would have told him to stuff his hundred quid. Jesus Christ, what a mess. Her father would kill her if he knew. And then that Russian witch, the one who called herself Inge Schreider, she was all the time after her because she suspected that one of the Russians, Sontag, fancied her; and the witch fancied him, the witch did.

It took Hastings some mild browbeating to make Joan Valero admit that she had actually done a few jobs for Kevin's employers in the past as well: buying books and magazines on political and military subjects and marking important passages, talking friends into joining the anti-nuclear movement, distributing leaflets against the deployment of American nukes in Europe . . . but that wasn't a crime either—she had done no harm, had she?—but she cursed the day when she had laid eyes on him, she did.

When he finally escaped from the talkative repenter, he

walked straight into Wells, who was impatiently waiting outside, to update him on the latest findings. Wells's report, based on the simultaneous interrogations in progress upstairs, confirmed most of Joan Valero's monologue. "You were right from the beginning, Chief," Wells announced solemnly, pausing for effect before he went on to tell him how he was right. The team, indeed, was an Intelligence-gathering unit of the KGB, dispatched under thin cover only for collecting unclassified information about Orloff's visit. The parallels—for once he skipped the laudatory "bastards"—explained the operation as one more example of the notorious mania of the KGB for mounting elaborate ventures merely to collect easily accessible information and to verify facts that were common knowledge. They had found all the tapes and files upstairs, Wells added, and three of the Russians were being kind enough to describe the operation down to its smallest details.

"They know they don't run any real risk," Hastings said. "We can prosecute them for illegal entry, nothing else." He frowned. "If we ever decide to prosecute, that is. What about liaison?"

"There was a routine connection with the local residence: a visiting professor from the East German Technikum in Leipzig, on sabbatical at the London School of Economics. He assured the contact with the Pankow Trade Mission, which is associated with Sovtorg."

"That wraps it up." And probably explained how Nigel Sykes had found out about the safehouse. He had extended the surveillance not only on the Russian institutions but also on the satellites as well. "Any weapons?" Hastings asked, as a matter of routine.

Wells shook his head. "They are too clever for that."

Hastings shrugged and walked out of the house. The

Russians had not killed anybody. He looked up. The lights on the upper floor had gone off already, and the break-in team had left, followed by the lab and investigation squads. The prisoners had been whisked away in unmarked cars. Across the street, a few blurred figures were sitting in a black Daimler equipped with an ostentatious aerial. Sir Nigel was still there, probably with Jim Brennan. And Peter Snow hadn't shown up. Could that be due only to wounded pride? Hastings wondered.

He walked down the steps. The sharp wind shrieked in the empty street and blew his foggy breath over the sweat that poured down his face. There had been one disturbing item in Wells's report. Two of the Russians had flown out of the country to Brussels the day before. No trace after that.

The blank wall was there again, as solid, as impenetrable as ever.

It was past 3:00 A.M. when the insistent rapping on the door woke Alexander Orloff. The old man laboriously struggled out of bed and reached for his woolen robe. He could hear the howling of the storm outside.

Wells, the assistant of Hastings, was standing outside. Behind him Orloff saw one of his Special Branch bodyguards, who had spent most of the night in a stiff-backed armchair propped against the opposite wall. His face was puffy, and he was rubbing his bloodshot eyes with his fists, like a little boy. "Yes?" Orloff said. His mouth tasted foul.

"Sorry to disturb you at this ungodly hour, sir," Wells said in an unusually civil voice. "Chief Superintendent Hastings would like a word with you. He is outside in his car. Could you please get dressed and come down? Awfully sorry for the inconvenience."

16

HASTINGS was waiting for him in the back seat of his car. The driver and Wells tactfully retreated into the hotel lobby, where black workers maneuvered huge vacuum cleaners, giggling at each other's jokes. Orloff bent over and slipped into the back seat. The smell of black tobacco lingered in the car, but for once Hastings was not smoking. He seemed singularly withdrawn and the old man had the impression that his heavy bulk had shrunk in size. He was hatless, and his big head was sunk between his shoulders. "They are all dead," he said without preliminaries. "All but one. Rodney Shaw. And we have no clues."

Orloff did not answer. He was trying to figure out the reasons for this conspiratorial nocturnal meeting in a parked car, with no witnesses. "We found Llewellyn yesterday morning," Hastings went on. "Drowned. He had been dead for a few days. It was no accident."

"Neither was Westlake's crash, I guess," Orloff said.

Hastings nodded wearily. "There is only Shaw left," he repeated, "and I must get to him before they do."

"But he left the country, didn't he?"

"He flew to Montreal last week," Hastings replied. "I have no jurisdiction over there."

Orloff cocked his head. "But you have good connections, haven't you? And your secret services are working hand in hand with the Canadians."

Hastings retreated into a long, brooding silence. "I can't reach him," he said finally. "We don't operate out of the country.

"But the Intelligence service can find him in a matter of—"

"I can't reach him!" Hastings declared, his voice heavy with contained anger. And it suddenly dawned on Orloff that Hastings did not want the Intelligence service to get to Shaw before he could. He also realized that Hastings had not driven to his hotel at the darkest hour of the night merely to recount his troubles to a former Russian spy. He wanted to ask him for something. Orloff recoiled, wrapping his coat around his chest. It was cold in the car and his breath was coming out in whiffs of white vapor. He raised his collar and tucked his gloveless hands in his armpits. Would Hastings dare? He wondered.

"And you see no way to dispatch any of your men abroad?" he asked, without looking at Hastings.

They were playing a curious duel, Orloff felt, with Hastings slowly approaching, circling around him, but not daring to state his demand in so many words. "I thought," he said slowly, deciding to play Hastings's game, "that you could request the assistance of any national police abroad."

"And scare the man to death?" Hastings snapped testily.

"He is running for his life. He is badly frightened. Any police inquiry would make him clam up. And vanish again."

"What did you have in mind then?" Orloff threw a quick glance to Hastings, but his face was in shadow.

"I was thinking of something unofficial, very discreet. Somebody who could make this man talk."

"I see," Orloff said. "Well, a good man could do that. If Shaw is still alive, of course. And if he is in Canada."

"You don't think he is in Canada?"

Orloff shrugged. In the silence that settled in the car, he heard Hastings's quick, shallow breath. He was uncapping a small vial he had taken from his pocket; he then hurriedly cupped his hand over his mouth. The lights of the car that emerged around the corner lit his distorted face with a sickly glare.

"Do you have family in America?" Hastings suddenly asked.

"No," he said, surprised at the turn of the conversation. "Not exactly."

"But you have somebody."

Orloff felt uneasy. "There is a middle-aged woman who is very dear to me," he said guardedly.

Again that heavy, tedious silence. "What's her name?"

"Nora," Orloff said, suddenly irritated.

"An American?"

"Yes."

"My wife's name is Barbara," Hastings said stiffly. "We have no children."

What did he want? A woman in an expensive fur coat walked out of the Churchill. She stopped by the brightly illuminated entrance to light a cigarette. Her face was pretty but heavily made up. Her long auburn hair was tucked inside her collar.

"Do you have Rodney Shaw's address?" Orloff asked.

"It's in the book. He lives in London." Hastings paused. "Why do you ask?"

The woman walked quickly to a blue Mini-Austin parked by the entrance. She had long, elegant legs.

"I think I'll go back now," Orloff said. "I am an old man, and I need my sleep."

Hastings was scribbling something in his notebook. He tore out a page and stuck it in Orloff's hand. "I am never in my office," he said, his voice almost apologetic. "That's my private number. You can always leave a message. Barbara knows how to find me."

As he got out of the car, Hastings leaned after him and rolled down the window. "It could be dangerous, you know. The man who is after Shaw is after you too."

"You said he was a bad shot," Orloff remarked dryly and hurried into the entry's rectangle of light, chased by the wind.

"He is not in Canada, is he, Mrs. Shaw?" Orloff asked very softly, very gently, his eyes glued to the distraught face of the plain, aging woman. Lynn, sitting stiffly on the edge of the sofa, was watching them in silence, her hands tightly clasped on her lap.

"What nonsense!" Sybil Shaw exclaimed, her voice shrill, her chin trembling with indignation. "Of course he is in Canada. I saw him to the plane myself. Here"—she gestured vaguely toward the Chippendale desk on his left—"I received a postcard from Montreal only this morning."

He got up and looked at the postcard, showing the St. Lawrence in artificial colors. The postmark, dated four days before, seemed genuine. The few routine formulas—

Dearest Sybil . . . Your loving husband, Rodney—were
written and signed by the same hand. It was too neat, too
tidy, a perfect alibi in obvious contradiction with the hysterical state in which they had found Sybil Shaw.

Orloff had reached Lynn in the late afternoon. He had
not been able to sleep after his odd encounter with Hastings.
The chief superintendent had played his game cunningly,
asking for his help without saying so, suggesting to him
what to do without admitting he needed him badly. He did
not care, he would have gone after Shaw anyway, and he
was glad he had at least the discreet support of Hastings.
Still, those strange questions about family and Nora and
that remark about his childless wife. They seemed so odd
in the mouth of the clumsy, tough man. "My wife's name
is Barbara." The whole conversation seemed absurd, almost unreal, when he thought of it in the sober light of
dawn.

Lynn had been reluctant to join him at first; but he had
insisted, stressing that Shaw held the key to all the murders,
and she had finally agreed to come. They found Shaw's
address in the phonebook and drove to his flat in Chelsea.
The police had been there already, Mrs. Shaw admitted
sullenly after Lynn convinced her to let them in. They
were very civil, she said, just asked a few questions and
left, apologizing for the intrusion.

Orloff laid the postcard on the desk. "I know he is not
in Canada," he said. "Please, Mrs. Shaw. Let me talk to
you. I am a friend."

The face of the elderly woman was flushed, her mouth
twitched nervously and her eyes were frightened, defensive.
"I don't have to listen to you!" she said loudly, and
looked around as if seeking help.

"Please, listen to him, Mrs. Shaw," Lynn said, reaching for the old woman's hand. Sybil Shaw withdrew it swiftly and shot a furious look at her.

"Your husband worked for the Russians in the fifties, Mrs. Shaw," Orloff went on. "You were stationed in Sofia, Warsaw, and finally Bonn."

"No, no," she shook her head vigorously. In her present state, she would deny anything. "That is not true. That's a lie."

"Your husband passed secret information to the Russians till nineteen sixty-two. After Philby escaped to Russia an internal board of inquiry found incriminating evidence against Ambassador Shaw. Four other diplomats admitted that they had served the KGB."

"That's not true," she repeated stubbornly. "My husband resigned of his own free will. He was not a spy."

"He was not a spy," Orloff agreed. "That's why they did not put him on trial. He was only asked to resign. The board established that he had been forced to cooperate with the Russians." He was guessing now.

She stared at him, clenching her teeth. Her lips were quivering. "They forced him," she finally admitted. "The Russians forced him. They threatened to publish proof that he had been a Communist in his youth. In fact he had at that time already collaborated with Soviet agents in England. They left him no choice."

"Of course," Orloff said. Lynn got up and went to the window. Night had fallen already and the street was deserted. On the upper floor someone was practicing the piano.

"Your husband had been blackmailed into working for the Russians," he said cautiously. "He was discharged from the Foreign Office. There was no scandal, just a quiet departure."

She nodded. Her resistance was waning.

"But he knew the names of the other diplomats involved in the scandal." Orloff looked up for her agreement, and she nodded again. "For almost twenty years nothing happened, and that sordid business seemed forgotten and buried."

He was looking over the woman's shoulder now, directly at Lynn who faced him, her back to the window. She was unusually pale. "But a few weeks ago," he continued, "a reporter dug out the material about Anthony Byroade, and he was assassinated. In the days that followed, your husband learned that Archibald Westlake died in a very convenient automobile accident, and Llewellyn disappeared from his cottage. I was attacked and wounded. Ambassador Shaw was the only one to see the pattern."

"There was that woman in France too," Mrs. Shaw said quickly. "She was also involved in a way, wasn't she?"

Orloff nodded. "So he told you about her." He leaned forward, toward the woman. "Your husband was badly scared, Mrs. Shaw. He was sure they were after him too. So he decided to escape."

"No!" she protested loudly, wringing her pudgy hands. "He had to go to Canada. He had to see some relatives of ours."

"Mrs. Shaw," Orloff said patiently, "we called the airlines before we came. Your husband made a rather sudden decision to go to Canada, didn't he? He reserved his seat the same morning and bought his ticket at the airport, in cash. One doesn't decide to go overseas on the spur of the moment. Just to visit relatives."

She stared at him in growing distress.

"Let me tell you what really happened. He said he was

223

going to Canada. He bought a ticket and flew to Montreal. He sent you that postcard, as soon as he arrived. But he knew that the people who assassinated his colleagues might follow him even overseas. So he left Canada for another country, where nobody would find him. Only you know where he is.''

"Who told you that?" she asked sharply, crossing her arms to conceal their trembling.

"Nobody. That's the way I would have acted if I were on the run.''

"And what do you want of me?" There was raw despair beneath the rudeness.

"I must meet with him, Mrs. Shaw. I must talk to him. Only if I meet with him, may I be able to save his life. Believe me, I can help.''

"No, you can't. Leave him alone. Please leave him alone.''

"Mrs. Shaw, if the police and the services of this country start looking for him, they will find him easily. I don't believe he has a passport under another name. The police have only to cable Mr. Shaw's name and description to Canadian immigration, and he will be located in a matter of hours. But the story might leak, his whereabouts could become known, and his life would be in danger again. Please, tell me how to find him, and we'll do our best''—he gestured toward Lynn—"to keep the police out of this.''

She shook her head.

"Mrs. Shaw," Lynn said and knelt beside her. She turned to Orloff. "Alex, leave us alone for a moment. Can he wait in another room, Mrs. Shaw?''

The woman nodded miserably. "My husband's study is at the end of the corridor," she said.

Ten minutes later Lynn called him back. Tears were streaming on the fleshy cheeks of Sybil Shaw. "He flew from Montreal to Frankfurt, rented a car, and drove to Bonn," she said in a wavering voice, her eyes focused on Lynn's compassionate face. Lynn held her right hand in hers. "Rodney has good friends in Bonn who are taking care of him."

"You must give us his address," Lynn insisted.

The old woman buried her face in her hands.

They hatched their plan later that night in a quiet Italian restaurant in Kensington. He had to leave the country as discreetly as possible in order to put some distance between him and the British secret services. He was convinced that when Hastings had come to see him, he was acting on his own initiative; he could expect that Special Branch wouldn't show too much zeal in delaying his departure. But if the Intelligence service got wind of his sudden voyage, they would stick to him, maybe even precede him, and blow his project.

"I have an idea," Lynn said suddenly, her eyes sparkling. "We're supposed to broadcast your last interview, live, in three days."

He nodded. "Thank God, yes."

"Nobody would expect you to leave England before, of course." She pushed aside her plate and leaned across the table. "Now, if we taped that interview secretly tomorrow morning, you could go from the studio straight to Heathrow and board a plane to Europe." As he frowned, puzzled, she quickly went on: "Any destination in Europe. Never mind, once on the Continent you can change planes and proceed to Bonn. You'll get there tomorrow evening at the latest. That would give you a few hours, more than enough to disappear and continue on your own.''

He scowled doubtfully. ''You can't tape an interview secretly, Lynn.''

She shook her head, her eyes twinkling in amusement but her chin stubbornly jutting forth. Exactly like her mother, he thought. ''Of course we can. We'll call it a rehearsal. Rehearsals are often taped, you know that. Ted will tell the personnel we had a lot of bad mail criticizing the camera angles and the sound of the last segment, so he wants to rehearse the next one. And on Thursday, we'll broadcast the tape, while you're away.''

''And you believe Ted will do it?''

''Of course he will.'' Again the mischievous smile. ''If I tell him to, that is.''

The next morning at 10:30, they recorded the last interview. Lynn was the only interviewer, as had been the case the first time. Ted watched the set from behind the cameras. Her questions were sharp and precise; she led him masterfully through the most dramatic stages of his spying career: Philby's great coups in the fifties; the deep penetration of the Intelligence service; the escapes of Burgess and Maclean; the January night when he had whisked Philby from a Beirut street and escorted him over the Syrian plateaus and across the wild wastes of Anatolia, all the way to the Russian border. Still, throughout the interview he had a strange feeling of detachment that bordered on indifference. Was it because of the adventure he was about to embark upon? Because of the feeling that by some strange twist of fate he was getting another, unexpected chance to relive the thrills, the fears, and the perils that had been his natural element a lifetime ago? A chance to face again the solitary challenge, the ultimate test of a battle of wits against a powerful, dangerous enemy, and reach for the coveted prize—a bundle of papers, a formula, a name? He was surprised at his own feeling of elation, surprised that the last seventeen years he had thought to be so fulfilling, so good, were suddenly paling in comparison with the forthcoming replay of his earlier life. Surprised and anguished, uncertain. You cannot teach an old dog new tricks, the saying went; but his old tricks were rising from the past, shadows of a life he had tried to forget, and did not want to, anymore.

Lynn did not see through him, did not sense his internal turmoil as she came to him once the interview was over. She was too preoccupied with herself, as he was to discover shortly, and glowed with a secret happiness. She then led him to her dressing room "just for a quick cup of coffee," as she said to his bodyguards, who remained on the set, watching the rites of the entertainment world that resided behind the TV screen.

Once in her dressing room, Lynn turned to him with a dazzling smile, and on a sudden impulse kissed him on the cheek. He liked the waft of her fresh fragrance and the brief touch of her lips on his skin. Her eyes were bright. "Ted moved in with me today, Alex," she announced. "This morning. He looks rather happy."

He managed to smile back. "I should be leaving," he said.

She tilted her head, her eyes wary. "You don't approve of that, do you?"

"Oh, I do approve," he shook his head, hating to cause her pain. "I just don't know how long it will last."

"But it won't, Alex." Her voice was very soft; her

face, quiet, mature. "It won't last," she repeated, "and I have no illusions about it. But I've got Ted now. I feel happy, and I intend to enjoy every minute of it. Who was it who said that life is nothing but a bank of happy memories? One day you cash what you deposited. I am still working hard on the deposits." Then, practical again: "Here you are: tickets, money, a letter of introduction by the network, just in case. You've got your passport?"

He nodded. "Where's my bag?" Lynn had smuggled from the hotel an overnight bag with a change of clothes and a shaving kit. He had left all his other belongings in the room to maintain the illusion that he was still in town.

"The bag is in the car already. Come."

She led him through a maze of corridors and a narrow staircase to a side door that opened into a back street. A car was waiting, its engine running. Ted Jennings suddenly materialized behind him. His handshake was strong, frank, and Orloff looked up at him in surprise. "Good luck," Ted said. Then, suddenly uneasy, he began a hasty retreat. "I've got to watch over your baby-sitters," he apologized lamely.

Lynn pressed his arm. "Take care, Alex," she whispered. He turned back and casually caressed her cheek with the tips of his fingers, then crossed the street and got into the car.

An hour later, he boarded a KLM plane to Amsterdam. When he walked through passport control, he caught a brief glance of a man in a tan raincoat, talking to a customs officer in a corner of the departure lounge. The man was standing with his back to him, enveloped in the faint odor of black French tobacco. But when he looked his way again, the man had disappeared.

At Schiphol airport, he caught a Lufthansa flight to Cologne. Shortly before midnight, he stood in front of a rustic cottage in the western outskirts of Bonn.

17

A SUDDEN ONSLAUGHT of wind bolting up from the Rhine
gripped his back in an icy embrace and disheveled his hair.
He stopped in the middle of the stone-paved path leading
to the house and looked back. Dark clouds were swiftly
creeping toward the pale moon, and the silver ribbon of
the river, down in the valley, had changed into a quavering
black mass faintly glowing in the distance. Still, the tidy
cottage in front of him looked extraordinarily peaceful
with its coquettish gabled roof, lace-curtained windows,
and a fragile wisp of smoke rising from the chimney. On
both sides of the path, the lawn was covered with an
immaculate blanket of snow. The only note of bad taste
was struck by two plump marble cupids impaled on stilts,
hovering over an elliptic frozen pond in the garden.

He pressed the bell under the discreet bronze plaque that
read VON HALBANS, and soft chimes tinkled in the house.
For a while nothing happened, so he rang again. Some-

thing stirred inside the house, feet furtively shuffled over carpeted floors, and a door moaned in the back. A grim apparition glared at him from the oblong strip of dark glass embedded in the door: a thin figure in black; a pallid, drawn face; a swaying halo of white hair. He involuntarily shuddered. This was the way a messenger of death should look. He took a step forward and realized that the sinister figure was his own reflection. It suddenly vanished, however, as light erupted in the black glass. The door slowly opened and he stepped inside, the stubborn cold enveloping him like a wet shroud, sticking to his numb body.

The man in front of him was tall, broad-shouldered but slightly stooping. His big head was completely bald, and the scrawny neck, the moth-eaten moustache, the loose folds of flesh on the sagging jaws were those of an old man. But the gray eyes were clear, the mouth firm, and the chin willful, aggressive. He was wearing a mono-grammed dressing gown over blue silk pajamas and elegant leather slippers. *"Guten Abend,"* he said politely, moving aside to let Orloff into the small vestibule. His right hand was stuck in his pocket. Through the open door behind the German's back Orloff could see an oak-paneled wall bathed in a wavering reddish glow.

"Guten Abend," Orloff replied softly. "Do you speak English?"

The tall man looked at him thoughtfully, as if he was weighing the question, then nodded. "Yes, I do." His voice was deep, well-bred.

"I am sorry to disturb you at this time of night. But you have a guest in your house, Mr. Rodney Shaw. I've got to talk to him. It's very urgent."

"You must be mistaken," the tall man said. "There is

no one by that name in my house." He paused, then added courteously: "Are you sure you've got the right address?"

"You are Mr. Von Halbans," Orloff said wearily. "You have been Ambassador Shaw's friend for many years. He is hiding in your house."

"Somebody must have misled you," Von Halbans said patiently. "I don't know what you're talking about. May I ask where you got that information?"

Orloff nodded. "I saw Mrs. Sybil Shaw yesterday, in London. I convinced her that I could help Ambassador Shaw, and she gave me this address. I am not connected with any official organization. My name is Orloff. Alexander Orloff."

The name did not seem to ring any bells. Von Halbans was watching him, his hand still stiff in his pocket, a skeptical frown wrinkling his forehead. "As I told you . . ." he began.

"You know Rodney Shaw, don't you?" Orloff asked bluntly.

For a second Von Halbans hesitated. "I—"

"It's no use, Helmut," a new voice said wearily. A gaunt, gray-haired man appeared in the open doorway. "I'll talk to this gentleman." He advanced, limping badly, and laid a friendly hand on the German's shoulder, then turned to face Orloff. "I am Rodney Shaw," he said. "What do you want?"

"My name is Orloff," he began, but Shaw nodded impatiently.

"I know who you are." He had a rasping voice and his breath was shallow, asthmatic. "I saw you on television in London. What do you want of me?"

"We are both in danger, Mr. Shaw," Orloff said. He felt the intent stare of Von Halbans, who had taken a step backward. "Somebody tried to kill me in London a couple of weeks ago. I'm still not quite recovered from the wound. I believe the same man killed some of your former colleagues . . . and is after you now."

"That's absolute nonsense," Shaw said, a little too quickly. "Why should anyone try to kill me?"

"I don't know. But you were the only one to see the connection between the murders, and you escaped before the killer reached you."

Shaw looked at him fixedly, indecision and anxiety deeply etched in every line of his meager face. He finally shrugged in resignation.

"How do you know it's a man and not an organization?" he asked. His small eyes gazed at Orloff suspiciously.

"I don't," Orloff admitted, "But I believe there is a reason for those killings. Those people must have known something, and died for it."

"I don't know anything," Shaw said stubbornly, his quick breath whistling in his sick lungs.

"You are the only one left," Orloff said. "Darcy has been shot. The police found Llewellyn, drowned. They established that Westlake's accident was murder as well. You must know something, even if you're unaware of it."

The mention of the dead men's names made Shaw hesitate. He looked angrily at Orloff, his narrow mouth twitching, and twice started to say something but changed his mind. He glanced at Von Halbans, seeking assistance, and finally gave in. "Will you step in, Mr. Orloff?" he said, and led the way inside.

The strange glow, Orloff realized as he followed Shaw into the vast sitting room, was the reflection of flames dancing in the marble fireplace. A Christmas tree, still unadorned, stood in the far corner beside a cardboard box full of trinkets, stars, and spools of golden yarn. On the walls were a few oil paintings representing hunting scenes. Rifles and muskets were displayed in an antique cupboard with glass doors. It was a masculine room, with no trace of a woman's touch. Shaw limped to a couple of brown leather armchairs facing the fire and sunk with relief into one of them. He was fully dressed in a dark blue suit, white shirt, and velvet bow tie, much too ostentatious.

Orloff turned back, toward Von Halbans. "I think you can put your gun away now, Mr. Von Halbans," he said softly. The big man stopped in the embrasure of the door, his face flushed with embarrassment. "I don't understand," he started.

"The gun in your right pocket," Orloff explained patiently. "I don't think you'll need it anymore." He turned back to Shaw.

"Helmut is a close and very dear friend," Rodney Shaw said. His smile was apologetic, revealing two bright rows of false teeth. "We were both first secretaries in our embassies in Warsaw in the late fifties. Later, when I was transferred to Bonn, we became real good friends. He retired from the service a couple of years ago."

Von Halbans appeared at Orloff's side, holding two bell-shaped glasses half-full with an amber-colored liquid. "That's cognac," he said gravely, and as Orloff opened his mouth to protest, he raised his hand and added quickly: "You need it, Mr. Orloff. You are frozen. Why don't you take off your coat?" The bulge Orloff had noticed in the right pocket of Von Halbans's dressing gown was still there. Von Halbans handed the second glass of cognac to Shaw, took Orloff's coat, and discreetly vanished. Outside, the low whine of the wind had risen to an angry howl.

Shaw painstakingly raised his bad leg to place it on the footstool in front of him.

"Does it hurt?" Orloff asked.

Shaw shrugged. "I'm supposed to say that one gets used to it. Well, I don't."

"A war wound?"

Shaw hesitated. "Not exactly, no. It happened during the war, but it was an accident. In Arnheim, one of our tank commanders was too eager to win the war. I was in the way." He touched his bow tie. There was something pedantic, calculated, in each of his gestures. "How's Sybil?"

"Distressed," Orloff said, unwilling to play a game of niceties. "She wanted to phone you that I was coming, but I talked her out of it. There is a slight chance that her telephone might be tapped."

"By whom?"

Orloff didn't answer, and took a sip of the cognac.

"You should know," Shaw said. "That's your line of business, isn't it?"

Orloff disregarded the sarcasm. "Yes, it is," he said simply.

An awkward silence broken only by the rising roar of the storm outside settled in the room. Orloff strode to the window. It had started snowing, a heavy downfall of huge flakes that the tempest sent whirling and eddying around the house. He returned to his seat and stared at the flames in the fireplace. "I must ask you what exactly happened between you and the Russians," he said. Shaw did not answer.

"It's important," he insisted, uneasy.

Shaw leaned back on the headrest and gazed at the ceiling. "I've never talked about it to a living soul," he said. Orloff let another minute pass, avoiding looking at the scared man beside him.

"When were you first approached?" he finally said to the burning logs.

There was another long moment of silence. Finally Shaw cleared his throat. "In Sofia," he said. "Nineteen fifty-two. I was second secretary in the political section of the embassy."

"Political? That's SIS, isn't it?"

"Among others," Shaw admitted, looking down at his glass.

"When did they contact you?"

"One morning in December, about six months after I arrived. I found a letter on the front seat of my car."

"You kept it locked?"

"Of course." Shaw was seized by a coughing fit, followed by pained, rasping respiration. He gulped his drink, struggled onto his feet, and limped to the small bar at the other end of the room. When he returned, his glass was full almost to the rim. His hand was shaking, and he spilled a few drops on the armrest.

"That letter," Orloff said, "it was in plain language?"

It took Shaw another minute to answer, but after some lame attempts to find refuge in silence and his drink, his story finally got under way. The letter had been rather short and straight to the point. "Welcome to the Popular Republic of Bulgaria," it had begun. "We proudly note that you have shared our ideals of socialism and Leninism since your youth." That statement was substantiated by precise details concerning his secret membership in the Communist party in Cambridge: the date of his adherence to the party, the code appellation of his cell, the names of his fellow members. Followed the call to arms. As he

237

would "certainly be willing to help the revolution," he was asked to visit the same afternoon, between 5:00 and 5:15 P.M., the Alexander Nevski Cathedral. A letter with detailed instructions for him would be taped on the back of the Cyril and Methodius icon in the small chapel behind the main altar.

He had not gone to the cathedral, of course, and for the next few days had seriously considered knocking on the ambassador's door to tell him about the letter and make a clean breast of his past. But, as a political officer, he knew too well the standard procedure in a case like his: he would be recalled to London immediately, struck off the maximum security lists, and never again appointed behind the Iron Curtain. His career would be switched onto a dead track. He might be sentenced to slow death: for instance, first secretary in Moputu; or, if he was lucky, get buried alive as representative to the World Health or Labor or some other nonsense organization in Geneva.

So he had kept quiet, hoping those who sought him would be deterred by his silence and leave him alone. But a week later another letter had come, then a phone call to his office, and finally he had gotten the unequivocal message: either he cooperated or his superiors would be presented with hard proof about his past allegiance. More than a month had passed since the first contact, and he knew now it was too late for making amends. Nobody would ever forgive him for waiting a month before confessing; nobody would ever believe that he had not yet cooperated with the opposition.

So he finally went to the dead-letter drop designated in their last letter. It had been, as far as he remembered, the Bulgarian National Museum at Boulevard Dondukov. The note with the instructions was slipped into his pocket while he lined up in front of the main entrance. And with that he started working for the KGB.

"How do you know it was the KGB?" Orloff asked casually.

Shaw looked at him sharply. "Who else could it have been?"

"Who else indeed," Orloff meekly agreed, sinking back into his brooding silence.

When he read the first note he was frankly relieved, Shaw admitted bitterly. All that they asked for was the unclassified news digest the press section was circulating weekly in the embassy. He didn't feel he was committing any crime when he stuck the small sheaf of papers between two loose stones in the Monument of the Red Army in Liberty Park. Only later was he to understand that they did not give a damn about the news digest. Their aim was to make him cooperate, get him involved. Once he had taken the first step, he was at their mercy, already a "spy," and they had acquired absolute control over him.

They supplied him with code-books and invisible ink, established a working code, and soon their demands started to pour in: They asked for detailed memos on his colleagues, classified SIS circulars, reports on the standard security regulations at the embassy and on the compartmentalization rules inside the SIS. They asked him to compile lists of all the SIS officials he knew in London and all over the world, including detailed biographical sketches of each and every one and his own estimates of their loyalty, efficiency, and ambitions. The next stage carried him deeper into the mire: He was instructed to substitute most of the reports provided by the SIS espionage networks inside Bulgaria with worthless fakes supplied by the Russians, while the originals were delivered to the KGB. By that time, he had no will of his own. There was no turning back, and he was unable to resist when they demanded his last secret: the names and addresses of SIS informers in Bulgaria.

"You knew them?" Orloff asked quickly.

"We had four independent rings in Bulgaria at that time. I knew the members of two of them, Periscope and Prelude."

Orloff hesitated before asking the next question. He was opening old wounds now, torturing an already broken mind. "What happened to them?" he finally asked, his voice very soft, very subdued.

"Nothing," Shaw said.

Orloff was erect on his seat, staring at him in disbelief.

"Nothing," Shaw repeated. "Absolutely nothing, at least while I was there."

"What are you talking about?"

He could not see Shaw's face. The flames in the fire-place had died, and blackness had gradually enveloped both of them. "It was strange," Shaw admitted. "Nobody was touched, and they continued to provide us with good reports as long as I ran them. I never heard that my networks were dismantled. Did you?"

"No," Orloff managed. "I never knew that you had been working for us."

"You were always very good at compartmentalization," Shaw remarked.

Orloff got to his feet. "But it doesn't make sense!"

"Doesn't it really?" Shaw asked, pouring himself another drink. "It does to me. I guess they wanted to protect me. If the networks were blown, I might have been exposed."

Orloff was shaking his head. "I never heard of anything

like that," he said. "It's common practice to capture networks, return them, and play them against their center. But leave them unscathed? Why? Didn't you ever discuss that with your case officer?"

The figure beside him shrugged in the half-darkness. "I never met him," said Shaw.

"Oh, come on," Orloff muttered angrily. He was standing behind his armchair, his fingers furiously digging in the supple leather. "What's that crap, Shaw? You never met anybody?"

"That's correct," Shaw said, and Orloff had the odd sensation that the man was taking pleasure in his disarray. "I never met a single one of them."

"And all the contacts—" Orloff began.

"I told you. All the contacts were made either by telephone—mostly from public booths—or by dead-letter drops. I never met, face to face, any KGB officer. Neither in Bulgaria nor later in Poland."

"Poland, yes." Orloff could not contain his sarcasm. "Tell me about Poland?"

"There's nothing to tell, I'm afraid. It was a repetition of the Bulgarian story, but on a larger scale. They had similar demands, I supplied similar material."

"And you never met your case officer in Poland either? You betrayed more networks, and they weren't touched either?" Orloff was burning with anger.

"That's correct. You have a quick mind, Comrade Orloff."

"And when you were transferred to Bonn. . . ."

"I was promoted to the rank of ambassador and transferred to Bonn in nineteen sixty-two. I was never bothered here."

"No calls, no drops, no letters in your car?"

"Nothing, as I said. It all stopped as suddenly as it had begun. It was like waking from a bad dream."

Furious, Orloff groped around the dark, unfamiliar room in search of a light switch. Shaw was lying his heart out. Or was he? What if he were telling the truth and the betrayed networks were neither returned nor destroyed? Was there any logic behind such strategy? He found the switch, and the room was inundated by dazzling light. Shaw scowled and stared at him with weary, slightly glazed eyes.

"How did British security get to you?" he asked, resentful at not understanding, unable to conceal his hostility toward the half-drunk man sprawled in his head-waiter's outfit before the dead fire.

Shaw shrugged indifferently. "A leak in Moscow, I guess. A KGB defector or some notebook Philby forgot in his drawer before he went to Russia. Who knows?" He gave a short, unpleasant laugh.

"And you told all this to the investigation committee? I mean the contact routine, the reports, the networks?"

"Yes, of course." Shaw propped himself up to a sitting position. His movements were uncoordinated, and his speech was slurred. Still, his narrative, which he now resumed with peculiar nonchalance, was consistent and precise. He had returned to London in late 1966, calm and serene after the four good years in Bonn. He was being considered for promotion, because the director of West Europe 1, Caute, had suddenly died of a heart attack. On January 17, 1967, he had been summoned to a Whitehall office "for a briefing" and had walked straight into the secret board of inquiry.

"Let's skip that part, if you don't mind," he said, looking sideways at Orloff. "All I can tell you is that the interrogation lasted for three and a half weeks and was a rather unpleasant experience.'' Shaw got up and limped purposefully to the bar.

"Who was on the board?" Orloff called after him. Shaw quickly emptied his glass, filled it again, and started his return journey holding his drink with exaggerated care, like an inveterate alcoholic.

"The board? Let's see. There was the director general of the Foreign Office, Ashley. The chief security officer as well; I don't remember his name. The secretary of the board was Jeremy Greenshaw. There were two people from the SIS, Jimmy Landsdale and another chap. And those two, Peter Snow and Nigel Sykes."

"Nigel Sykes? He was in the SIS already?"

"No, of course not. He had just been appointed director of MI-5." He chuckled. "He and Snow were building a flourishing cat-and-dog relationship. Sykes became chief of the SIS only in nineteen seventy, if I remember correctly." He pursed his lips and bent over his glass.

"And after the inquiry? Why weren't you put on trial?"

Shaw slurred his way through what he called "the pinnacle of his private ordeal." He had been asked to tender his resignation in twenty-four hours, he said. Ashley, the Foreign Office director had taken him to another office for a tête-à-tête. The old boy had been very harsh with him. If it had depended on him, he had said, he would have had him tried and convicted, and would have rejoiced to see him rot in prison for the rest of his life. But the service had been riddled with scandals: Burgess, Maclean, and now that bloody Philby. The government had therefore decided to spare the country another traumatic experience. "He said he would have gladly asked for my head," Shaw quoted, waving his empty glass, "but under the circumstances he would have to settle for my letter of resignation, and may I roast in hell.''

"Still . . ." Orloff started, but Shaw interrupted him with an imperative flourish of his brandy glass.

"Jimmy Landsdale told me a different story, though.''

"Landsdale?''

"The SIS chap. He said they still hoped that the KGB might try to get in touch with me in England, so they wanted to keep me free and available. A sort of bait, you know.''

"But the KGB didn't get in touch with you?''

"No, never.''

Orloff felt a chill settling over his body. It was the cold in the room, or maybe his fatigue. He crouched before the fireplace and hopelessly prodded the ashes with the long, thin poker, searching for a still glowing ember. He shivered. "During the inquiry," he slowly said, "did you meet the other diplomats involved?''

"The other culprits, you mean?" Again the repulsive, drunken chuckle.

"Yes.''

"I didn't meet anybody," Shaw declared. "It was all very hush-hush, very cloak-and-dagger, you know.''

"So how—''

"Patience, my dear chap, I'm coming to it. That was strictly personal, and highly irregular.'' He burst out in laughter again. "Highly irregular.'' Shaw stretched back on his chair and yawned luxuriously. "I knew the secretary of the board, Jeremy Greenshaw. He had served under me in Bonn. After all that was over, he came to my office to pick up my letter of resignation. Then he told me, swearing me to secrecy, that there were four other diplomats, all of them Cambridge graduates, who had also been interrogated and fired, for similar reasons. He gave me the names. Byroade, Westlake, Llewellyn, and Darcy.''

"You knew them?"

"Of course I did."

"You were in the same cell in Cambridge?"

The question, for no apparent reason, seemed to irritate Shaw. "What difference does it make?" he said sharply. "I knew them, that's all."

"Did you meet them after the inquiry?"

"I met nobody after the inquiry," Shaw grunted, his irritation growing. "I retired and went into finance and minded my own business."

"And you never saw them again?"

Shaw turned to face him with the exaggerated movements of a drunk. "I read in the paper that Byroade and that French woman—Benedetti—had been murdered, and that Westlake had had an incident. I got worried so I tried to call Llewellyn and Darcy. I got the answer."

"So you panicked," Orloff concluded, "and you caught the first available flight."

Shaw shrugged, contemplating his empty glass. "I should have brought over the bloody bottle," he said.

Orloff took a step toward the bar, then changed his mind. Shaw's usefulness seemed to have run out for tonight, maybe even for good. He did not need his help anymore to guess the rest of the story.

Prostrate again in his chair, Shaw was breathing heavily. Orloff watched his glossy eyes slowly close, succumbing to the liquor. His hand went limp, dropping the glass, which shattered on the floor. The noise did not affect him. His mouth slackened, and a gurgling noise came out of his throat, quickly changing into regular snoring.

In the hall, Von Halbans was waiting, Orloff's overcoat

neatly folded over his arm. He helped Orloff put it on. His brow was puckered in thought, and he avoided Orloff's eyes. He seemed on the verge of speaking but apparently lacked the courage. Finally he drew a deep breath. "I don't know what all this is about," he said, his face red with embarrassment. "He must be under great strain. Don't judge him too harshly, Mr. Orloff. He is a good man, believe me." He added quickly: "I called a taxi for you. It should be here by now."

"Does he often get drunk like that?" Orloff asked, buttoning his coat.

Von Halbans nodded. "Every night, since he arrived."

As Von Halbans opened the door for him, Orloff turned back. "Get him out of here," he said. "If I found him, somebody else could. They'll kill him if they ever get to him."

Von Halbans stared at him with shocked, disbelieving eyes. "Who would want to kill him?" he murmured. "He is just a harmless old cripple."

"Get him out," Orloff repeated. "Wake him up, dress him, and take him away."

Only when he was out in the storm, trudging in the snow toward the waiting cab, did he realize that he still did not know *who* wanted to kill Rodney Shaw.

In the early morning he reached a decision.

He had spent the rest of the night in his hotel room, unable to sleep, haunted by the strange encounter with Rodney Shaw. He had gone through Shaw's narrative over and over again, seeking a clue, a hint, a key to the enigma that obsessed him. Shaw's disclosures had been stunning indeed, and he instinctively knew they were like the mixed pieces of a puzzle. Arranged in the right order they would spell out the identity of the killers. But in spite of all his efforts, the pieces did not fall into place, and the riddle remained unsolved.

The bleak light of dawn brought with it a bitter sensation of failure as a sudden numbness, coupled with physical exhaustion, descended upon his tired mind. He was an old man, and the eventful night had drained every drop of energy from his weakened body. He had to admit defeat. There was nothing more for him to seek in Bonn; there was no reason to go back to London either.

Reluctantly he had to concede that there was only one man on this earth who could, who might, give him the answer. As a matter of fact he had known that from the very moment Lynn had broken to him the news of Byroade's death. But he had been reluctant to plunge back into his past, open the sepulchre of his former life, stir the ghosts that followed him along this last leg of his journey on earth.

The telephone was on the small marble-topped night table, beside the bed. Twice he picked up the receiver, and twice he hastily laid it down. It was like committing a sacrilege, raising a soul from the dead. He feared this last step just as he had secretly, unconsciously feared it from his first day in London. He had tried to avoid it, striving to manage by himself but haunted without respite by the same face, the same voice, the same brain that held the answer. There was no other way, he said to himself. His private quest for his faceless enemy had reached a dead end. He had to make that call. Did Hastings understand this too? Was that the reason he had set him on Shaw's trail to Europe? Gambling on his past, hoping he would take that last step? He reached for the phone, for the third time.

"I have to place a long-distance call," he said to the operator. "London."

Lynn sounded sleepy, and from the whispers in the background he understood she was not alone. Ted, of course. He felt a twinge of unexpected jealousy.

"Alex?" Her warm, sensuous voice filled the receiver. She paused a second. "Where are you? Are you all right?"

He did not answer the questions. Before she went further, he spoke urgently. "I want you to do something for me, Lynn. I want you to go to this address." He quoted it from memory, painfully aware that he was parting with his last private secret, the only detail he had not disclosed to the CIA during his exhaustive debriefing, the only bit of information he had concealed and carried with him for seventeen years. A small secret it was, his private link with a rejected past, rather a sentimental memento; still, at times it had seemed to him a sort of trump card that had given him, he hated to admit, an odd illusion of power, of liberty.

She repeated the address; it was in the East End. "Go to that house," he repeated. "An old couple is living there. You will give them a message. Tell them Robin needs an urgent meeting with his friend next Friday night."

"That's Christmas Eve," she said.

"Yes. Robin needs a meeting with his friend at the first lady's place. Will you remember that?"

"What does it mean, Alex?" Lynn seemed disturbed.

"Please don't ask. Trust me. The first lady's place."

She repeated the message. His hand was trembling, and cold sweat formed on his forehead. "If anything goes wrong," he said, "or if the meeting is not possible, send me a telegram in care of General Delivery in Berlin."

"Berlin? Are you in Berlin?"

"Take care," he said, and the line went dead.

As he was about to replace the receiver, he heard a soft click—or perhaps it was his imagination.

Assured, suave, oozing charm from every pore, J.J. Kraft helped her take off her coat, pulled up her chair, poured her a glass of wine, ordered their lunch, then smoothly leaned forward, sizing her up with an admiring smile. "You are much more beautiful in real life than on the screen, Miss Kennan," he drawled in his deep southern accent. "It is a real privilege for me to lunch in your company."

She smiled in return, very much on her guard. The charming blond Casanova who faced her was the chief representative of the CIA in London. He was not an undercover agent; his main function was to assure the liaison with the British services; his name figured in the diplomatic repertory as one of the political officers in the American embassy. She had had no trouble finding him, thanks to Jack Oppenheim, the *New York Times* correspondent in London. "Keep your distance, lady," Jack had said, chuckling, when she had told him she wanted to meet Kraft. "That guy is a sex machine." He had told her about J.J.'s secret passion for women, whom he picked up mostly at the parties for embassy staff and local friends that he and his unsuspecting wife would throw at any possible occasion. "He won't let an opportunity like you pass him by." Then he had added, growing serious: "But don't be deceived by appearances. He is tough, he is clever, and has a brilliant record. He just surfaced two years ago. They say he planned quite a few coups when he operated undercover in South America."

Kraft agreed to meet her as soon as she phoned him at

the embassy. He invited her to lunch at the White Tower. He was very handsome indeed and knew his way with a woman, she admitted to herself as she watched him now over the rim of her glass; still, the thoughtful, calculating stare of his cold blue eyes stood out in striking contradiction to the pleasant, easy smile illuminating his attractive features. For a moment she wondered how he would react if she told him that barely an hour before she had brought a secret message from a former Soviet mole to his contacts, who might still be working for Moscow Center. She had done it after a long, painful hesitation; and she had done it only because she trusted the old man and couldn't believe he might do anything to betray her confidence. The woman who had opened the door of the decrepit house in the East End hadn't asked her in, just stared at her suspiciously from the obscurity of the narrow entrance, which was enveloped in the stale smell of old walls, old furniture, and old age. She was dressed in shabby black trousers and a loose checkered pullover, its original colors faded. Her sparse hair was clean and neatly combed, though, and her eyes, magnified by her thick glasses, twinkled with intelligence. Lynn couldn't say if she was English.

"I come on behalf of Robin," Lynn had said, feeling utterly foolish.

The woman's expression hadn't changed; she had turned back and whispered something, and a man, also quite old, with a bald head and long scrawny neck, had materialized at the door, peering at her over the woman's shoulder. Lynn had told them about Robin and his friend and the first lady, and they had both nodded without a word.

"Is there no answer?" she had asked, but the old woman had quickly closed the door, and Lynn had found herself alone in the street again. Alone and suddenly furious.

Jesus, a couple of weeks ago Alex Orloff had been for her a stranger, even an enemy, and today she was serving as his courier, passing his messages to some old-time spies engaged in who knew what secret activity. Her anger flared again now, as she realized that it was for Alex, and for him alone, that she was meeting Kraft.

"So what's new in the Company?" she said, refusing small talk, hoping that the unexpected question would stop Kraft's hungry examination of her face and body.

He didn't even blink. "Are we here to talk shop?" he asked, faking mild surprise. He didn't even bother to deny that he was a CIA man. "I thought this was a purely social occasion, Miss Kennan."

"I wanted to talk to you about Alexander Orloff," she said, unwilling to beat around the bush. "Off the record, of course, and not for publication in any form."

He impassively watched the Spanish waiter who brought their food, then checked the tenderness of his steak with his fork. Visibly satisfied, he looked at her again. "Alexander Orloff," he repeated distractedly. "He is some relative of yours, isn't he?"

"He was the first husband of my mother," she said. "Now come on, Mr. Kraft, you know that, don't you? I'm sure you know every detail of Orloff's life, and you must have vetted me too."

His smile broadened. "Touché!" he exclaimed, seeming genuinely amused. "You're right, of course, I know about him and about you. So, what do you want me to do about the first husband of your mother?" He deftly plunged his knife into his steak. "And," he added, raising his fork, "it's J.J., okay?"

"Do you know that Orloff is in Germany?" she asked.

He shrugged. "I know that he left the country a few days ago. Why?"

"I think his life is in danger, and you're not doing anything to protect him."

He looked at her pensively. "We are talking shop then," he established sadly. He didn't want to take her seriously, she realized, and that made her even more furious. "How is your sole?" he asked.

She pushed her plate aside. "Please don't patronize me, Mr. Kraft. I am serious."

"I guess you are," he said slowly, reaching for the wine bottle. At least she had succeeded in wiping that amused smile from his face. "All right, let's be serious. My answer is yes on both counts. Yes, I know that Orloff's life might be in danger. Yes, we are not doing anything to protect him."

"Why?"

"Why should we?" Kraft's most effective weapon was his sincerity, she realized. "We allowed Orloff to come to this country. We got assurances from the British police that they would guarantee his protection. Which they did."

"Which they did so well that he was shot and almost killed a couple of days after he landed here."

He shook his head, leaning backward. "Miss Kennan, even the best security measures cannot cope with an assassination attempt, and you know it. Especially when the man in question deliberately eludes surveillance, as Orloff did. Still, after the shooting the security measures were tightened, and as far as I know no further attempts were made on his life."

"How come that . . ." she started, but he raised his hand. He was dead serious now.

"Nobody asked him, though, to get involved in the

Byroade affair, is that right? Nobody asked him to play Hercule Poirot and chase spies and killers. The deaths of Byroade and the others were not his business. You flew with him to France, and you did it at your own risk. You say he is in Germany now. Why? We didn't send him there. You say he is in danger. I believe you. But it doesn't concern us, do you understand? We didn't send him to Europe for that.''

''Why did you send him to Europe, then?'' she asked.

He didn't answer immediately, preferring to concentrate on his food. But she felt he was trying to shape his thoughts. ''We didn't send him,'' he finally said. ''He agreed to come to this country to appear on television, and his trip coincided with our interests. We wanted to focus opinion on the ruthless methods of the KGB and on their attempts to undermine Western society.''

''Are your methods better?'' she interjected.

He lit a cigar. ''That's beside the point. As far as I am concerned, yes. We are the good guys. You may agree or not.'' He blew some thick gray smoke off to one side. ''I don't care. Orloff's coming here served our interests. We gave him protection. He was alive and well when he sneaked out of this country. With your help. Anything he does now, in Germany or elsewhere, is none of our business. Am I making myself clear?''

''You don't really care if he gets killed over there, do you?'' she said bluntly. ''If the KGB kills him, that would prove your theory, that you are the good guys and they are a bunch of murderers, right?'' She felt utterly helpless, faced with the coldly logical answers the man before her was reciting like a computer. ''As a matter of fact, you will be damn pleased if he is killed, won't you?''

He looked at her blankly, then turned backward, waving his cigar. "Check, please," he said to the waiter. As the Spaniard started to say something, he cut him short. "No. No dessert."

Part Three

18

THE LUFTHANSA STEWARD who served him a ham and sausage snack on the flight to Berlin was a supple, strikingly handsome young man. His wavy hair, delicately curved lips, and most of all his mannerisms reminded Orloff of Guy Burgess. He had been one of his first recruits and certainly the most bizarre: brilliant and volatile, boastful and cynical, blazing a trail of charm across the British ruling strata, fomenting scandals and living by them, a pathetic symbol of the decadence of his class and country. Orloff had pampered him, used him, but never really trusted him. Deep inside Burgess there was something utterly false and basically unreliable. "You dig deep down there," Kim had once said of Burgess, "and all of a sudden you reach the moving sands." Not that he had not been useful. Burgess had brought in tow the bashful Blunt, a confused aesthete with wonderful connections, who was to become the real survivor of the ring; and Burgess had kept, by his charm and attractions, the brooding, unstable Maclean inside the organization; he had been an excellent courier to Philby on the Continent in the thirties and later had opened for him the doors of the SIS. But his soul, once exposed, had appeared to be so tortured, so scarred, that Orloff had instinctively recoiled in spite of the overwhelming charm, the easy nonchalance, the intriguing, fiercely independent mind. He had had his glimpse of the moving sands one night at Cambridge, when Burgess, for no apparent reason other than an inherent urge to impress, had described to him the ghastly experience that had been haunting him since his childhood.

He had been a boy of thirteen, Burgess recounted, spending a vacation with his parents at West Meon Lodge, when in the middle of a mild September night he had been wakened by horrible screams and cries for help. The voice was his mother's and he had darted to his parents' bedroom, where an appalling sight had unfolded before his eyes: his mother, naked, was writhing and screaming under the inert nude body of his father. When he approached, he discovered to his horror that his father was dead, victim of a heart attack while he was making love to his mother. He had expired while still deep inside her. In a frenzy the boy had pulled and tugged the warm, heavy cadaver of his father, till he had managed to tear it away from the hysterical woman. Then he had run away, delirious.

Many years later, at Cambridge, when he had laid his soul bare before Orloff, Burgess had admitted he had relived that horrendous experience over and over again, and always remembered it with disgust and torment.

Orloff's doubts about Burgess were proven correct. In 1951 Philby suddenly had sent him from Washington, where they were both stationed at the time, to warn Donald Maclean in London that he had been identified by the FBI and MI-5 as a Russian spy. Maclean was about to be arrested and had to leave England immediately by an escape route already laid out by Orloff. But instead of passing on the message and quietly blending in with the scenery, Burgess had panicked and joined Maclean in his escape to Russia. That had been an irreparable mishap. The inquiry into Burgess's actions and whereabouts just before his clumsy flight, and into his closest connections, had cast the first doubts on Kim. A swift coverup in which he, Orloff, was the main moving force had succeeded in watering down the suspicions and assuring Philby a reprieve for a few more years; but it had been Burgess's blunder that finally brought Kim's downfall and disgraceful escape across the Turkish border. And with Philby gone, Orloff's own crackdown had been only a matter of time.

"Will you please fasten your seat belt, sir?" The German steward was attentively leaning toward him, the candid smile of Burgess lighting up his handsome face.

They landed at Berlin Tegel airport in a driving rain.

Christmas was everywhere: in the gaily decorated evergreens in the big arrival hall, the huge posters and neon signs wishing the passengers happy holidays, the red-costumed Santas distributing presents to the children. Throngs of Berliners in their Sunday best were happily greeting arriving relatives. All the big hotels were fully booked, the attractive blond hostess at the tourist information office regretfully pointed out. But he was not interested in a palace, and booked a room in a small modest hotel off the Kurfurstendamm. He said his name was Stephen Fletcher. Once out of the terminal, he took a cab to the main post office. "Wait for me here, please," he asked in broken German. The driver, a moustachioed Turk, looked him over suspiciously before deciding he could take the risk.

As Orloff approached the GENERAL DELIVERY sign, he glanced around him. The place was full of people lining up in front of the counters for parcels and telegrams. He handed his passport to an elderly employee reading an old copy of *Welt am Sonntag*. "Herr Alexander Orloff," the old man pompously announced, staggering to his feet and disappearing into an office, the open passport in his hands. In a moment he was back, waving a large manila envelope. "Will you sign here, please, *mein Herr?*" he grinned toothlessly, pushing a badly thumbed ledger toward Orloff.

But Orloff stood very still, his eyes glued to the envelope and a sudden chill crawling up his spine. The envelope wasn't the kind used for telegrams; it hadn't been sent from England either. Beside his name, written in block letters, it carried a German stamp representing Cologne Cathedral. The post mark was Berlin. It had been posted in this city, in his name, to an address only Lynn knew. Lynn and the people who had tapped her phone. The click he had heard when he had phoned her from Bonn had not been the fruit of his imagination. When he had vanished from London they had focused their efforts on Lynn and had intercepted his phone call. They had heard his message as well, but that did not bother him. His enemies were in Berlin now, waiting for him, probably watching him at this very moment.

The old employee was staring at him, his head cocked, a puzzled frown on his emaciated face. Orloff stiffly took his passport and the envelope, which was surprisingly thick, and signed the ledger. His heart was pounding, and frenzied thoughts were rushing through his mind. He was too old for this kind of game, he couldn't cope with the tension anymore. They might be here stalking him, waiting to spring the trap when he picked up his letter. But they wouldn't kill him yet, not here, not with all these witnesses around, and the two armed policemen who had mounted watch over the exits ever since the last Baader-Meinhoff incident. They would follow him to a quiet street or to his hotel, where they would be running no risks.

He slowly put his passport and the folded envelope into his inner pocket. His only advantage was that he had a cab waiting outside. If he managed to reach it in time, he might still have a chance.

He stepped leisurely to the right, where a group of people were clustered together examining a colorful collection of stamps in a glass case. Sheltered by the crowd, he threw a casual glance over his shoulder. There was nobody by the exit now. He suddenly turned back and darted toward the glass door, his blood pulsating wildly at his temples. *"Entschuldigen Sie Mir,"* he mumbled, colliding with a fat woman who sailed into his path, carrying a heavy parcel. He heard an angry exclamation behind him and a heavy thump, but did not look back. The policeman by the door, a stocky, sallow-faced man with a spruce reddish moustache, scowled at him but did not try to stop him. He crossed the wet sidewalk, almost tripping, and got into the cab. "To the Adler Gallery, on Potsdamerstrasse," he ordered the driver. He was sweating profusely.

As the cab made its tortuous way through the heavy midday traffic, he leaned back, breathing heavily. His leg muscles were aching and a weight was crushing his chest. He had not seen anybody following him, but then, if his pursuers were well organized, they would certainly have positioned somebody in a car outside. He turned back, staring through the film of water that blurred the view from the back window. In the rain, all the cars looked the same, anonymous dark shapes looming behind yellow headlights. He would never be able to tell if his cab were being followed. And, too, there was also the more sophisticated method of a front tail—one or more cars moving ahead of the taxi, keeping it in their rearview mirrors.

Once in the hotel he would be safe, he assumed. The girl at the tourist desk would not remember him, and even if somebody got his hands on the list of today's bookings, he wouldn't be recognized under the name of Fletcher.

He had known about the Adler Gallery for years. He had visited it often in the fifties and early sixties on his frequent trips to Berlin. Adler had a constant supply of valuable paintings and Orloff seldom left the gallery empty-handed. It had been the perfect cover for the real purpose of his visits: quick, smooth contacts with his East Berlin courier.

The Adler Gallery had another priceless advantage: a second exit on Kleiststrasse.

The cab stopped in front of the illuminated entrance. They were alone in the street. He paid the Turkish driver, threw a last look over his shoulder, where a silver Mercedes was turning the corner, and stepped into the gallery.

Two hours later, soaked to the bones and utterly exhausted, he walked into the glum lobby of the Schwarzwald Hotel. His feet and hands were numb with cold and fatigue. He had crisscrossed Berlin a half dozen times. From the moment he entered the gallery, his overnight bag in his hand, he had not stopped moving. He had left the gallery by the back door; taken more cabs, one after the other;

walked into two all-day cinemas; breezed through a couple of Aschinger restaurants; taken the underground to the Bundes Platz and back; and even chanced a walk in the deserted Tiergarten. But at least now, as he signed the name of Fletcher in the guest register, he was sure that he hadn't been followed.

Only when he had locked and bolted the door of his room, which overlooked a drab, narrow street, did it occur to him that he might have got it all wrong, that the strange incident with the manila envelope could have a totally different meaning.

The people who were after him did not have to post that letter. His face was well known not only in England but all over Europe. His televised interviews had been broadcast in every country, and most papers had printed his photograph at least once. If somebody was stalking him, waiting for him to show up at Berlin General Delivery, he did not need to hear his name, see his passport, or watch him actually accept his letter. The envelope did not help his pursuers. On the contrary, it could only alert him by arousing his suspicions. They could simply lie in wait for him in the main post office, close to the general delivery counter. If there was nothing to be picked up in his name—and he had not expected a thing, actually not even a telegram from London—he would not suspect that they were closing on him.

The envelope, therefore, had been posted for some other purpose.

Puzzled, he took it out of his pocket and ripped it open. It contained several photocopies held together with a paperclip. As he extracted them from the envelope, two black-and-white snapshots slipped and fell on the threadbare carpet. He bent over and picked them up. The first one was of a baby in diapers, scowling at the camera, tiny hands reaching upward. He turned it over. A neat inscription had been jotted on the back in red ink: "The girl at the age of four weeks. February 27, 1956." The second photograph showed an older baby with fair hair, splashing in a small bathtub and grinning toothlessly. The inscription read: "Age fourteen months. March 30, 1957."

His bewilderment growing, he took a couple of steps toward the window. The dull December light fell on the papers in his hand. The topmost one was a birth certificate in the name of Lynn Mary Kennan. It had been issued in Berkeley, Alameda County, California. It was dated January 30, 1956.

It couldn't be.

A sharp, violent pain suddenly shot through his chest, and he swayed on his feet. Sweat popped out on his forehead and, as he wiped it with his sleeve, he felt the tremor in his arm. He pulled the paperclip from the sheaf of documents, tearing a piece from the second photocopy. It was the marriage license of Virginia Carlisle, born Fielding, to Samuel Kennan. It was dated October 17, 1955. He threw it away, and the paper fluttered to the floor. The next document was one he remembered only too well: a copy of a divorce certificate issued in London on July 29, 1955 and establishing the divorce of Virginia Carlisle, born Fielding, from Alexander Carlisle.

He stood by the window, a wave of heat rising in him, a sledgehammer thumping in his chest. The dates were running through his mind, inexorably settling in a chronological pattern. It couldn't be.

But beneath the divorce certificate there was one last document. It was not a photocopy. It was a typewritten note, very short, very impersonal. "Lynn is not 26 years old," it read. "She is 27. She was born six months after your divorce, but she does not know it. Virginia divorced you when she found out that she was pregnant. Kennan married her and gave the child his name. That was Virginia's condition. She did not want her child to be a spy's daughter. Lynn was never to be told."

And under all that, in big block letters: LYNN IS YOUR DAUGHTER.

He backed away from the window and slowly, cautiously, settled in the only armchair in the room. It was hard, uncomfortable, covered with faded chintz. Lynn is your daughter. Your daughter. He was suddenly swept by a surge of fury. They had found him and were trying to stop him with another dirty trick. After failing to kill him, after failing to thwart his investigation, they were now trying to stop him with the allegation that Lynn was his daughter. The message was more than clear: If you want to protect your daughter, drop your investigation. The papers were fake, of course.

Or were they?

He went down on his knees and collected the documents that were spread over the carpet. He scanned them once again, attentively examining the stamps, the signatures, the reference numbers. He could find no flaw, not at first sight anyway. Something in the official language and the formal clichés made him think of a verdict read in a dispassionate tone by some court clerk.

The phone was on a small table by the window. He fumbled in his wallet till he found the folded piece of paper with the hastily scribbled phone number.

"All the lines to London are busy, sir," the weary voice of the hotel operator said. "It's Christmas Eve."

"I know," he said. "Please, keep on trying. This is an emergency." The phrase sounded to him forced, artificial.

"I shall try again," she said indifferently. She didn't believe it was an emergency.

Dusk was quickly settling outside. Down in the street, an elderly woman in a long black coat was walking quickly, bent under her umbrella. A little girl in red cape and hood merrily galloped behind her, giggling and waving a huge package tied with bright ribbons. She triumphantly jumped in the middle of a puddle, splashing water all over and screaming with delight. The old woman turned back, said something to the child, and grabbed her little hand.

A wave of static suddenly filled the receiver. "I think we have London for you, sir," the operator said.

"Thank you. Thank you very much."

He heard the characteristic twin rings. The phone was picked up immediately at the other end, and a woman's voice said rather anxiously, "Hello?"

"Good evening. May I speak to Chief Superintendent Hastings, please?"

There was a moment's silence. "I'm afraid that he is not available," the woman said. Her voice was unnaturally strained.

"Could you please tell me how to reach him? I am calling from abroad, and it's rather urgent."

"Who is calling, please?"

He hesitated. "My name is Alexander Orloff," he finally said.

"Oh yes. I'm sorry, Mr. Orloff. He expected you to call. But you can't reach him now. He is in the hospital."

"The hospital?" He paused, confounded. The receiver was moist in his hand. "Is there something wrong? Anything happened to him?"

Another silence. "No," the woman said in a muffled voice. "My husband had to undergo several tests. It was . . . it was rather unexpected."

Hospital tests on Christmas Eve? It doesn't make sense, he wanted to say, but he didn't. "I am sorry, Mrs. Hastings. Please wish him a prompt recovery. And Merry Christmas."

He hung up. Something was wrong, of course, he could feel it. But there was nothing he could do. Hastings was out of the picture and could be of no help. He was alone again and had to proceed as planned. There was no other way.

He leafed through the small tourist brochure he had picked up on the reception desk when he had checked in. He reached for the phone again and dialed the concierge. "I want to book a number seven tour," he said.

"Just a moment, sir." The voice was strikingly similar to that of the reception clerk, and he suspected the same man was in charge of both functions. "You mean the night tour and dinner in East Berlin, sir?"

"Yes."

"There has been a small change, sir. Tonight, it's a Christmas Eve dinner in East Berlin. It would cost you twenty marks more. Is that all right?"

"That's fine."

"You've got a valid passport, of course."

"Yes."

"American?"

"That's right."

"It's all set then. They will pick you up in the lobby at seven-fifteen. Return at eleven-thirty."

A gust of wind discharged heavy raindrops on the window. In the darkness that invaded the room, the papers strewn on the small table dissolved into a dirty white

267

smudge. The face of the little girl on the photograph—
"age fourteen months" became blurred, then finally faded
in the shadows.

LYNN IS YOUR DAUGHTER. By the time he went
down to the lobby, the four words had turned into an
obsession. The document ploy was a blatant disinformation
scheme meant to paralyze him, to make him abandon any
further course of action out of fear that something terrible
might happen to his daughter. Routine KGB practice.
Could Kim have done that? To him? Kim knew how much
he had wanted a child; he even joked about it once, in
London. Would he use that knowledge against him now?
There were rumors that he had reorganized the disinformation
department of the KGB, developing a masterly talent for
sophisticated forgeries. Still, he couldn't suppress the question that kept echoing over and over again in his mind:
could it be true? Could Lynn really be his daughter? He
desperately tried to discard any distracting thoughts and
concentrate on the mission ahead, but a part of him revolted,
reaching into the past, mercilessly delving into his most
painful memories.

It was true that Virginia had decided to leave him
suddenly, and had stormed through all the divorce proceed-
ings with a sort of frenzied urgency. Was it because she
had found that she was pregnant? She had told him that
she was divorcing him because she found his code-books
and the tiny transmitter concealed in the attic, because she
had discovered her husband was a spy. Still, on a couple
of earlier occasions, she had dropped hints that made him
suspect she knew much more about him than she cared to
admit. Knew but pretended not to. And the crash marriage
to Samuel Kennan barely four months after their divorce.

Samuel Kennan had been totally enraptured by her, since he had met her at that Halloween party the year before; his professorship at Oxford had actually turned into a disaster, and the poor man had made a fool of himself, chasing Virginia all over London, declaring to her his all-consuming love. They had not taken him seriously, though, and had turned the whole affair into a private joke. "He is a dear man," had been the kindest words Virginia had for Kennan, which in her vocabulary signified she did not feel for him anything but benevolent pity. And all of a sudden this divorce and the abrupt departure—more of a flight, actually—to the other side of the world, to a stolid existence in Berkeley. Virginia, that bubbling, effervescent bohemian, eccentric and self-centered in the extreme, mesmerized by her own art and vibrating with contagious vitality . . . suddenly becoming the subdued, self-effacing wife of a mediocre political scientist, plunging into the gray anonymity of middle-aged campus wives?

Virginia's face on the day of their divorce emerged vividly from the past, that strange look she wore, the message he felt her eyes were trying to convey to him. And then there was Lynn's story about Virginia's quarrels with Kennan, his own name turning up in their bitter clashes, the drinking, the suicide. For a suicide it had been, he had no doubts about it now.

When had he first learned about Lynn's birth? Three or four years later, he recalled. His letters to Virginia had been returned unopened; and then in 1967, when he had phoned her sister, Marjorie, he had learned that she had had a daughter with Kennan.

LYNN IS YOUR DAUGHTER. Would he ever know for sure? He could fly back to the States, check the records at Berkeley, unearth the original documents. And, if he found out this was true, what would he do? Would he ever find the courage to reveal the truth to Lynn? And brand her with his own mark of Cain?

"Herr Fletcher?" The reception clerk must have been calling Orloff for quite a while, for when he came out of his reverie he noticed the strange, reproachful looks of the other guests in the lobby. "The bus is here, sir. You'd better hurry."

He found an empty seat at the back of the tourist bus, close to the rear exit. The bus was half-empty, as he had expected it to be. One would have to be an inveterate masochist, he mused, to forsake the temptations offered on a Christmas Eve by the lascivious, hedonistic city of West Berlin for the dubious recreations of its eastern counterpart. Out of habit, he quickly scanned the faces of his companions, as he walked to his seat. There was a group of Americans wearing white plastic badges showing a cross decorated with flowers. Most of them were old, rather taciturn people conversing in low voices. Some fundamentalist church, he guessed, that had chosen Christmas to bring the message of Jesus across the wall. They suited his own purpose rather well, providing him with a fine cover. Only when the bus set out on its journey, and the tour guide started blabbering his trite jokes about Berliners and women, did he hear a few scattered protests in the bus's dark interior. It turned out that there were a couple of Frenchmen and a few Portuguese on the bus as well, probably Communists who were determined to celebrate Christmas on friendly soil.

At the Hilton and the Schweizer Hof they picked up some more Americans and a noisy Italian tribe. The stout guide—a Bavarian, to judge by his accent and his striking resemblance to Franz Joseph Strauss—passed down the aisle and collected the passports. He didn't even open the passports, and Orloff judged it wiser not to give him his real name; the guide probably didn't have a list of his passengers' names anyway.

He retreated into his corner, removed his hat and laid his burning forehead against the icy window. The same strange stupor descended upon him again, pulling him back in time to a shadow world of suppressed memories; of frenzied nights, forgotten embraces, a lithe body, and a husky voice. A world so abruptly transformed by the toothless laughter of a fair-haired little girl.

He felt a surge of gratitude to the naughty Italian brats whose sudden screams jolted him back to the present. They were running up and down the aisle of the slowly moving bus, two small boys and a tiny girl with enormous black eyes, jumping on the empty seats and pressing their little faces against the windows. The bus was heading down the Kurfurstendamm now, as if drawn into the vortex of a psychedelic whirlpool. The large avenue was blazing with multicolored lights, cascades of gold and silver, the glittering signs of restaurants and nightclubs, mutating billboards. Electric Santas were drowning their beards in huge steins of beer; red and gold flags were fluttering in the wind; neon Christmas trees glowed with shiny trinkets and plastic baubles. Over the roof of a penthouse restaurant floated a gallery of gigantic balloons, representing the Holy Family, the three wise men, a cow, a sheep, and a jolly little donkey.

Black, gutted, and haunting, the ruined Kaiser Wilhelm Church sailed suddenly by them, a remnant from a past the fat city of Berlin was doing its best to forget. The children's shouts faded away as the dark mass of the Tiergarten emerged. The bus was moving faster now, rocking them not too gently as it sharply veered to the left and to the left again. And there it was, as immovable as his memories, the dreary Friedrichstrasse; the ruins gaping at them with thousands of scarred, hollow eyes; the wall; and the old battered sign: YOU ARE NOW LEAVING THE AMERICAN SECTOR.

He didn't feel any particular emotion when they reached Checkpoint Charlie. He was perhaps running a risk of mortal danger by crossing into East Berlin, straight into the lion's den. Or was he? The KGB had grown much smarter since the days when butchery was its choicest method. They had never admitted that Alexander Orloff had been a Russian spy. Moscow had reacted to his interviews with a short communiqué, dismissing his revelations as ''base CIA propaganda.'' They wouldn't dare harm him in any way or arrest him now that he was so well known all over the world. His notoriety would grant him ironclad credibility. They wouldn't risk their recently acquired respectability for the dubious prize of an old, worthless spy whom nobody really cared about.

The worst they could do, he concluded, would be to refuse him entry into West Berlin. But the two Vopos who boarded the bus—the obese, grizzled sergeant and the youthful buck-toothed officer—contented themselves with a quick walk down the aisle and some stiff nods. Three Communist-youth girls, shivering in their thin white blouses and red scarves—he had watched them take off their coarse woolen coats in the guards' booth—got on the bus now and presented each tourist with a tired rose, a propaganda brochure about the wonders of the People's Democracy, and some bashfully murmured Christmas greetings. The Portuguese and the French applauded enthusiastically. One of the Frenchmen made the inevitable remark that in the

West such a thing could never happen, but here they cared about people. His well-trained family shouted unanimous approval.

The bus slowly moved forward past the giggling Communist girls who stomped their feet on the sidewalk and waved them good-bye. They were now in East Berlin.

On top of the Brandenburg Gate, the restored Quadriga Chariot, drawn by four fiery stallions, blazed like pure gold. Along the Unter den Linden, the Armory, the Neue Wache, and the Princess Palace were poorly illuminated in a half-hearted attempt to match the glittering universe lying beyond the wall. The massive, graceless city hall building was festooned with large strips of red cloth stamped with patriotic slogans. The worried face of Chairman Honecker inspired tepid Communist zeal in his nation from his fifteen-foot-tall portrait. In front of the city hall a huge Christmas tree was glowing with countless electric bulbs, its top crowned by a shining, five-pointed red star.

The bus pulled to a stop beside a crowd of young people loudly shouting and jesting under the frozen stare of the Volks Polizei. "Ladies and Gentlemen!" Their guide was addressing his flock. "Will you please get off the bus now? We are expected at the Ratskeller, in the basement of the city hall. We shall be served a special Christmas dinner with unlimited beer." He marked a pause, expecting their cheers, and, when none came, hastily resumed: "Afterward we'll have the privilege of watching a show of typical German folklore."

An old woman's voice in the front of the bus squeaked briefly, and the guide vigorously nodded into his microphone: "Yes, Madam, we'll be mixing with East Berliners who are also celebrating Christmas in the Ratskeller." The American group hummed their satisfaction.

Orloff meekly followed the other tourists across the crowded sidewalk and down into the picturesque old cellar. The enormous place was half full already. A Bavarian band in Tyrolean green hats and lederhosen was playing merry tunes led by an old, wiry accordionist. Groups of people clustered around several long tables were joking and singing, while young country girls in dirndls were sweating their way through the crowd, carrying huge steins of beer. The tourists fanned into the vast hall, taking over several tables. A stone-faced maître d'hôtel, helped by the tour guide, solemnly counted them as they passed by.

Orloff didn't take a seat, but instead casually drifted across the hall. On the other side, the singing was louder. He found the door to the restrooms, climbed the adjoining staircase, and emerged on the Alexander Platz again. He plunged easily into the merry crowd. Two boys in green Windbreakers and a fat girl wrapped in a red shawl ran past him. The girl turned back and shouted something at him. He caught the word *mädchen*. The boys laughed loudly. He smiled uncertainly and made his way down the avenue. Farther down, he crossed the street and glanced warily at the city hall building. The dinner wouldn't be over before eleven. He was on his own at last.

A police van was parked down the road beside a tawny new building. In the dark interior, cigarette tips were glowing. Two Vopos were standing outside eating sandwiches out of paper bags. They didn't step aside as he approached and he squeezed his way along the wall, catching the sharp odor of onion as one of the Vopos brushed against him, munching noisily.

When he turned the corner into Alte Schönhauserstrasse, it started raining. A gentle, whispering rain it was, touching his face in hesitant caress, softly rustling the shrubs that lined the deserted sidewalk. Dim light filtered onto the street from curtained windows. A furtive sound, barely discernible beyond the murmur of the rain, made him veer back sharply. On the opposite sidewalk, a tall, stooping man and a skeletal woman were trudging in the other direction, walking a sleek hound. He watched them till they turned the corner. He remained all alone in the quiet street, surrounded by immobile shadows. After a few more steps he stopped again, haunted by a peculiar sensation. He couldn't be being followed, not here. He had slipped away from the MI-5 surveillance in London; during the few days he had spent in Bonn, he had changed hotels several times, using different names. He had examined his fellow passengers aboard the flight to Berlin and hadn't found anyone suspicious. Still, there had been the envelope at the post office. Somebody knew he was in Berlin. And somebody might be expecting him here, in East Berlin.

Before he reached the house, he stepped into a dark porch and stood there for a long moment, holding his breath. But the street stretched before him, cold, secretive, and deadly quiet.

She had resumed using her maiden name. LILY HARTMAN. read the plastic-coated card pinned to the door. He knocked. She opened almost immediately, as if she had been waiting behind the door, in the gloomy vestibule, expecting his arrival. She had grown old, and her raven-black hair had turned sparse and gray. The effervescent vitality was gone from the face. The once full, sensual mouth was bitterly pinched. Her chin was strong, as before, but the golden specks were no longer dancing in her black eyes. She had been so lovely, so unique, when he had first met her in Vienna, back in 1934.

"Hello, First Lady," he said, attempting a quick smile.

She smiled back, and just for a fleeting instant did the tiny dimples flourish again in her withered cheeks. But she did not offer her face for a kiss. She stepped back stiffly to let him in, and he sensed the cold reserve in her bearing. She motioned toward the living room.

"How are you, Lily?" he tried.

"Fine. *Wunderbar*." She didn't seem to mind that he knew she was lying.

"It's been a long time."

Unresponsive, she smiled nervously. She was wearing an austere gown of a black fabric, buttoned up to her neck. She shivered slightly and he preferred attributing this to the damp cold that permeated the house.

"Is he here?" he asked.

"Poor Alex," she said unexpectedly. He walked into the obscure living room. He could hear the pendulum of an old clock and the steady thud of the rain on the window. He turned back, but Lily had disappeared. And then he discerned a movement in the shadows.

"Kim?" he said uncertainly.

"S . . . sit down, Alex," a voice whispered, and he recognized the familiar stutter of Kim Philby.

19

THE ROOM WAS COLD AND DARK. The light of a single lamp, mellowed by a beautiful hand-painted shade, glowed in a far corner. The bare wooden floor squeaked under his feet. He discerned the contour of a large, low sofa against one wall and cautiously sat down, unbuttoning his coat. The seat was hollow, the springs of the sofa having expired long ago. A thin carpet, apparently as old and threadbare as the sofa, was spread in front of him, its pattern a blur of faded pastel colors. As his eyes adjusted to the darkness, he noticed that the room was very sparsely furnished. On his side, there was nothing but the sofa and a rectangular, glass-topped coffee table. Across the room, a pair of legs stretched from an armchair set beside the gas stove, which radiated a faint bluish haze. Two large paintings hung behind the stove, but all he could see from his position was their massive gilt frames and some indistinct smudges of brown and gray. A couple of chairs stood on either side of a narrow cupboard against the right wall.

A match flared briefly and a whiff of sharp, unfamiliar tobacco floated across the room. Orloff wondered if Kim had turned off the lights and displaced the furniture on purpose, aiming to establish a stretch of no-man's-land between them. A protective moat, dark and hollow and more eloquent than words, to keep them apart.

"Why don't you turn on the light?" Orloff said, irritated.

For a moment nothing happened; then an orange globe came to life in front of him, shedding dull illumination on the figure seated in the armchair. Philby's face had thickened with the years: the nose was heavy, the jowls rounded; his features had lost their firm, energetic expression but were still handsome. His hair had turned white. He was wearing it longer now, and its smooth sheen made him look rather distinguished. Some thin white strands descended behind his ears, brushing over the loose collar of a dark blue turtleneck. He was dressed in a light gray suit of plaid pattern, very British, and a pair of black, thick-soled shoes. His girth had swelled, while his large, flat chest had somehow caved in between his slackened shoulders. Old age was gaining on him, too.

He couldn't bear the silence, nor the fixed gaze of Philby, who was drawing on his pipe perhaps a trifle too eagerly. "Thank you for coming, Kim," he said. His throat was oddly contracted.

"I owed you." Philby's voice was cracked, weary, yet so much the same.

"You owe me nothing."

"Of course I do. Since that night when you smuggled me over the Turkish border."

"Don't be silly," he countered, irritated. He didn't want the meeting to be a settlement of debts.

"That makes twenty years and eleven months," Philby pointed out stubbornly. "All that time, there has been an unpaid debt between us."

Orloff didn't answer. The hectic events of that nightmarish week in January emerged from the past with terrifying clarity: the defection of Anatoli Golitzin, chief of the KGB bureau in Helsinki; his stunning revelations, which led to the arrest of two hundred Russian agents, among them George Blake, one of the best moles in SIS Orloff had ever had. And there followed his frantic cables to MOSCOW: GET PHILBY OUT. GOLITZIN KNOWS ABOUT HIM! And in response, Moscow's enigmatic silence. Didn't they care about Philby anymore? Were they ready to sacrifice him? Or were they hoping that their wonder boy, the elusive Pimpernel of modern espionage, would fool everybody once again and save his hide? Philby was in Beirut then, still working for the SIS under the cover of a correspondent for the *Observer* and the *Economist,* supplying Center with priceless material about the anti-Soviet intrigues of the CIA in Lebanon and Syria and their grand scheme to subvert Egypt's Nasser. Center wouldn't easily give up their best agent, close friend of Miles Copeland from the CIA, and companion of the SIS area chief in Beirut, Andrew Laird. But Orloff knew the noose was inexorably tightening around Kim's neck. Kim knew that too, feeling like a trapped animal in the treacherous city of Beirut, drinking himself unconscious each night.

And finally, that night of diluvial rain, when the red signal from Moscow had arrived. GET HIM OUT. He was to learn later that Center had intercepted a CIA message from Langley Woods to London, confirming the joint project to arrest Philby. Or liquidate him on the spot if capture was impossible. Orloff had flown to Beirut on January 23, and gotten hold of Philby that same night, when he was on his way to a dinner party given by Glen Balfour Paul, the unsuspecting first secretary of the British embassy. The escape Mercedes with the hastily forged papers was waiting at Rue Verdun. They had driven non-stop for forty-eight hours, across the Syrian border, north toward Turkey. Then another two days on the winding mountain roads and finally down to the Russian border. And his last memory of Kim, a lonely, vulnerable figure barely managing to remain on his feet—he hadn't stopped drinking the entire trip—uncertainly waving a last good-bye before sneaking into the black shadows beyond Dogubayazit. Twenty years and eleven months.

Kim's dry voice brought him back to the present. "I was rather amused," he was saying, snuggling comfortably in his armchair by the gas fire, "by your choice of a meeting place. Quite amused indeed." His voice was cold, detached, and not amused at all. "It was bloody clever, Alex, picking my first wife's house. I guess Berlin was the only place for us to meet without me crossing to the West."

Orloff nodded. The empty space between them was like an invisible barrier. Their private Berlin wall. "I knew you and Lily had remained friends. You were always fond of her. I thought her house would be ideal. Have any trouble getting here?"

"No, I didn't," Philby said with arrogant firmness that meant yes, he had trouble coming. "Why did you want to see me, Alex?"

He couldn't talk to him about the Byroade affair, not like this, not to this cold, hostile figure entrenched behind

a wall of arrogance. He had been secretly dreaming for
years of this encounter. Old men tended to get weak,
overly sentimental, Nora had once said to him. Perhaps.
There were so many things he wanted to say but couldn't.
Not to this man who surrounded himself with shadows and
silence to check his approach. There were so many phrases
and questions he had rehearsed in his mind on the way
here, but now they seemed to him utterly ridiculous, out of
place.

"There were several things that happened in London,"
he said vaguely.

"London. Oh yes." The indifference was studied. "I
hear you've become a television star in London lately."

"I couldn't go to London otherwise." He decided not to
mention Lynn. Not yet.

"Of course," Philby agreed, his sarcasm raw, aggressive.

Orloff felt a surge of anger. "Wouldn't you have done
the same?" he threw back, raising his voice. "Don't you
crave London? Don't you dream of returning? If only for a
few days, Kim?"

Again the dry impersonal chuckle. "How many times
did I tell you, Alex, what the trouble was with you? You
always were a hopeless, incurable romantic. You still are.
You wanted to see London again before you died, didn't
you? A last nostalgic voyage into the past. Even if the
price is a public crucifixion broadcast live on television."

Orloff didn't answer, and Philby went on: "And what
did you find when you got to London? Let me tell you.
Nothing. It's all gone, Alex. They are all dead. Burgess
and Maclean and Blunt, and my women and yours as well.
Even that world we fought against isn't there anymore.
What's England nowadays? Nothing but a bad joke. A
toothless old hussy singing 'Rule Britannia' at streetcorners

and peddling souvenirs to Japanese tourists. Sending armadas to the Falklands to play the mighty empire again. When I think that we sacrificed our lives to defeat her! Take the fortress from within, remember? She went to pieces without our help. And we are gone too, Alex. We belong to the past. There was nothing for you to do in London. No sentimental journeys.''

"There is no place for us in Moscow either," Orloff said.

"For you there isn't," Philby said heatedly and abruptly fell silent. "You know," he said after a while, "I never expected you to turn up in Moscow. You were born homeless and you'll die homeless. The eternal stranger. You could serve Moscow only from afar. You were a devoted Communist only as long as you didn't come too close and didn't have to confront the flaws and the contradictions." He got up and the dim light silhouetted his slightly arched body and his sagging shoulders. "Still," he said in a milder tone, a tone of genuine wonder vibrating in his voice, "you were a genius. Or rather those who sent you were. If you had been different, less human, less vulnerable, I doubt you would have charmed me and Guy so easily."

"Was it worth it, Kim?" Orloff asked in a low voice. But Philby wasn't listening, or pretended not to be.

"You changed our lives, do you know that? A twenty-two-year-old boy coming from America like a harbinger of fate and taking over our destinies. You were irresistible in those days, Alex. You simply enticed us. You played your pipe, and we followed. I've often wondered what would have happened to us if we hadn't met you. Something disgustingly dull and frustrating, I guess."

"Was it worth it, Kim?" he asked again, more forcefully.

"They still call me a traitor, don't they?" Philby remarked with sudden vehemence. "I read all the London newspapers. I also saw the tapes of your interviews. In England I am still the traitor, the enemy. The one who sold his soul to the devil."

Orloff was taken aback by the explosion of bitterness. He peered into the half-darkness, but Kim's face was turned away from his, his eyes in shadow. "Does it surprise you?" Orloff managed.

"No. N . . . no, it doesn't." When Philby was upset, he couldn't control his stammer. "I don't care about them. N . . . not a bit. They're nothing but a bunch of bloody hypocrits. A traitor, am I?" He got up from his chair, and his heavy shoes thumped on the parquet. "If I were a writer or an academic, I would have ended respected and admired, even if I had helped communism tenfold more than I did as a spy. Look at Koestler and Sartre and Malraux. Nobody called them traitors. Sartre went about preaching communism almost till his death and remained revered, worshiped by the very system he strove to destroy. Malraux and Koestler repented and became twice as admired as they were before. Who is the real traitor, Alex?" He was now pacing restlessly between the cupboard and the window. "The one like me who sticks to his beliefs and goes into exile? Or the one like Koestler, who betrays them, recants, and by doing so becomes a symbol to admire and emulate? I shall go down in the history of England—not that I mind—as a mole, a traitor, a despicable spy. And Sartre, who did for communism more than you and I ever did, who invented the most farfetched arguments to justify Stalin's crimes, is considered one of the greatest men of all time! What did De Gaulle say when some right-wing nut suggested arresting Sartre? "You don't arrest Sartre. *'Parce que Sartre, c'est aussi la France.'*

Sartre is, in a way, the embodiment of France." He fell silent as abruptly as he had flared up, and stopped in front of the window. He stood there motionless for a long moment, then said without turning back: "What brought you over, Alex? Why this call from the dead?"

"I came to ask you a question," Orloff said. He rose with effort from the sofa and joined Philby by the window. The rain had stopped and the night was suddenly very still. He looked at Kim's profile, struggling with the question that haunted him, fearing the reply that could destroy his last illusion. The illusion that this awkward, embittered old man was still in a way his only friend.

"Kim," he said softly, "did you ever double-cross me?"

The question was so unexpected, so odd, that Philby winced and sharply turned to face him. He looked much older now, with those deep lines on either side of his glum mouth, and the wrinkled pouches sagging beneath his eyes.

"What is that supposed to mean, Alex?" Kim's voice was low, almost a whisper.

"I want to know if at anytime during our work together you double-crossed me," Orloff repeated quickly. "I don't mean that you could have betrayed me to the British, of course. What I need to know is whether or not you ever acted behind my back. If you reported to Moscow Center without my knowledge. Or if Center ever got directly in touch with you and instructed you to carry out a certain operation without informing me."

"If you ask, it means you suspect I did," Philby said slowly, obviously still digesting the question. His eyes were guarded, calculating, and he almost imperceptibly moved back. "Now why do you think I would have done that?"

"A thousand reasons. Compartmentalization. Orders from Center through your emergency channels to establish direct contact with an agent. In order to protect his identity, I'd say. Or your own initiative, Kim. You had, as I remember, several quite brilliant ideas that I vetoed. You might have laid your hands on a priceless piece of information or discovered a unique source. Perhaps you didn't want me to prevent your exploring the lead further; or maybe you wanted no intermediaries along the way."

Philby was frowning, lighting his pipe again. Out of old habit, he carefully replaced the spent match in its box, looking up at him through the wavering wisps of smoke. "Let's say I did," he said evenly. "Why should I tell you, Alex? Any good reason why I should tell you, of all people, what I did or did not do on orders from Center?"

Orloff had anticipated Philby's question. "Because I don't believe, in spite of all that happened, that you would send a killer after me. You're still with Center, aren't you, Kim?"

Philby had retreated into his dark corner again, smoking in silence. There was a bottle—cognac, Orloff guessed—and a glass, maybe two, on the floor beside him, and now and then he heard the gentle clinking of glass on glass, followed by the languorous flow of the liquid. Kim didn't offer him a drink; he would have refused it anyway. But the characteristic sounds of his friend steadily consuming his bottle were oddly reassuring; together with the intermittent glow of his pipe pulsating in the darkness, they proved at least that Kim was there, with him, listening to his story.

He spoke for a long time, cautiously shaping his thoughts,

choosing his words with care. He was tense, uncertain, reluctant to return to his own corner and fit into the decor that Philby had designed for him. Thus, he remained standing by the window, repeatedly running the back of his hand against the cold glass. He narrated his surfacing two months before: his trip to England; the deaths of the four diplomats, the Arab boy, and the Frenchwoman; the attempt on his life. He was sure Philby knew most of the story, but, after asking a few questions in the course of his account and encountering a deadly silence, he didn't expect an answer anymore. He got no further when he mentioned the secret list of Mary Ellis. So he continued on, dispassionately describing Hastings's strange initiative and Shaw's stunning revelations in Bonn. He even went through the ordeal of the manila envelope, describing in painful detail the photographs, the documents, the hinted threat. LYNN IS YOUR DAUGHTER. "That's a fiendish plot, Kim," he said, departing just this once from his controlled, factual account. "Genuine or not, those papers have not been collected by an amateur. This is the work of an organization."

Philby, surprising him finally by departing from his silence, had spoken: "You care for the girl."

It was not a question but a statement of fact, and Orloff didn't have to answer. And thus his story came to an end, sealed with Kim's stinging words.

"What is the meaning of that, Kim?" he asked, unable to endure another spell of silence. "Did you run that network behind my back? I must know. I can take it, but I must know."

"And you must know if it was I who cooked up that bloody story about your Lynn," Philby added, gulping down his drink.

Orloff made two steps toward the armchair where the smoldering cyclops eye of Philby's pipe was slowly dying, its ominous red glow obscured by black ash. He felt his whole body tensing in anticipation. He had come all the way here for this answer. He had to learn the truth, as terrible as it might be.

Kim took his time, and Orloff suspected he was doing it on purpose, perversely pleased to see his visitor at his mercy, playing a humiliating cat-and-mouse game.

But he was not prepared, not in the least, for the low, dry cackle that suddenly broke through the dark. Philby was indulging in a kind of private, amused chortling laced with an undertone of admiration. "I would not have believed this in a thousand years," he said, without trying to conceal his wonder. "Don't you see what this means, Alex?" The dry cackle again. "You have been fooled, of course, but not by us. Don't you see?"

"No, I don't," he said woodenly, torn between relief and anger. "I must have lost my touch. I must have gotten rusty after all these years. Why don't you tell me, Kim?"

"How bloody clever," Philby went on and clumsily struggled out of his chair. "No, Alex, I am afraid you will have to figure this out for yourself. You have all the pieces of the puzzle, I'd say. Quite wicked indeed. And to calm you," he went on mockingly, crossing the no-man's-land between them, "you can go home assured. Your onetime friend didn't betray you. That's what you wanted to hear, isn't it?"

Philby led him to the somber vestibule and stood in the poor yellow light, his empty glass in his hand, the tired eyes clouded. "Why don't you go back to America and hang up your boots, Alex?" He was not teasing him anymore but had adopted the weary, patient tone of an

287

older, more experienced man. "You are too old for this kind of game. That story is another kettle of fish. It doesn't concern you. Go home, if you have one. And to your woman, if you have one."

The glass-paneled door on the right opened and Lily appeared in its frame, fixing Orloff warily with her black eyes. He remembered Vienna forty-nine years before, as he had stood like this between them, making the introductions. "Lily, meet my friend Kim. Kim, beware, this woman is dangerous. I am desperately in love with her." Her easy, infectious laughter and Kim's momentary confusion. He had needed her beside Kim then; he had to get them married. He still hadn't been sure that Kim would make it. And so he had decided to smuggle a Communist, a believer, into Kim's very bedroom. Darling Lily. Kim and Lily had parted, but she was still on Kim's side, only the alliances were reversed.

"You'd better hurry," Kim said to him. "It's getting late."

"Good-bye, Lily," he said. She nodded, holding her black gown against her meager chest. Philby didn't offer his hand. It dawned on the old man that all three of them knew they would never meet again in this life. He turned up his collar. "One last question, Kim."

Philby looked at him tolerantly, his face softened by the liquor.

"You know who shot me," Orloff said very gently.

Philby looked through him, a vapid smile spreading on his face. "Do I? What makes you think so?"

"Don't play that game with me, Kim," he said wearily. "We are too old for that, as you said. You recognized the man I described, didn't you?"

Philby shrugged, his movements oddly disjointed. "What did you say the chap looked like?"

"A short man with a beaked nose, Adam's apple, scar under the left eye. Good with a knife, medium shot, expert at accidents."

"Scar under the left eye?" Kim frowned. He was not so drunk after all. "There was that boy in London, long time ago. Not with our house. With the others. I think they called him Henry." He nodded to himself. "Yes, it sounds like Henry to me. Good old Henry." Kim chuckled once more and opened the door, making Orloff face the blackness of night once more.

"You have been fooled, of course, but not by us. . . ." Orloff struggled with these words all the way back, as he hurried in the cold drab streets toward the towering city hall. The city seemed totally desolated, an icy desert he was crossing again on his return journey from his past. What did Philby mean? You have all the pieces of the puzzle, Alex. Your onetime friend didn't betray you. But if not Kim, if not Center, who? Quite wicked, Kim had said. And laughed.

Alexander Platz was empty now, the youngsters having gone to celebrate elsewhere. The Vopos, with their cars, had vanished as well. It was strange, he thought. But the tourist bus was still there, and he went back into the cellar by the same route he had left it. A pleasant-looking woman in her middle years but dressed like a little girl, with short skirt and pigtails, was halfway through a witty monologue, and the crowd was bellowing with laughter. At the far side he saw the Bavarian guide bent over the table of the Americans, apparently translating the *bons mots*.

* * *

As nobody was paying him any attention, he took a corner seat at a smaller table not far from the exit. The two other men seated at the table were too drunk and too busy exploiting the obvious endowments of their female companions to even spare him a look. A dark-haired waitress, her flushed face moist with perspiration, placed a mug of frothy beer before him. He sat still, stonily watching the show up to its very end, then walking like a robot behind the other tourists back to the bus. You have been fooled, Alex.

Later, he could swear he didn't remember the ride back; passport control at Checkpoint Charlie; the slow progress through the congested, festive streets of West Berlin. He came out of his torpor only when the guide gently touched his shoulder. "The Schwarzwald Hof, *mein Herr*." For a moment, he stood alone in the street, then crossed the small lobby, nodding absently to the night porter, and started climbing the stairs. He reached the second floor, and stopped to catch his breath. And it was at that very moment, when he was leaning against the corridor wall, gulping air in quick, painful gasps, that the pieces of the puzzle started moving, forming into a pattern, smoothly sliding into their slots. It was only then that the ugly, devious scheme flashed before his eyes, so strange, so cynical, and yet founded on an implacable, blood-chilling logic.

He managed to take a few steps and remove his key from his pocket. His mind was still flooded with scores of unanswered questions. He unlocked the door and stopped in his tracks as a scene of déjà vu suddenly hit his senses. A room, dark and cold. A dim light in one corner. An immobile figure in an armchair facing the door. An unfamiliar odor of rough tobacco.

He turned on the lights.

"I am in Berlin for the conference of the NATO Intelligence chiefs," the swarthy, lean man said conversationally. "I thought I'd drop over for a chat. My name is Nigel Sykes. We've never met before—or have we?"

20

HE STOOD with his back to the door, staring at the chief of the Intelligence service. He couldn't speak for a long moment; febrile thoughts were whirling through his mind. He was not prepared for this encounter. Still, he felt, the eerie affair in which he was immersed was now unfolding according to its inner, devious logic.

"How did you get in?" he finally asked. It was a pointless question. The night porter downstairs had greeted him quite naturally. Sykes must have used the classic trick: as soon as he had discovered that Orloff was in this hotel, he must have booked a room for himself. They could have spotted him at the airport upon his arrival and watched him make his hotel reservation. An organization like the SIS could cover all the possible entry points into Berlin—airports, railroad stations, highways. They must have been close to him everywhere he went, maybe even in East Berlin. He thought of his cab driver, and of the couple walking their dog in the rain in front of Lily Hartman's house. Still, Sir Nigel's coming into the open in his room meant the hunt was over. They had closed in on him for the confrontation.

Nigel Sykes was patiently watching him through narrowed eyes, his head tilted sideways. He had certainly aged since Orloff had first seen him in 1965. Blunt had pointed Sykes out to him at the opening session of Westminster, in the public gallery of the House of Commons. He was already deputy director of MI-5, Blunt had said, and the word was that he aimed "across the Park," which meant he coveted the helm of the SIS. He was a man of burning ambition, Blunt had added, fiercely lobbying his way to the top, using both sly strategy and muscle to get what he wanted. He had even succeeded in obtaining a private audience with the queen. Nothing could stop him, current opinion would have it, certainly not that poor Peter Snow.

"What do you want?" Orloff said. "Is this a courtesy call?" Sir Nigel's mouth twitched slightly; he seemed amused by the term.

"You can call it that," he said with ease. He was wearing a three-piece charcoal suit, a silk shirt, and a discreet dark blue tie. "A courtesy call," he repeated, then unhurriedly got up from his chair. Very much in control of himself, he stepped to the window across the room. Taking his cigar out of his mouth, he gently pulled the curtain and cast a sweeping look outside. Then, carefully replacing the curtain, he asked in the same soft voice: "And how is our dear Kim doing? It must have been a touching reunion."

Orloff felt a sudden lassitude permeate his body. He took a step forward. "I should have assumed you were tapping Lynn's phone.'' He wondered if they had found Shaw.

"But of course." Sykes turned to face him, settling in a half-sitting position on the jutting windowsill, his ankles crossed, the big brown hands resting on his thighs. The lean black cigar hung loosely from the corner of his mouth. "We recorded your message, we made sure it was delivered—and I figured out the rest. You had only one friend, Philby; and there was only one first lady in his life. We knew Lily Hartman was living in East Berlin. She is in the film industry now, isn't she? A producer or a censor . . . no matter. Anyway, I had a nice reception committee waiting for you in Berlin. You did your best to shake them, but. . . ." He spread his arms in mock apology. "I must compliment you on your valiant efforts. But you can't really fight an organization, Orloff. Methods have improved since your days." He looked around him in a rather theatrical way. "Now, where did I leave my matches?" He picked up the expensive fur coat that was nonchalantly thrown on the bed, and went through its pockets. "Here we are."

"Will you stop clowning?" Orloff shouted at him, suddenly flaring up. He couldn't stand the grotesque, artificial show. "You're making an awful fool of yourself."

Sir Nigel looked up, relighting his extinct cheroot. His smile had vanished. "You shouldn't have gone to meet Philby, Orloff. That was a mistake."

"Was it really?"

"For mistakes like that people pay with their lives, you know." Sykes wasn't joking anymore. "If Philby talked to you and if you are clever enough. . . ." He fell silent, his unfinished phrase dangling in the air like an unspoken verdict.

Orloff wearily peeled his coat off his shoulders, hung it in the narrow cupboard, and pulled a chair from behind the small desk. The last act in his quest was going to take place in this shabby hotel room. And he had all the time in the world.

"I should have guessed from the start," he said, watching Nigel Sykes resume his seat directly in front of him. "The murder of Byroade with the electric Avenger. Typical KGB weapon. The attempt on my life with a Tokarev. Standard KGB weapon again. The KGB signature was everywhere, left for everybody to see. A little bit too obvious, don't you think? I should have guessed it had been done on purpose. The murderer wanted everybody to think that it was a KGB operation. But it wasn't."

"How clever." The Englishman's voice was heavy with irony. He was neatly clipping the tip of a new cigar with a tiny gold cutter, looking quite serene; but Orloff had the feeling he was putting up a front. "And how did you find out," Sykes asked, raising his eyes, "that it was not the KGB?"

"I had my first doubts in the hospital." Orloff was speaking openly, determined to lull Sykes into a feeling of ease. "When Mrs. Byroade came to me with her story. And later in Paris and Cannes. When I knew for sure that it was the same man who in nineteen fifty-two had hired that French tart, Corinne Benedetti, to entrap Byroade, and then returned, thirty years later, to kill her. Her, and Byroade, and me. Moscow Center doesn't operate that way. We never blackmailed Communist sympathizers with French prostitutes. We never used prostitutes; it was too risky. If the woman was an agent, somebody reliable—perhaps. But a common whore from the street? It just didn't fit."

"So you came up with the mole theory," Sir Nigel remarked.

"You seem to know everything I did and said in England."

"Let's say almost everything," the SIS chief confidently pointed out. "That's elementary, don't you think?"

Orloff shrugged. "It doesn't matter really. Most of your colleagues have been after me since I landed at Heathrow."

"The mole theory," Sykes reminded him gently. Behind his suave front, the man was stubborn, holding onto his prey like a bulldog.

"Yes." Orloff was speaking openly, shaping his thoughts as he delved deeper into his narrative, dispelling the last doubts and question marks. "I thought that Byroade and the others had been recruited by a veteran mole, someone like Philby in his time. Maybe someone using the resources of the SIS to carry out his private operation as Philby had. He might have had recourse to some rather unorthodox methods to establish his network. Blackmail, for instance. And once I was there, and the skeletons were suddenly coming out of the closets, the mole had embarked on a killing spree, desperately trying to cover his tracks." He paused briefly, hearing footsteps in the corridor and the drunken giggle of a woman. He waited a few moments before resuming. "Still, for a while I was at a loss. How could there be a mole left from my time without me knowing about him? All our agents in the parallel services and in the Foreign Office were my responsibility. And yet, out of the blue appears a bunch of former spies whom I had never heard of. That was a fact. They had spied, they had been caught, they had confessed. So why the killings? For a sole purpose, of course—to prevent me, at all costs, from meeting those people."

"But you thought the KGB helped the mole in the killings," Sir Nigel offered.

"Certainly. I thought Center wanted to defend the mole or protect some vital secrets from exposure. And I might never have learned the truth, if I had not met Shaw."

For the first time, surprise flashed in Sir Nigel's eyes. "You met Shaw," he slowly said.

"That was a small failure of yours." Orloff felt oddly reassured. "I left England without your knowledge, and for just a few days you lost my track, didn't you?"

But Sykes didn't answer, the swarthy face impassive again.

"You see, Shaw told me something very strange. He said that the most important Intelligence reports he handed over to his case officers were never used. The networks he betrayed were never touched. That made me think that perhaps it was not the KGB after all."

"Still, you thought that Philby had the answer," Sir Nigel objected.

"I thought there was one last, remote chance that Philby had put in place another network of agents without my knowledge. It was a very slim chance, but I could not rule it out. Shaw had been out of the game for years; his information might have become obsolete long ago. He was a broken man, an alcoholic, running for his life. He might have misled me, unknowingly of course. On the other hand, I know Kim Philby. He is a vain man. He enjoys the feeling of power. After the Burgess and Maclean fiasco he might have decided to build a parallel network. And to keep it as his private secret in order to maintain his status. He might have foreseen that sooner or later he would have to escape to Moscow; and he didn't want to arrive there as a refugee, empty-handed. He wanted a dowry to bring along. Maybe that's why the networks had not been operative for years. Philby might have been saving them for a rainy day. When he finally escaped to Russia, he might have left somebody behind to run his Foreign Office ring.''

''And that somebody panicked when the confrontation between you and Byroade was announced,'' Sykes said thoughtfully. ''You would have maintained that Byroade didn't work for you, the Byroade case would have been reopened—and the mole might have been exposed.''

Orloff nodded. ''That was my assumption. That's why I thought the mole was so hurriedly silencing his former agents, one after the other.'' He paused. ''But in London nobody succeeded even in approaching that mysterious mole. So that left me with one last possibility.''

''To get the answer from Philby,'' Sir Nigel said. He leaned forward, and Orloff noticed that his hand holding his cigar was unsteady. ''Philby's answer was negative, I presume.''

Orloff didn't reply.

''What was his answer?'' Sir Nigel pressed on, a new note of urgency slipping into his voice.

''His answer was clear enough,'' Orloff said slowly, ''for me to realize that there was only one other solution left. If it was not the KGB—which automatically excluded any Eastern European service—it had to have been an inside job.''

''That's what they say in America when they fail to crack a bank robbery.'' Sir Nigel's smile was forced, and the narrow, sardonic face had grown very tense.

Orloff couldn't suppress a dry smile. ''Exactly. I've been looking for the robbers everywhere, while the real culprit was the chief cashier.''

Sykes looked at him blankly.

"There is only one man," Orloff said, holding Sir Nigel in unwavering focus, and for the first time certain, absolutely certain that he had reached the truth, "one man who was once an MI-5 officer, who had served on the board that investigated the five diplomats, and who later reached a position that enabled him to have them tracked down and killed in England and abroad. And abroad," he repeated with emphasis.

"Is that so?" Sykes's façade was peeling away, like an actor's discarded makeup.

"What intrigues me still, Sir Nigel," Orloff said softly, "is why you did it. As we both know, you ran the entire operation from the start."

"Don't you think you are going too far?" Sykes said calmly, a well-mannered man casually talking his way through a mundane conversation. "It's very kind of you to cast me in the role of the mole, but I'd like to remind you that things like that don't happen in real life. I've also read all those books; still, you should know that not all SIS chiefs are necessarily Soviet moles. Why in heaven should I spy for the KGB?"

"I never said you spied for the KGB. I know you haven't, and I know you aren't a mole either. There was never any mole in the SIS after Philby. Still, it was you who did it. Not your service but you, personally. And now that I know, I think I can get the proof in no time."

He was bluffing of course, but to his surprise Sykes nodded matter-of-factly. "You're right of course, there is no use denying it. It was my operation, and I don't mind telling you about it. Actually, by coming to your room tonight I committed myself." He took his cigar from his mouth and pensively contemplated its glowing tip. "I am quite willing to tell you about it, Orloff." He shrugged. "But this knowledge is going to harm you, not me."

Orloff was watching him, speechless.

Sir Nigel put his cigar in the ashtray beside him and rubbed the bridge of his nose with his thumb and forefinger. "It all started in your days, Orloff. Imagine this rather junior officer in MI-5, British counterespionage, thirty years ago. He is a young man, quite gifted and rather ambitious," he continued, a self-deprecating smile briefly touching his face, "freshly transferred from the Palestine colonial police, burning with desire to distinguish himself, but hopelessly handicapped by background, hierarchy, experience, and social status."

Orloff looked up in surprise. Such frankness seemed alien to Nigel Sykes's nature. Someone like Nigel Sykes didn't strip himself bare in front of a stranger. Except when he knew for certain that the stranger would never be able to repeat what he heard. A tiny alarm screamed at the back of Orloff's mind, and he was abruptly jolted into a state of alertness, all his senses awake, apprehensive.

"Burgess and Maclean have just defected to the Soviet Union." Sykes was spinning his story, obviously enjoying himself. "Philby is suspected and cleared, but we still have the feeling that there are other Russian spies operating inside the system, in the SIS and the Foreign Office. The junior officer is among those charged with the investigation. He proposes to his superiors several projects aimed to flush out any other Russian agents buried in the Intelligence community. These plans imply, of course, a rather active participation of MI-5 in the operation. But the Foreign Office and the Intelligence service refuse. No thanks, they say. They won't let those plebeians from MI-5 invade their private domains. They'll carry out their own investigations.'' He paused and looked straight at Orloff to get his reaction.

''That means—''

''That means that they will never catch the culprits, of course. They wouldn't even dare to question the probity of a blue-blooded English diplomat. The old-boy network would protect its own at all costs.''

Sykes picked up his cigar again. ''The junior officer has a sudden idea when he discovers, in the MI-5 archives, an old file about suspected Communists. The file comes from Cambridge. Does that ring a bell, Orloff?''

The secret list of Mary Ellis, Orloff thought bitterly. Of course. If there was a copy, there should also be an original somewhere. It suddenly struck him that the Cambridge list, the first success he had achieved in his career, had also become, in a rather oblique way, the first success of the man in front of him.

''The junior officer checks the list,'' Sykes went on. ''He finds that nine of the former Communist sympathizers are in the Foreign Office now, some of them serving as liaison officers with the Intelligence service. And then he decides''—the temptation obviously becoming irresistible, Sir Nigel paused for effect—''to make some of them his own agents inside their respective services.''

Philby had been right. It was wicked indeed. ''So he blackmails them into working for him,'' Orloff interjected, ''making them believe they are spying for the KGB.'' At last he had discovered Nigel Sykes's motive: his private hunt for the Communist moles, but far more than that—his ruthless, obsessive drive for power, even if he had to destroy certain people's lives in the process.

''Precisely.'' A car stopped outside, and Sir Nigel was by the window in three catlike strides. After a moment he turned back, leaning against the wall and crossing his arms. "It was very easy, you see. The junior officer had to take only a few of his colleagues into his confidence to start the operation."

"Didn't it ever cross your mind," Orloff asked candidly, "that what you were doing was illegal?"

"Illegal?" Sykes affected astonishment. "Good God, man, we were trying to clean the service of spies and enemies of Britain. Is there anything more legal than that?"

Orloff preferred not to pursue that subject any further. "How did you get in touch with your agents?" he asked. "The diplomats, I mean. All those contacts in Sofia, Warsaw, Prague—"

"That was the easy part of it," Sykes said. "All we needed was a few trips every month across the Iron Curtain to where they were stationed. We just volunteered, each in his turn, for courier assignments. At the time, Foreign Office couriers were regularly accompanied by security agents."

"And once in place, what did you do?"

Sykes shrugged. "We didn't even meet any of our private moles." He smiled. "A threatening letter or a phone call was enough to scare them into cooperating. Sometimes they were inside calls, from within the embassy." He chuckled. "And for quite a few years they supplied us with everything we could ask for. First-class material."

"But Anthony Byroade did not succumb so easily."

Sir Nigel nodded. "Yes, he was rather tough. But we needed him. For a while most Intelligence communications between Eastern Europe and London came through his hands. We had to know exactly who handled his material

303

in London, and how. The receiving end in London. That was one of the main weak links.''

Yes, Orloff thought, of course. ''The receiving end'' had a name: Cyril Hambro, the man Philby had recruited and Maclean had planted in the satellites department of the Foreign Office. He supplied Philby with priceless information till his sudden arrest. When he was exposed, Philby was stunned. He couldn't understand how his cover had been blown. The answer lay across the room now, in the self-satisfied smile of Nigel Sykes. Mysteries were suddenly clearing, brilliant coups of MI-5 against his networks were emerging in a new light.

''And we finally got good old Byroade,'' Sykes was saying.

Orloff nodded. ''Sure. By sending good old Henry to Paris to set Byroade up with Corinne.''

''Who told you about Henry?'' Sykes stiffened. Just for an instant the suave façade vanished, revealing a mean, violent visage. But his reflexes were quick, controlled. His body relaxed and the ironical smile was back on his lips. ''Oh, never mind. There was no way to carry the project through without sending one of us into the open, so Henry had to do it.''

''And it was a success of course,'' Orloff said.

Sykes eyed him suspiciously, looking for a sign of irony. ''Yes, it was a success,'' he finally said. ''And I'll tell you why. Nobody in the Foreign Office or at the SIS would ever have dared to spy on our own respected, trustworthy, and loyal diplomats, ambassadors and attachés.'' His voice was mocking, harsh, with a vulgar undertone.

''But you did.''

''Oh yes,'' Sir Nigel confirmed. ''And I was right.''

The revenge of the colonial policeman, Orloff thought.

How sweet it must have been for him to discover and later prove that those golden boys, the pride of aristocratic Britannia, the brightest lads of Eton, Harrow, and Oxbridge, were nothing but despicable spies. And how rewarding for him to break into their exclusive club and erect his own castle in their forbidden spheres.

"My agents," Sykes was saying, his face flushed, his defenses down, "supplied me with all the information I needed. From their reports I knew all about the service, who was doing what and how, who was supposed to be weak and corruptible, who was vulnerable, who was likely to become a subject for KGB recruiting. With all that information flowing into my hands, I got results, Orloff. I defeated you over and over again. I succeeded in pinning down John Fleetwood and Cyril Hambro in nineteen fifty-four. I exposed the double dealing of Finch in nineteen fifty-seven. I caught Sommers red-handed the same year. That's why he committed suicide. I actually expected him to be seduced by some Russian hussy. With a wife like his, and given his sexual appetite, it was bound to happen. As soon as we discovered the leak in the Moscow embassy, I knew exactly who my man was." He crushed his cigar into the ashtray, turning and pressing it viciously, as if he was grinding Sommers to dust. "I was also the first to suspect that the Poles had broken the Black Code of our embassy in Warsaw; and finally I was the one who re-opened the investigation against Philby in nineteen sixty-two." He stopped, his last sentences ringing with the solemn tone of a lawyer who rests his case, confident of the final outcome.

Sykes was enjoying himself immensely, Orloff realized. He was relishing the unique opportunity, once in his lifetime, to describe his brilliant game of deceit to another master of the trade. To confess all of it, to stun his audience, and still escape unruffled.

"With your permission," Orloff said coldly, "I'll take over from here." His voice was very old, very tired. "You did indeed get excellent inside stuff through your private network. I can testify to that. I know now how we lost Hambro and Fleetwood and Sommers. And there must be a few others you didn't mention. But," he continued, disregarding the self-satisfied nods of Nigel Sykes, "as the French saying goes, '*L'appétit vient en mangeant.*' While you were devouring those treacherous red spies, you developed a quite healthy appetite, didn't you? And very soon you—or, if you prefer, the 'junior officer' we were discussing—realized that he could use the Intelligence reports from the Soviet bloc for his own benefit. That was the second stage of the Cambridge Communists affair. So our hero instructed his agents to substitute, henceforth, worthless material for their reports, while he went to his superiors claiming that he had a secret new source behind the Iron Curtain. He scooped up the reports from the networks run or supervised by Shaw, Byroade, Llewellyn, and whoever else and presented his astonished chiefs with priceless information. That's how he climbed the ladder in such record time, got transferred to the SIS, and finally took over the chief's seat. How patriotic, Sir Nigel!"

Nigel Sykes stared at him speculatively for a moment, then shrugged indifferently. "Nobody was harmed. I did not betray the country or the service. The Russians never learned about our networks behind the Iron Curtain. I climbed the ladder, as you say, and cleaned the service. When my informers were not needed anymore—I mean Byroade and the others—they were quietly discharged and pensioned. Is anything wrong with that?"

"Nothing. Except that almost twenty years later, when I was on my way to England, a young woman, a journalist—"

"Your daughter, you mean."

The jab scored painfully, but he pretended to ignore it. "A journalist stumbled upon Anthony Byroade. And you panicked. You understood that, if I confronted him, I would soon find out that neither he nor the four other diplomats ever worked for us. And a thorough investigation might lead to you. Think of the scandal! The chief of the Secret Intelligence Service had been spying on the other services under the cover of a KGB ringleader. Blackmailing innocent people into carrying out his dirty work for him. So you had to kill all of them. And Corinne. And me, of course. It was either that or shameful disgrace for you. And who knows? Maybe even long years in prison. You were ready to do anything on earth to save your hide, Sir Nigel."

Nigel Sykes was watching him, head bent, a vacuous look in his narrow eyes.

"So you got your killer out of mothballs to do the dirty work for you. Where is Henry now, Sir Nigel? Somewhere in Berlin, I suppose. Waiting."

Sykes stared at him without speaking and an ominous silence settled in the room.

Displaying his remarkable self-control once again, Sir Nigel straightened up. He picked up his coat and pocketed his matches. He went into the bathroom and came back with a handful of tissues. He spread them on the windowsill, emptied the ashtray in their middle, then rolled them into a soft, round ball, which he also put in his pocket. His movements were easy and confident. He turned to Orloff. "I'd say that you've summed up the affair correctly. I should be going now."

307

Orloff stared at him in bewilderment. "And you don't care about what I might do with this story?"

Sir Nigel smiled suavely. "You are not going to do anything with it, Orloff. Do you think I would have talked to you if I had any reason to expect you would tell anybody?"

"Well," Orloff said, taking a deep breath, "you'd better know that I came to Germany on the advice of one of your good colleagues, Chief Superintendent Hastings. He knows where Shaw is, and he'll hear the truth very soon."

But Sykes was shaking his head, and the strange glint in his eyes spelled a mixture of amusement and condescension. "Hastings is dying in a London hospital, Orloff." He gave a quick, unpleasant laugh. "For once a death will have nothing to do with me. A juicy cancer, they say. As far as Shaw is concerned, you shouldn't worry about him either. Henry stopped in Bonn on his way here. I have good reason to believe that Shaw won't talk. You were right again about Henry, though. He is in Berlin. Waiting, as you said."

He put on his coat. "Meanwhile, you are going to stay in your room, Orloff. And keep very quiet. No letters, no messages, no phone calls. You want your daughter to live, don't you? That depends on you.

"If you dare to speak, nobody will believe you. You haven't got a shred of evidence, and besides you are an old, used-up spy. But Lynn will die. She will die even if you only talk to her." Sykes glanced at the telephone on the night table. "Even if I only suspect that you have let her know. I have quite a few people from my service watching you. They don't have the foggiest idea what it's all about, of course. They have been dispatched to Berlin to watch a former KGB spy who reportedly defected to the

West seventeen years ago but has just sneaked into East Berlin to meet Kim Philby. That's all they need to know. But they will report to me, and I still work with Henry."

He was about to put on his gloves but at the last moment changed his mind, stepped to the desk, and picked up the manila envelope. He took out the documents and flipped through them, his forehead wrinkled. "It took us a couple of weeks to unearth all this. You don't want her to die, do you, Orloff?"

"She is not my daughter," he muttered angrily. "Those papers are forged and you know it."

"No, they are not," Sir Nigel said, throwing them on the desk. Lynn's birth certificate fell to one side and slowly fluttered down, noiselessly settling on the carpet. "Actually," Sykes added, "it's beside the point. You like the girl, don't you? You wouldn't want her to come to any harm. Sorry, Orloff."

At the door he turned back one last time before slipping out of the room. "It's curtains for you, I'm afraid," he said, and was gone.

21

ALONE in his room, he turned off the lights and dragged the armchair to the window. He pulled the curtains wide open, letting in the faint, dying light from the street. A few snowflakes were fluttering in the wind, swaying like falling leaves. It was all unreal, a strange dream, a delusion. He settled into the armchair and closed his eyes. Nigel Sykes was right, of course. It was beside the point whether the documents in the envelope were real or fake. He knew he would protect Lynn at all costs.

Slowly, almost peacefully, he realized that he had reached the end of the road. Curtains, Nigel Sykes had said, and he meant it. They couldn't take any risks, not now that he knew. They couldn't let him get away with their secret. And Lynn's life depended on his death.

He looked at his watch. The luminous dial showed two A.M. They would not be long now. It would most certainly be good old Henry. Nigel Sykes couldn't have more than

311

one or two accomplices in this affair. They would probably wait a little, long enough for Sykes to get away and establish his alibi. Then they would come for him, with some museum piece like a Tokarev or an electric Avenger. Another KGB killing.

The phone started ringing—short, strident screams—but he did not pick it up, only watched it silently until it stopped. Lynn might have found out where he was. She might be calling. And he could not answer. They were undoubtedly tapping the phone. They would not hesitate to kill her if they even suspected that she knew their secret. He was trapped by his feelings for her. Philby wouldn't have hesitated, of course; at that moment he would already have been holding a press conference. But then Philby was not an "incurable romantic" like him. Sykes, too, had found his soft spot. He was going to die. There was nothing he could do, nowhere he could go. Checkmate.

It dawned on him that he actually didn't mind dying. He had no port to sail back to, no home he could call his castle. Russia was dead for him, England hostile, America indifferent. Nora had gone to her son in Colorado; she would not come back to him, not after all the notoriety. And Lynn was too busy building a career and a love affair. He would only be an embarrassment to her. Philby had been right once again. He was the eternal stranger, carrying his exile like the plague, and there was no place for him in the whole world to cure his cursed malady.

He peered down into the street. A heavy snow was falling, noiseless, ghostlike, gently covering the dirty sidewalks, surviving on the glistening car hoods. Berlin would look like a legend tomorrow. And somewhere in a luxury hotel suite Nigel Sykes would savor his first cloudless morning in a long time. With Orloff dead, he would be safe again, the real winner. And nobody would ever know.

All of a sudden, he grew very still. Something was wrong, utterly wrong with his reasoning. He had overlooked a capital point. And so had Nigel Sykes. They had both behaved as if nobody else but them knew the truth. They had ignored the most dramatic event of that night: a third man had been initiated into their secret.

The third man.

Philby.

Philby knew.

Philby had guessed a few hours before, at Lily Hartman's place. "You have been fooled, Alex, but not by us. . . . Quite wicked indeed. You have all the pieces of the puzzle, Alex. . . . That boy in London . . . not with our house, with the others. . . . Good old Henry."

And Philby was still with Center.

In a recent issue of the *London Times* he had read an article about Philby. He had metamorphosed the KGB, the article said, from a crude bunch of clumsy thugs into a sophisticated machine run by urbane, bright, highly educated young men. He had remodeled the service, given it allure and cunning. And he was still one of its most inventive, most original planners.

It occurred to Orloff that Philby might have been quite willing to meet him but had thought it wiser to give the opposite impression. Perhaps it had been Philby's hand that pulled the invisible strings making his venture into East Berlin so smooth and easy. The perfunctory passport control at Checkpoint Charlie, the presence—and then the disappearance—of the Vopo buses and guards at the city hall. Yes, that could have been Philby's hand at work. He had the feeling that, drunk or not, Philby had not been disappointed by their meeting, by the story he had told him.

Orloff's instincts were suddenly rushing madly ahead, far ahead of his thoughts, projecting on the screen of his imagination the stunning pictures of what might happen. Of what was bound to happen now that Philby knew. He had inadvertently offered him the ultimate trophy, the prize they had both coveted for forty years and failed to win. Good God!

He could imagine Philby at that very moment, sitting on the floor cross-legged in his bedouin fashion, whispering into the telephone in Lily Hartman's dark apartment. Only it wouldn't be dark anymore but blazing with lights; couriers would be running in and out; and Kim would be feverishly dictating his messages. To East Berlin station, and by scrambler relay to Moscow, and then top-red to the resident in London. Moscow Center in Dzerzhinski Square would be aglow with lights, while harried operatives checked old records, indexes, files and white-coated technicians punched on their keyboards the secret codes of the computerized archives. England—services—MI-5 personnel—field agents—1950-1963. Before the night was through, Philby would know the last name and address of good old Henry. Henry from MI-5 of course ("not with our house, with the others"). Once he knew the name, he unknowingly discovered the chink in Sir Nigel's armor.

The images in his dazed mind were succeeding each other with lightning speed. He could foresee in fragmentary flashes the sequence of events that would occur in London in a week or two. Whom would Philby send? The soberly dressed gentleman from an insurance company in the City? The florid country attorney, bearer of "good news"? . . . Perhaps a bashful, elderly schoolteacher, an old childhood friend, or even a retired major, a former army buddy from the Coldstream Guards? Going from one address to another, milking the landladies, politely inquiring about his good old friend Henry till he found his present address and learned his routine. And then the snatch in the middle of the street, very quiet, very discreet: two men, one on each side, two backups, a car, a hand with a syringe. And the short, bald, scar-faced Henry waking up in a safehouse in the outskirts of London. Then the lights, the blows, the threats, the drugs. And the breakdown. "They always talk," his instructor for the refresher course at Lubyanka had once said matter-of-factly.

Next image: the dismay and the wild emotion when Henry would whisper the name of his master. The emergency meeting at Center with the Politburo envoy, and Philby reporting. The decision to go ahead. The choice of the team. The means of escape. The countdown.

And finally, the "chancy" encounter with Nigel Sykes at the Marlborough Club or at the entrance of L'Etoile restaurant, perhaps even on a staircase in Whitehall. The polite bow of the deferential stranger, the puzzled smile on Sykes's face. "Sir Nigel? What a fortuitous coincidence. I don't believe you know me, but I just saw Henry, good old Henry. He sends you greetings from Maldon." Or Hertford. Or Bonn. Or perhaps Berlin. And the trap will have been sprung.

Yes, Philby could do that. He would lay his hands on Nigel Sykes. Orloff was swept with a strange, perverse satisfaction. The ultimate revenge. Unwittingly, Philby would avenge his death. The absurd had no limits.

Espionage, he thought in wonder, works in strange arabesques. He would be dead already, and by his death he would present the KGB that he had deserted with its biggest catch ever: the chief of the SIS in person. Litvinov would have been proud of me, he said to himself. Sir Nigel would become a Russian spy. By sheer blackmail. The game he practiced so well from the other side.

He had no power to prevent that. And even if he had, why should he? Why should he save the British SIS? Western Intelligence? He was a man without a country, home, or friends. Unable to be a patriot, and thereby unable to become a traitor.

He got up one last time, tore the manila envelope and its contents to pieces, and flushed them down the toilet. Lynn would never know. Then he settled back in his chair. On a beach in Fort Myers a doctor had told him once that before death there is a strange illumination of the face of the dying man, a sudden smoothing of the wrinkles. A reflection of inner peace, like the one he was feeling now. In a hospital bed in London, Hastings was dying. Had he guessed Sir Nigel's role? He wondered. Was that the reason he had sent him to Bonn?

In Chelsea, Lynn was enjoying a fleeting spell of happiness in the arms of a stolen man.

Here, in Berlin, Sir Nigel was having his first peaceful night in months, while on the other side of the wall Kim Philby was already planning his destruction.

There was nothing left for Orloff to do. He was just an old spy in winter. The time had come, as Kim had said, for him to hang up his boots.

He leaned back in the armchair, watching the ethereal snowflakes dance for him over the sleeping city, waiting for his executioner.

BESTSELLING BOOKS FROM TOR

☐ 58725-1 *Gardens of Stone* by Nicholas Proffitt $3.95
  58726-X   Canada $4.50

☐ 51650-8 *Incarnate* by Ramsey Campbell $3.95
  51651-6   Canada $4.50

☐ 51050-X *Kahawa* by Donald E. Westlake $3.95
  51051-8   Canada $4.50

☐ 52750-X *A Manhattan Ghost Story* by T.M. Wright
                                                   $3.95
  52751-8   Canada $4.50

☐ 52191-9 *Ikon* by Graham Masterton $3.95
  52192-7   Canada $4.50

☐ 54550-8 *Prince Ombra* by Roderick MacLeish $3.50
  54551-6   Canada $3.95

☐ 50284-1 *The Vietnam Legacy* by Brian Freemantle
                                                   $3.50
  50285-X   Canada $3.95

☐ 50487-9 *Siskiyou* by Richard Hoyt $3.50
  50488-7   Canada $3.95

Buy them at your local bookstore or use this handy coupon:
Clip and mail this page with your order

TOR BOOKS—Reader Service Dept.
P.O. Box 690, Rockville Centre, N.Y. 11571

Please send me the book(s) I have checked above. I am enclosing
$_____ (please add $1.00 to cover postage and handling).
Send check or money order only—no cash or C.O.D.'s.

Mr./Mrs./Miss _____

Address _____.

City _____ State/Zip _____

Please allow six weeks for delivery. Prices subject to change without
notice.

MORE BESTSELLERS FROM TOR

☐ 58827-4 *Cry Havoc* by Barry Sadler $3.50
    58828-2   Canada $3.95

☐ 51025-9 *Designated Hitter* by Walter Wager $3.50
    51026-7   Canada $3.95

☐ 51600-1 *The Inheritor* by Marion Zimmer Bradley $3.50
    51601-X   Canada $3.95

☐ 50282-5 *The Kremlin Connection* by Jonathan Evans $3.95
    50283-3   Canada $4.50

☐ 58250-0 *The Lost American* by Brian Freemantle $3.50
    58251-9   Canada $3.95

☐ 58825-8 *Phu Nham* by Barry Sadler $3.50
    58826-6   Canada $3.95

☐ 58552-6 *Wake in Darkness* by Donald E. McQuinn $3.95
    58553-4   Canada $4.50

☐ 50279-5 *The Solitary Man* by Jonathan Evans $3.95
    50280-9   Canada $4.50

☐ 51858-6 *Shadoweyes* by Kathryn Ptacek $3.50
    51859-4   Canada $3.95

☐ 52543-4 *Cast a Cold Eye* by Alan Ryan $3.95
    52544-2   Canada $4.50

☐ 52193-5 *The Pariah* by Graham Masterton $3.50
    52194-3   Canada $3.95

Buy them at your local bookstore or use this handy coupon:
Clip and mail this page with your order

TOR BOOKS—Reader Service Dept.
P.O. Box 690, Rockville Centre, N.Y. 11571

**Please send me the book(s) I have checked above. I am enclosing
$_____ (please add $1.00 to cover postage and handling).
Send check or money order only—no cash or C.O.D.'s.**

Mr./Mrs./Miss _____

Address _____

City _____ State/Zip _____

**Please allow six weeks for delivery. Prices subject to change without
notice.**